The 10 p.m. Question

The 10 p.m. Question

Kate De Goldi

CANDLEWICK PRESS

The author gratefully acknowledges the assistance of
Creative New Zealand for the writing of this novel.

Thank you Sally, Peter, Tosca, Frank, and Coco, for your wonderful
hospitality and friendship, which got this novel cranking.

Thank you Bella, for the art of waving, and Bonga Swetso!

———————————

Copyright © 2008 by Kate De Goldi

First U.S. paperback edition 2012

The Library of Congress has cataloged the hardcover edition as follows:

De Goldi, Kate, date.
The 10 p.m. question / Kate De Goldi. — 1st U.S. ed.
p. cm.
Summary: Twelve-year-old Frankie Parsons has a quirky family, a wonderful
best friend, and a head full of worrying questions that he shares with his mother
each night, but when free-spirited Sydney arrives at school with questions
of her own, Frankie is forced to face the ultimate 10 p.m. question.
ISBN 978-0-7636-4939-5 (hardcover)
[1. Questions and answers—Fiction. 2. Worrying—Fiction. 3. Family life—New
Zealand—Fiction. 4. Eccentrics and eccentricity—Fiction. 5. Schools—Fiction.
6. Agoraphobia—Fiction. 7. New Zealand—Fiction.]
I. Title. II. Title Ten PM question
PZ7.D33944A12 2010
[Fic]—dc22   2009049726

ISBN 978-0-7636-5848-9 (paperback)

12 13 14 15 16 17 BVG 10 9 8 7 6 5 4 3 2 1

Printed in Berryville, VA, U.S.A.

This book was typeset in Berthold Baskerville.

Candlewick Press
99 Dover Street
Somerville, Massachusetts 02144

visit us at www.candlewick.com

For Luciana and Jack,
at the heart of it all

ONE

Tuesday, February 14

Tuesday the fourteenth of February began badly for Frankie Parsons. There was no milk for his Just Right. There was no Go-Cat for the Fat Controller, so the Fat Controller stood under the table meowing accusingly while Frankie ate his toast.

The newspaper hadn't arrived, which meant Frankie couldn't take a headline and article for Current Affairs and so would earn one of Mr. A's sardonic looks. Nor could he check the weather report for humidity. Humidity levels were important to Frankie, for two reasons: One, a cricket ball swung rather trickily and lethally when the air was heavy, which was a good thing. Two, ants appeared in droves when the temperature was warm and the atmosphere thick, which was a very bad thing. Frankie nursed a special hatred for ants.

So, Tuesday the fourteenth began badly and continued that way. Frankie's sister, Gordana, had swiped the last muesli bar and the only crisp apple; there were no water bottles; the Cling Wrap had run out; there was no bus money in his mother's wallet, so Frankie had to search for a nail file in order to prize out ten-cent pieces from the emergency pink china pig.

A nail file was always hard to find in Frankie's house and today was no exception. He located one, finally, in the yellow first aid container, which lived in the laundry with his carefully arranged earthquake kit (twelve two-liter water bottles, two sets of spare batteries, enough baked beans, tuna, toilet paper, and Go-Cat for a week). By which time it was 8:05 a.m. and, furthermore, the pink china pig was ominously lightweight. Someone had been there before him. On Saturday, when he'd last checked, the pig had been quite heavy. (Frankie shook her regularly, an almost involuntary but comforting gesture whenever he passed the hall bookcase, which was where the pink pig lived, beside the *National Geographics*.)

Frankie suspected Louie. His brother lived away from home now, but he came for dinner and laundry several times a week and was always on the hunt for small change. There were no stray coins lying on shelves or bedside tables after Louie had been around.

Nothing made Frankie madder than a lightweight pink china pig. He relied on that pig. Experience had taught him that precisely when he needed it most, his mother would not have cash in her wallet. Nor would his father. But the pink pig — the repository of everyone's unloved ten-cent pieces — generally had a bellyful of coins.

Except today, February the fourteenth. Today there was only one dollar and thirty cents — fifty cents short of Frankie's bus fare to school, which meant he would have to borrow from his friend Gigs. Who wouldn't mind, but that wasn't the point.

"This house doesn't work!" Frankie called up the stairs. He stuffed his exercise books, lunch bag, and sneakers into his backpack. Then he stood very still and mentally perused the school day. This was his habit each morning. It was so he wouldn't forget anything. He was really very organized.

Math (protractor, calculator, yes). Reading (*Hicksville*, yes).

Language arts (*Concise Oxford,* yes). PE (shorts, sneakers, yes). Cricket at lunchtime (bat, ball, box, yes). Lunch (*soft* apple, cheese-and-peanut-butter sandwich, carrot, lemon cake, secret-chocolate-hidden-behind-the-rice, yes). Art (pencils, ink, sketchbook, yes). Science project (glue gun, statistics sheet, black paper, double-sided tape, Stanley knife, yes, yes, yes, yes, *yes*).

"A bad workman always blames his tools," said Gordana. She came thumping down the stairs in her flat-footed, truculent, morning way. Gordana maintained she wasn't a morning person. In Frankie's private view, his sister was a no-time person, not morning, afternoon, nor evening. The less he saw of her the better.

"Whadda you mean, a bad workman?" he said, and instantly regretted it. He really didn't know why he ever responded to Gordana. It always ended badly. Every day, he told himself to ignore her, and every day, he ignored himself instead.

Face it, Gigs had told him. You hate her. It's official. And mutual. Your sister is your enemy. Stop consorting.

"It may be *your* fault if the house doesn't work," said Gordana.

"How could it be?" said Frankie. "I'm the *child.*"

"And there you have it," Gordana snapped. "A *child* is precisely what this house doesn't need anymore."

"No bickering, please," said Ma. She said this automatically whenever she came into a room containing Frankie and Gordana. It was usually necessary, she said.

"We need cat food," said Frankie. "And *human* food."

"And food for Frankie," said Gordana with a smirk.

"And money," said Frankie. "And new batteries for the smoke alarm."

"Oh, good *God,*" said Gordana. "Not the smoke alarm thing again."

"I'll ring Uncle George," said Ma. "He's shopping for the Aunties."

The Aunties. A sudden and familiar heaviness settled over Frankie. It was as if someone had fastened large marbles to his entire body. Of course. Why not? Tuesday the fourteenth began with no cereal and it would end with a surfeit of aunts. Perfect.

"Oh, good *God*," said Gordana. "Count me out. I'll be at Ben's." Ben was Gordana's boyfriend. He had a buffed body, a nifty wrist action, and absolutely no aunts. It all seemed quite unfair to Frankie.

"Bye," said Frankie funereally. He kissed Ma on the cheek. She smelled morningish, a mixture of Coal Tar soap and toast. After school, she smelled of baking—a fusion of melted butter, toasted almonds, nutmeg, and vanilla essence. He liked both smells.

It wasn't Ma's fault about the Aunties. The entire American military couldn't have kept them away. They came every second and fourth Tuesday and stayed for dinner and cards. Sometimes it was too much for even a reasonable boy.

"Have a good one," said Ma.

"Fat chance," said Frankie. But he closed the door gently behind him. He would have liked to slam it, but Gordana did more than enough slamming for everyone in their house, and it always made Ma jump.

Gigs was waiting at the top of the Zig Zag. He was leaning against the Forsythes' fence, reading a comic and pulling at his right eyebrow. He always did this when he was concentrating. There was a tiny bare patch where he'd overworked the habit.

"Better hurry," he said, not looking up.

"Financial emergency," said Frankie. "You got a dollar?"

"Sure." Gigs always had spare money. His house was awash

with coins. Twenty-dollar bills spilled from his father's pocket. Or so it seemed to Frankie.

They walked slowly down the Zig Zag. It was a steep path, overhung with ferns and other greenery, which made it pleasantly cool in summer, but damp and treacherously slippery in the winter months.

Frankie and Gigs had an invariable routine on the Zig Zag.

At the third corner, they gave a swift pat to Mrs. Rowan's cat, Marmalade, who was always sitting on the letter box. Marmalade was an elderly bundle of fluff and very inoffensive (just like Mrs. Rowan, Gigs said; Mrs. Rowan was old and kindly and had something of a beard).

At the fifth corner, they took turns slamming shut number 41's letter box, which was, inexplicably, always open to the heavens and the weather. They had been doing this for five years, ever since Gigs arrived in the neighborhood and they began walking to the bus stop together. Every afternoon, the lid was up again, and every afternoon, they closed it once more. It was an enjoyable little game between the boys and Mrs. Da Prini, who lived at number 41. At least, Frankie assumed Mrs. Da Prini found the game enjoyable. He and Gigs found it extremely satisfactory.

Just before the tenth corner, they prepared themselves to ambush Ronald, the bad-tempered dachshund who lurked beside his owner's picket fence, ready to yap at unsuspecting pedestrians. Ronald's owners were nice enough, but their pet was a loser and thoroughly deserved everything he got.

"What a dumb dog," Gigs said, bending down. He said this every day as he and Frankie crouched and inched their bodies around the tenth corner. That was the pleasing thing about ambushing Ronald. It worked every time because Ronald never learned from the past. He seemed never to expect the two boys to burst around the corner and let rip a machine-gun rattle of fearsome boy yaps, though they'd been doing this at the same time, twice a day, for nearly three years. Ambushing Ronald never failed to make them laugh like hell.

"We'll know we're practically dead when we don't want to do old Ronald," said Frankie.

"Does that mean we'll actually be sad when he dies?" said Gigs. He leaped up on the Ernest Burrows Memorial Seat, balanced briefly and daintily on its upright back, then jumped down to the thirteenth zig. Frankie followed. They did this every morning, too. The Ernest Burrows Memorial Seat allowed a view of a cascading garden of succulents on the gentle hillface opposite, but Frankie and Gigs had never actually sat on Ernest Burrows. He was merely their launching pad for the canter down the remaining four zigzags and along the riverbank to the bus stop.

"Imagine Ronald's effect on stress levels," shouted Frankie. He lobbed the bus stop cricket ball up over the bus shelter to Gigs on the other side.

"Sky-high," Gigs called. He cupped his big freckled hands ready. They were like the firm but flexible petals of an aging tulip.

Stress levels were a recurring topic of conversation between the two of them just now. They had an acute and quite professional interest in stress, because it was the subject of their ingenious — and completely secret — Science Fair project. Their project would, Gigs confidently predicted, beat all other Year Eight entries, which were were all wire and battery units, or plant habitats, or tidal river patterns, the usual old stuff. Their project was so novel, it would enchant the judges at school, the judges at the regionals and the nationals, and probably the world.

They had conceived the project together over the summer, but Frankie claimed the original moment of inspiration. He had been watching Uncle George in the weeks before Christmas — a period when Uncle G's work was particularly hectic and consuming. Sometimes after dinner Uncle George would settle his substantial frame into the cushioned green sofa. He had a particular way of not relaxing when he was seated in an easy chair or on the sofa. His feet tapped, his arms jerked, his head was up and alert like a rotating periscope. He twitched and barked and generally disturbed anyone else's attempts to idle and lounge.

"Keep *still!*" ordered Gordana, smacking his arm. "You're ten times worse than the Harding twins." (The Harding twins were Gordana's regular babysitting charges. According to her, they were human hurricanes. Looking after the Harding twins was enough to prostrate Gordana for an entire day.)

The only thing that ever settled Uncle George, Frankie noticed over the weeks before Christmas, the only thing that stayed his perky head and flailing limbs, the only thing that shut up his constant talk, was the Fat Controller. When the Fat Controller leaped weightily upward and planted her big body in Uncle George's lap, a strange quiet settled over them both. Uncle George's hand kneaded the Fat Controller's head, tickled her ears, and played over her massive back, and the Fat Controller spread her considerable length and width over Uncle George's legs. At the same time, a liquid calm seemed to seep through Uncle George's normally electric self.

"It's like a drug," said Ma admiringly.

"Stress buster," said Louie one time. Which was the moment Frankie had his inspiration.

It was Gigs who refined the idea for the purposes of the Year Eight science project. Gigs was a great organizer. He liked to draw up lists and charts and graphs and spreadsheets. He liked to underline. He liked to assign tasks. Their own task, he said, was to sit people down and measure their pulse rate, stick a cat in their lap for five minutes, then measure their pulse again. They would do ten people each, he said, which would give a good range.

They had borrowed a digital sphygmomanometer from Gigs's dad. As well as blood pressure readings, it had a pulse rate counter. That was the best part—attaching the sphygmomanometer cuff to people's arms and watching it balloon when they pressed the start button, listening to the rising whine of the machine. It sounded like a light plane taking off. So far, the statistics were 80–20 in favor of a cat's beneficial effect on adult stress. The only person who disproved the hypothesis was Gigs's stepmother, Chris. Her pulse rate went stratospheric whenever anyone put a sphygmomanometer cuff on her.

"You'll have to put that in the experiment," she said. "That's a margin of error, or something."

"No problem," said Gigs. He had a special column on their spreadsheet for this sort of thing—people who got asthma from cats, people who got scratched in the course of the experiment, people who freaked out at sphygmomanometers.

"You should be an accountant," Frankie told Gigs. "They like spreadsheets."

"Or a general," said Gigs. "They use spreadsheets to deploy troops. They just feed instructions into the computer and bingo. They don't even really need to be there."

That was the thing about Gigs. He could imagine being a general and not worry in the least about army training, or war, or getting wounded. Or ants in the hot countries. Gigs saw the bright side of everything. It made him a good person to be around.

"Come over after school," Frankie called as the bus rounded the hospital corner. He lobbed a last ball over the shelter. "It's Aunties."

"Hot damn!" said Gigs. *Hot damn* was his latest phrase. He'd picked it up from some country song. "Will there be brandy snaps?" According to Gigs, they never had cake or biscuits because Chris was too busy with the little kids.

"Probably," said Frankie.

"You stress-tested the Aunties?" asked Gigs. He dug in his pocket for money and dribbled one-dollar coins into Frankie's open hand. "Don't spend it all at once," he said, just as his father did.

"No," said Frankie, stepping up to the bus stop pole. For some reason, he'd entirely failed to try the Aunties with the sphyg-momanometer. He felt minutely cheered. Testing them would be a laugh, especially if Gigs was there. He had a way with the Aunties, which Frankie had admired often.

The bus roared to a halt. Cassino, their bus driver, prided himself on a full-speed, accurate stop — the brakes singing, the air seizing, the doors sucking open precisely in front of the waiting passengers. Frankie and Gigs held their breath every time, anxious that Cassino should maintain his own high standards. In five years, he hadn't failed them.

Cassino was big and brown and had an impressive boa constrictor tattoo running the length of his left arm. Like Frankie and Gigs, he was a creature of habit; every morning, as he took their coins or slotted their bus cards, Cassino said the same thing.

"And the code word is, fellas?"

They took turns inventing the code word. You could never use the same one twice, and Cassino had a phenomenal memory for repeats.

"Lorikeets," said Frankie. He often did birds. He knew a lot of wacko bird names. Tomorrow he planned to roll out *kittiwake,* and the day after, *wigeon.* He was still debating about Friday; it would be either *lily-trotter* or *capercaillie,* which were both names that made him smile.

"Fair enough," said Cassino, which was what he always said — even when Gigs had been on a bodily excretion theme and had worked his way from *not* to *earwax* to *bile* to *toe jam* to a grand finale of *feces.*

They rolled down the aisle to their usual seat, the left corner of the long bench at the back of the bus. Frankie and Gigs had been sitting there for years and no one had ever argued against it — except Bronwyn Baxter, who'd taken it into her head last year to challenge the arrangement. They'd worn her down, though, and driven her to the front of the bus by talking Chilun in a constant monotone from the other end of the bench seat.

Chilun was a code, a complicated language spoken by only two people in the world. Frankie had invented it one dull summer and then taught it to Gigs. It was a mixture of pig Latin, inverted syllables, truncated words — and bits of Russian.

Frankie and Gigs found Russian hilarious. Sometimes for a good laugh, they listened to Ma's old tapes from her Russian study days. In class, Frankie could always make Gigs (and himself) crack up by whispering, *"Feodor, Feodor, rastsluy menya, da po zharche,"* across the desk. It meant: Feodor, Feodor, kiss me more passionately.

Frankie enjoyed languages. Their different sounds and patterns interested him, and his ear seemed to sort out their mysteries quickly. He was the best in the class at French, and he'd picked up a bit of Italian from Mrs. Da Prini, too. He knew the word for *bird* in eight languages. Inventing Chilun had been easy.

Gigs wasn't interested in languages, but after four years, he, too, had pretty much mastered Chilun. It was the ultimate nonviolent weapon, Gigs reckoned. If you talked in Chilun long enough and repeated an offending person's name at regular intervals, they eventually got fed up and moved out of earshot. Gigs used it all the time against his twin brothers and little sister. It was useful on the phone, too, Frankie had found, especially when Gordana was hanging about. (Nynodimus was Gordana's Chilun name, though, amazingly, she'd never caught on. Chilun just brought her out in a rash, as the Aunties would say.)

"So," said Gigs, taking out his breakfast. He always ate breakfast on the bus, an arrangement he had made with Chris. He could stay in bed every morning until the last possible minute—and thereby avoid his siblings—as long as he ate a decent breakfast on the bus. A decent breakfast, according to Chris, included a BLT (with egg) and a milk drink and fresh fruit. Chris's BLTs were top heavy with bacon and avocado. Her smoothies were excellent, too. And her definition of fresh fruit encompassed canned peaches. The Parsons certainly had great baking, but Gigs's breakfasts always made Frankie a little envious.

"The Aunties," continued Gigs, through a mash of pig and vegetable. "We should do them during the card game—they'll be super stressed. Shotgun Alma."

Alma was the eldest Auntie and Gigs's declared favorite. Frankie, who was deeply fond, really, of all the Aunties, also secretly favored Alma. She was enormously fat and very funny; she smoked small cigars called cheroots and drank whiskey and liked to gamble on all her card games. And when she'd had quite a lot of whiskey and a winning hand at crib, she sometimes demonstrated her ancient ballroom-dancing skills.

For someone so hefty, Alma was surprisingly light on her feet. The flesh around her middle and arms shook alarmingly when she bossa novaed. Sweat gathered in the folds of her chins, and her breath came fast and rattling. But her feet tripped and darted as daintily as any slim-line ballerina. Frankie found an Alma dance routine peculiarly mesmerizing.

Alma'd had dozens of boyfriends in her time, but none of them, she maintained, had been good enough dancing partners to marry. It was Frankie and Gigs's private view that all Alma's boyfriends had run off for fear of being squashed.

When he was in the mood, Frankie found Alma a riot.

On the whole, he really wasn't in the mood today.

"Okay," he said. "You can do Alma and I'll do Nellie and Teen. But we'll have to factor in who's winning and how much they've had to drink. And hopefully it won't prejudice the judges." (Ms. Oates, the Junior Dean, was one of the school judges, and Frankie knew for a fact that Ms. Oates didn't approve of alcohol.)

"Man, your Aunties put it away, don't they?" said Gigs in perfect imitation of Uncle George.

Put it away they certainly did. Uncle George had said to Frankie once that the Aunties were the last great lady drinkers in the Western World. And he was all for it. Uncle George loved the Aunties. It was a match made in heaven, Frankie thought. They were all four of them boisterous and loud and optimistic, with big appetites for food and fun.

He sighed and stared out the window at the river, at the ducks gliding, apparently happy, on the lit-up surface. Food, fun, and fast hands of cards were great, and, really, he liked them as much as Uncle G. But there was so much else to think about and no one except him seemed to bother doing the thinking.

Worms, for instance. Frankie was pretty sure the Fat Controller had worms, which meant that he, Frankie, probably had worms, too, since the Fat Controller slept on—and often *in*—his bed at night. Frankie found the idea of worms almost as revolting as ants. He'd mentioned the worm possibility several times to Ma but she insisted the Fat Controller was fine. He'd have to deal with it himself, he supposed—get money from Uncle G, buy the worm tablets, and make everyone in the house take the dose along with himself and the cat.

Then there was the smoke alarm. The batteries had passed the use-by date and were certainly dead by now. He'd asked Uncle George a thousand times to get new ones but, as usual, Uncle George kept forgetting. So Frankie would have to do it himself.

Also, school camp was coming up and he just knew the house would go to rack and ruin if he went away. No one would remember rubbish day; no one would get the right groceries; no one would vacuum or wipe the table properly and ants would gather, for sure. Gordana would stay at Ben's too much and Uncle George would work late and Ma would have no one to talk to or to run errands.

Also, there was a strange rash on his chest that was starting to greatly preoccupy him. He'd ask Ma about it tonight but he knew pretty much how the conversation would go:

"Honestly, Frankie, I'm sure it's just heat or something, or a tiny insect bite—definitely nothing serious. . . ." And then Frankie would lie in bed trying to believe Ma but dwelling on all the things the rash could be: scabies, ringworm, flea infestation, meningitis, dengue fever, malaria, cancer, Ebola virus . . . The list was potentially endless. . . . And then, he would have to ask Ma again the next night, and the next. And finally she would say, "Would you feel better if you asked the doctor?" and he would nod sheepishly, and Ma would feel bad that she couldn't take him but she would ask Uncle George, and Uncle George would say he couldn't till next Friday because he was up to his eyeballs and it looked exactly like a heat rash to him, anyway, so Ma would ask Gordana and Gordana would say, oh, good *God,* was he *always* going to be such an incredible *freak*?

The bus was picking up speed now, down Memorial Avenue, past his grandmother's old house, past Centennial Park, where he and Uncle George had bowled thousands of balls, past Bava's, where they'd always bought their ice creams. Those were the days, Frankie thought—when Uncle George had time to bowl two hundred balls and eat a three-scoop cookies 'n' cream afterward. He sighed again. Maybe he'd just go to the doctor by himself. Why not? He was twelve. He didn't need a child minder.

"Want some?" said Gigs, offering him half an apricot.

Frankie chewed the fruit slowly, enjoying the plump sweetness, and mentally added apricots to the ongoing grocery list in his head, which frankly—ha!—he was rather tired of having to compile on behalf of everyone else.

"You watch any *Get Smart?*" Gigs asked. *Get Smart* videos were their favorite thing just now.

"Tried to," said Frankie. "But Gordana was practically having phone sex with Ben right beside me on the couch."

"Really?" said Gigs.

"No, not really, just kissing crap. And loud."

"Nothing new."

"No."

And that was another thing: Gordana. Frankie didn't really care that his sister was habitually rude and mean to him, but he did care that she never did *a thing* around the house. All the work fell his way these days—getting the groceries, delivering stuff for Ma, picking up library books, buying birthday presents for the relatives. It was so *unfair.* And, as far as he could see, extremely unlikely to improve. Gordana'd leave home next year, he just knew it. Like Louie. She'd move in with Ben or Christa or Tamara or one of her forty-seven friends (she'd counted them)—but she'd swing back home for laundry and dinners. He sighed yet again.

"Could you *stop* that?" said Gigs. "You're just like Chris. She's always sighing and doesn't even know she's doing it. She sighs when she's eating, when she's reading, when she's looking something up in the phone book . . . the phone book especially. The minute she gets it out of the drawer, she starts this massive sighing campaign."

Gigs had finished his breakfast now. He put away his plastic containers and bottles and settled back to read his comic book. Frankie surveyed his best friend's freckled face with fondness, and envy.

Gigs *never* seemed to worry. His life was a steady, tidy progress from one activity to another. He would have a task (breakfast, say; or getting his watch fixed; or doing his trombone practice; or buying an ice cream; or finishing a math project) and he would just *do* it. He didn't think about the nutritional value of the breakfast or the ice cream (Gigs never worried about fat intake). He didn't stress about his math ability, or his chances for Boys' College next year, or his batting average, or whether blowing a sustained forte passage on the trombone might accidentally trigger a brain hemorrhage.

There were no detours or distractions, nor interruptions by any of a catalog of pressing problems. Gigs didn't worry about his household, his parents, his health, his safety, his future, the probability of earthquakes, terrorism, global warming, or McDonald's taking over the world. He was a funny guy, and a smart one—and the smartest thing about him, in Frankie's view, was that he never, ever, *ever* worried.

Frankie dreamed of having such a disposition. If only you could win a temperament like that in Lotto, or get it through mail order, or bid for it on Trade Me.

* * *

The bus came to another precisely judged stop outside the midtown terminal, where a number of the kids at Frankie and Gigs's school boarded. Cassino had a comment or a quip for everyone — except, of course, the Kearney twins, Seamus and Eugene. They'd been getting the cold shoulder from Cassino for nearly a year now — ever since they'd set fire to the seat nearest the back door.

Cassino was a kind and easygoing guy, everyone knew. He let kids eat on his bus and sing loudly and even get physical; he let people on for free if they'd mislaid their cards; he often waited for kids in case they were running late. But even Cassino had his threshold, and damage to his bus was something he neither tolerated nor forgave. Gigs and Frankie reckoned it'd be a cold day in hell before Seamus and Eugene cracked even a faint smile from Cassino. Earning Cassino's permanent wrath, Frankie thought, ranked as one of life's least bearable punishments.

"Wasim Enegue arcnarum multiplicitum et feralum?" Gigs muttered. (Eugene Kearney's zits are growing in number and size and repulsiveness.)

"Gigantum Saccum et maladits personalitonium," said Frankie. (Too much McDonald's combined with an evil personality.)

Frankie slumped in his seat as an alternative to sighing. He didn't really feel like analyzing his schoolmates in Chilun. Usually it was a great way of passing the last half of the bus ride to school, but this morning his litany of worries was causing an irretrievable gloom to settle on him, heavy as a saturated beach towel.

It was strange the way this happened. He'd noticed it before. One week he'd be bouncing along relatively happily, only a couple of minor problems bothering him. A week or two later, the problems would have burgeoned and multiplied until the list of matters to solve dominated his thoughts and none of his usual pleasures could give him a scrap of comfort.

He sank lower in the seat and frowned at the semicircle of rolled-up bus tickets describing the wide arc of the seat-back in front of them. There were hundreds, jutting like white porcupine quills from the gap between the seat leather and the aluminum frame. He and Gigs had been building the quills for four years now and it was quite a sight. It was another example of Cassino's extreme tolerance; he'd never mentioned the bus ticket stash, but he'd never interfered with the display, either.

"February the fourteenth," said Gigs suddenly. "Hot damn, it's Valentine's Day. We might get cards."

"Fat chance," said Frankie with infinite pessimism.

"Norbo B, Norbo B," whispered Gigs. This was their Chilun name for Bronwyn Baxter. Gigs was convinced that Bronwyn Baxter had her eye on Frankie.

"Shuddup," said Frankie. "I don't believe in Valentine's Day. Loada crap."

Months later, remembering that moment, Frankie would smile to himself. He liked to go back over that little exchange, drawing it out, remembering his bleak mood, enjoying the before and after. Having declared his disgust with Saint Valentine, he was just preparing to submerge himself fully in his slough of despond when the new girl got on the bus.

Months later Frankie liked very much to remember that February the fourteenth had begun badly and shown every sign of becoming a real horror, but—as the benefit of hindsight proved—it marked, ultimately, a turning point in his mood and fortune, because at 8:36 a.m., the new girl boarded Cassino's east-west school bus.

The new girl tripped up the steps in her beige Ugg boots, flashed a bus card, gave Cassino a wide smile, tossed her long, hefty dreads—*dreads!*—and strolled down to the rear of the bus, where Gigs Angelo was ruminating on the possibility of valentines and Frankie Parsons was prostrate and maudlin on the brown bench seat.

The new girl was smallish and round and had a very tanned face. She wore jeans and a bright red T-shirt, which read *You gonna? I'm gonna.* She wore gold hoop earrings, and a tiny diamond stud in her left nostril.

"Is this the dormitory, or can people actually *sit* here?" she said to the slumped Frankie. Her voice had the faintest of accents.

"I'm Sydney," she added. "Can you believe this is my fourth school in nine months? No? I'm having trouble with it myself. Want a salted licorice?" She held out a small brown paper bag, and the bangles on her hand made a brief musical rattle.

"Ta," said Frankie, raising a languid arm and digging in the bag. He looked at the black pebble candy, then put it in his mouth. It was as odd as its donor, but he quite liked it.

"You?" said Sydney, passing the bag over Frankie to Gigs, who was staring a little defiantly at her.

"No, thanks," said Gigs. "Hate that stuff."

Sydney sat down and Frankie slid up the seat until he was quite straight again. Gigs gave him a look.

"Nogis golody callistus freakano. Dispatchio presto," he said. (What colossal nerve. Have to get rid of her fast.)

"My dad sent me this stuff," said Sydney. "From Holland. You can get it here but I don't like to rain on his parade. Not a bad breakfast substitute, if you're in a hurry. Which I usually am."

"Nollis gannat negey comadonatus," said Gigs, staring straight ahead at the bus ticket quills. (Lordy, she's a talker.)

"Good *scheme*," said Sydney, pointing to the quills. "A bus installation. I like it. Urban art." She leaned into the seat, examining the quills. Then she sat back and rolled up her own ticket, correctly fashioning the point in the particular way Frankie and

Gigs had pioneered years ago. She wormed the new quill carefully into the seat gap and smiled around at Frankie.

"Nozdoreeshna!" said Gigs. (Oh, my *God*!) His voice had a distinct tone of outrage.

Frankie looked at Sydney and back at Gigs.

"Glasnostov aginwia plovik?" (Are you going to answer me, or what?)

"Is he actually speaking Russian or just being an idiot?" asked Sydney. She pulled a shuffle and earphones from her bag. Her bag, Frankie noticed, was covered in drawings and words. It looked old and well worn and loved. He looked up at the bag's owner.

"So," she said. "He's speaking Russian or something and you're completely mute. Once again, I hit the jackpot. Why is it I never end up at schools with *normal* people? Could you even tell me your name?" She bulged her eyes at Frankie. They were black eyes, with dark lashes. Her raised eyebrows were thick half-moons.

"Frankie Parsons," he said, and surprised himself by holding out his hand. He could feel Gigs stiffen beside him.

"Frankie Parsons," repeated Sydney, taking his hand. She gave him the trademark wide smile. "Sounds like a country and western singer. Or a mafia boss. Or a famous tennis player."

"Nozdoreeshna!" said Gigs again.

Frankie let go of Sydney's hand and tried a small smile. He felt suddenly and inexplicably cheerful.

"So," he said, and picked up Sydney's shuffle, surprising himself once more. "Nice machine. Wouldn't mind one of these. My brother's got one, too. Are you planning to stay very long at this school?"

* * *

"A fruitcake," was Gigs's judgment as they walked into school.

He had been heavily silent for the remainder of the bus ride, his silence louder and louder, it seemed to Frankie, the more he and Sydney had chatted. Silence was the major indicator of Gigs's fury, Frankie had found over the years. Though Gigs Fury was, in fact, a rare thing and Frankie himself had seldom earned it. Gigs reserved fury almost exclusively for his siblings. He'd been silent for more than a week a couple of years back, when Dr. Pete and Chris had announced that they were having another baby.

Frankie threw the cricket ball toward the ceiling of the locker room and caught it one-handed.

"Throw downs?" he said.

Gigs walked toward the door, cupping a hand behind him. Frankie threw.

"Let's hope she's not in our class," said Gigs, taking the ball expertly.

But of course she was. When Frankie and Gigs came into room 11, Sydney was standing beside Mr. A at the front of the classroom, surveying her surroundings with open interest, smiling broadly at kids as they came through the door.

Frankie was rather admiring. Most kids would have been restless and nervous on their first day in a new school. Most kids would have looked a little pinched and shy. Most kids would have been staring at the floor, or at a vague point in the distance, avoiding the eye of anyone in particular.

"Okay, friends and Romans," said Mr. A in his customary way, when everyone was more or less seated and the noise was subsiding. "Lend me your ears, please. Shut up and listen up. This is Sydney Vickerman. Please make her welcome. Show her the ropes. Ask her sympathetic questions. Tell her about yourselves—"

"If you can get a word in edgewise," muttered Gigs.

"Sorry, what was that, Gigs?"

"Nada," said Gigs.

"Try not to interrupt the teacher when he's in full flow, there's a good fellow. As I was saying—tell Sydney about yourselves, share your books where necessary, and your lunch if you feel so disposed . . ."

He thrust his hand toward Sydney. "*Bienvenue à salle onze,* Sydney."

"*Merci beaucoup,*" said Sydney in a faultless French accent. "*C'est bien.*" She shook his hand with vigor.

"*Très bon,*" said Mr. A, grinning. "A rival for Frankie."

"Oh, mervil yerks," said Gigs, in his ridiculous French accent. "Just what we don't need. A foreign language expert."

"You seem to be suffering from an uncontrollable urge to express yourself this morning, Gigs," said Mr. A. "Could I offer you some gaffer tape? A small gag?" Gigs looked stony.

He was no happier a few minutes later when Mr. A directed Sydney to the seat beside Frankie at the Pepys table, where Frankie sat with Gigs, Solly Napier, Esther Barry, and Vienna Gorman. It was the obvious place for a new person; there'd been a spare seat at the Pepys table since Fletcher Armstrong had left at the end of last year.

Gigs scowled, anyway. And scowled further when Mr. A assigned him to computer duty for the morning. A Gigs scowl was an arresting thing, Frankie thought. His normally cheerful, plump face creased up like a malevolent cushion; his freckles seemed to gather and darken.

Mr. A wasn't finished, either. He confirmed what he'd been threatening since last year. Their upcoming projects would *definitely* involve new working partners. Gigs banged his *Concise Oxford* on the desk in disgust.

Frankie wasn't wild about this development himself. He and Gigs always worked together. They did their best work that way. It was a fact. Frankie had done a French project with Fletcher last year and that had been all *right,* but not as good as working with Gigs. He and Gigs worked like a perfectly oiled machine, a machine powered by two different but complementary brains. They were pistols. Unrivaled. Everyone knew it. Not least, Mr. A.

"Mustn't let you wallow in your comfort zones," said Mr. A, over everyone's protests. "You won't be working with your mates when you're out there in the urban jungle. It'll be a lottery most of the time. Sometimes you'll work with people you don't even *like.* You have to be adaptable, you have to be ready for change and challenge, you have to be—"

The class let out a collective groan, knowing what was coming.

"Yes, yes, *yes,* you have to be . . . *counterintuitive!*"

Before he'd become a schoolteacher, Mr. A had been a probation officer and a prison psychologist. Until he'd burned out.

"Singe marks all over me," he'd say, holding out a hairy forearm.

"Can't you see?" He'd lift up his hair, show the weathered skin on the back of his neck.

Mr. A's hair was dead white and shoulder length, cut like a Roundhead soldier's. (That was how Uncle George had described it after he'd met Mr. A at the first parent-teacher meeting two years ago, then shown Frankie a picture of Oliver Cromwell and Frankie had seen his point.)

"Looks pretty battle-hardened, too," said Uncle George, reporting to Ma. He meant Mr. A's scar, which was the most startling thing about him. It was like stuck-on Plasticine, bleached and leathery, snaking diagonally down the left side of his face, from eye to earlobe.

There were many stories circulating at Notts School about the origin of Mr. A's scar: he'd been in a motorcycle accident; he'd fallen through a window; his wife had thrown a broken plate at him; a deranged prisoner had gone for him with a knife. . . .

"Maybe he just had cheek cancer," Gigs suggested once. (Frankie hadn't even known there was such a thing, and he'd added it to his long list of terrifyingly possible diseases.)

"The simple truth," said Mr. A. "When I was fifteen, I fell out of an apple tree and onto a nasty piece of corrugated iron, which meant thirty stitches. And a face like a recovering pirate."

Somehow, Frankie and Gigs doubted it. They favored the deranged prisoner story, though Mr. A said deranged prisoners were generally a figment of the lurid collective imagination. He talked like this a lot.

"Offenders have nothing on the preadolescent," he said to room 11 from time to time. "Take your average school—a cesspit of deviousness. You guys demand all my counterintuitive skills."

Being counterintuitive was something Mr. A had brought with him from prisons and probation service. It meant going against your immediate and natural instincts, thinking cleverly before you acted. *Acting, not reacting*—that was Mr. A's mantra. Being counterintuitive was practically his religion.

"You know, he's not a Mormon or a Catholic or a Muslim, he's a Counterintuitor," Frankie said to Gigs.

"Or a Counterintuitivist," said Gigs.

"Or a Counterintuitivationist."

"Or a—" But here they ran out of steam.

According to Mr. A, his job was to enlarge their vocabularies and teach them how to get on with people—with the whole of the rest of the world, in fact. Even the people they didn't like. *Especially* the people they didn't like. If it killed him, he said, they were all going to leave his classroom knowing some words longer than two syllables *and* how to think their way through tricky relationships.

Of course, how to sing a lot of songs from start to finish was important too, he added. Also how to write a coherent sentence, how to research history, speak another language, and throw a ball well. These things undoubtedly made for the completely rounded person, said Mr. A, but vocabulary and counterintuitiveness were the first two commandments in his classroom.

Frankie thought a spot of counterintuitiveness might come in handy just now with Gigs. What he *felt* like doing was fashioning a paper dart with "What's wrong with you, knob-shine?" written on it, and aiming it at Gigs's chest. But it would probably aggravate his mood.

Instead, he sketched a comic strip of Seamus Kearney trying unsuccessfully to spell *knob-shine* and Bronwyn Baxter trying to strangle him. A magpie dive-bombed the two of them. Underneath, he wrote *B and S: a marriage made in hell.* He folded the strip into a dart and sent it gently across the table to Gigs.

Gigs opened the dart and gave a glimmer of a smile.

Sydney giggled. "Good drawing," she said. "Do you take art as an elective?"

"Yeah," said Frankie, pleased. "What're you taking?" He watched Gigs drawing something to send back.

"Writing," said Sydney. "I'm pretty good at writing."

"Love yourself, why don't you?" said Solly, from across the table.

"Just stating the facts," said Sydney. "I'm hopeless at everything else—changed schools too often."

"How come?" said Frankie. "Your dad get transferred?"

"He lives in Holland," said Sydney. "Nah, my mother's a nomad. She gets a rash if she stays in the same place too long. But, she's promised to stay here at least a year. She's promised on my grandmother's grave. My sisters can start school and I can finish at least one project."

"Enough, Pepys!" Mr. A called from the front of the classroom. "Concentrated work for fifteen minutes, please. Usual drill—definition and sentence. Then we'll talk book projects."

Gigs's dart came wafting over to Frankie. It had FYEO in black marker on the wing. FYEO meant "for your eyes only." He opened it slowly, turning it away from Sydney.

"Hey," hissed Sydney, "you want to do this book project with me? He told me about it before class." She gestured toward Mr. A. "Sounds good. I'll write and you can do the artwork."

She beamed at him. Her eyes nearly disappeared when she smiled, Frankie noticed.

"Um," he said, scanning Gigs's message. It was a cartoon in Gigs's primitive but distinctive style—stick figures and exclamation marks with legs harassing everyone. Everyone in his cartoons had an identifying feature. For instance, the Frankie character always wore a cricket cap, the Mr. A character had a scar jutting horizontally from his face, and the Seamus Kearney character had a head shaped like a pumpkin.

There was a new character in this cartoon. A stick figure with preposterously pointy breasts and a head of writhing snake hair. A torrent of letters was tumbling from her large, open mouth, and helmeted exclamation marks were dragging her away to a police van. The Frankie stick figure was wiping sweat from his brow and muttering, "Lucky escape, lucky escape."

"Um," said Frankie, quickly crumpling the paper. Out of the corner of his eye he could see Gigs smiling.

"Um . . ." He was finding it hard to think straight.

"Spit it out," whispered Sydney loudly. "You want to or not? Be good."

What *was* good, Frankie thought, suddenly clear about something, was the way she said exactly what she wanted. It was unusual. It was refreshing. She wasn't like any girl he'd ever met before. Or any boy, come to that. She didn't seem to care what people would think. She spoke her mind, as they said in books.

"Um," he said for the fourth time.

She bulged her eyes at him as she had on the bus.

"Okay," he said, putting the balled paper in his pocket and not looking at Gigs. "Okay, but can it be about birds? I'm best at them."

"No problem," said Sydney, opening her dictionary and getting down to work.

Very busily not looking at Gigs, Frankie opened his *Concise Oxford* and stabbed the open page with his finger.

Perplexed: per·plekst, *ppl, involved in doubt and anxiety about a matter on account of its intricate character; bewildered, puzzled.*

It really was *uncanny*, Frankie thought, keeping his eyes resolutely on the tip of his pen as he copied the definition. It was downright odd how often the Word of the Day seemed to actually be about his life. He speculated about a sentence.

He was extremely perplexed by the unusual behavior of his best friend.

He tried another stab just to see what would happen.

Vexed: vekst, *ppl, distressed, grieved, annoyed, irritated . . .*

Frankie banged the dictionary shut. It was too weird.

He knew his friend was very vexed because his normally cheerful face was creased and cross-looking.

He opened the dictionary and tried a third time.

Portal: por·tal, *n, an entrance to a place, or any means of access to something.*

That was better, Frankie thought. He glanced across the table. Gigs, with head down, was scribbling.

The portal to the Tower was as high as a house and decorated with ferocious gargoyles. Ravens circled overhead. . . .

Frankie sighed. But why was life always so complicated?

"So," said Frankie, "how was your day?" He lay down beside Ma, on top of her duvet.

Ma put down her book. She was reading Crime and Punishment *by Fyodor Dostoyevsky, which Frankie happened to know was her second favorite Russian novel. Her absolute favorite was* Anna Karenina *by Leo Tolstoy. Ma had wanted to call Frankie Leo, but there was already an L in the family.*

"Pretty good," said Ma. "Eight cakes, three slices, and a new biscuit. Albanesi. White wine, olive oil, flour, and castor sugar. Strange but nice."

Frankie stared as usual at the painting hanging beside Ma's bed. It was dark and a little menacing and not at all the kind of picture Frankie would want to look at as he went to sleep, but Ma was devoted to it. A ghostly woman with long yellow hair stood, waiting, beside a four-poster bed hung with transparent draperies. The brushwork was so fine you could make out each strand of the woman's hair and the strain in her whitened knuckles.

"So," said Frankie, still looking at the painting. "We got this bird flu handout at school."

"That's good," said Ma. "Good they're distributing information in schools."

"And this house hasn't got any of the stuff we need," said Frankie. "Except what's in the earthquake kit."

"What do we need?" said Ma.

"Heaps," said Frankie. "Practically everything. Flour, tea, tinned

fruit. Surgical masks. Rice. Panadol, plastic gloves, more baked beans, medications—"

"We'll talk to Uncle G," said Ma.

Not for the first time Frankie wondered what the ghostly woman was waiting for. Or whom.

"Do you think it will happen soon?" said Frankie. "Bird flu?"

"Probably not," said Ma. "Good to be prepared, though."

The bedroom door in the painting was slightly ajar; a soft light showed in the adjoining room. Sometimes Frankie thought he could detect a shadow in the light. Maybe it was the woman's husband, or her child. Or her maid. Or a highwayman. But probably highwaymen didn't come into houses; probably they stuck to the highways.

"'Night, then," said Frankie. "You really think it won't happen soon?" he said from the doorway.

"I really think it won't happen soon," said Ma. She glanced at the clock on the bedside table. "Ten-oh-two p.m. You're so punctual, Frankie."

"Ha, ha," said Frankie.

He closed the door quietly.

TWO

Tuesday, February 28

Frankie and Gigs were climbing the Zig Zag, the eternal afternoon slog. It was hot. Crushingly hot, said Gigs. Punishingly hot, said Frankie. Mercilessly hot, said Gigs. Barbarously hot, said Frankie. Gigs matched him step for slow step around the fourth corner—thinking feverishly, Frankie could tell.

Even the ferns looked hot, Frankie thought. Kind of limp and exhausted. His feet were damp and gritty, his pack impossibly heavy.

"*Malignantly* hot," said Gigs, punching the air.

"You win," said Frankie, glad to give up. It was far too hot for adverbs.

"Shall we do Upham's?" said Gigs. Upham's was the local swimming pool—the Charles Upham Memorial Baths, to be exact. Frankie and Gigs went there as often as possible in the summer. They didn't actually swim much; they just spear-dived off the deep end for white stones, and ducked each other a lot.

When they were much younger, Louie had taught them to cannonball, but the pool attendants had threatened Louie with a life-ban for bad role-modeling and they'd had to stop. Upham's was the best way Frankie knew for cooling off, despite Louie's recent assurance that riding a motorbike down Tram Road, naked except for soaking wet jeans, was better still.

But Upham's would be unbearably crowded today, Frankie thought. And last Saturday when they'd been there, he'd had his annual unsavory collision with a Band-Aid. There was nothing more revolting in Frankie's view than freestyling your way, innocent and blissful, into the path of a used Band-Aid. In Frankie's private hierarchy of squeamish experiences, the casual caress of a stained Band-Aid was right up there with accidentally catching sight of writhing maggots in a forgotten rubbish bag. He'd had to get out of the pool immediately last Saturday and lie on his towel in the sun to recover.

And it was double bad luck having a Band-Aid collision, Frankie found. It always set him off obsessing about all the other unpalatable things that could be floating one's way in the pool: scabs, boogers, pubic hair, earwax, horrible egg-whitish strings of snot . . .

Uncle George said it was just as well Frankie hadn't been around in the old pea-soup days, before swimming pool filtration. Upham's had been called The Lido then and it had been so full of crap, it was impossible to see the bottom. Not seeing the bottom wasn't really a problem, though, Uncle George said breezily; he didn't remember minding in the least. They'd all caroused quite happily, he said, no problem, until the day someone had felt that body on the bottom. . . .

Frankie shuddered. He hated that story. The body had been a child's. That child's body had given him bad thoughts for weeks. He'd had to creep down the hall night after night and stand by Ma's side of the bed, mentally reciting cricket test statistics, just to calm down. Mostly now he managed not to think about the body, but Band-Aids could wreck things in a moment.

30 :

On the other hand, his school shirt was sticking to his back, and a sweat drip was winding down his hairline. That first dive into the deep end was a beautiful thing.

"Let's do it," he said to Gigs. "I'll see if Ma needs anything first. It's Aunties. And Louie's birthday."

"Bonga Swetso!" said Gigs, punching him on the arm.

Frankie punched him back with equal enthusiasm. Gigs had been saying "Bonga Swetso" with monotonous regularity since the Aunties' last visit. Bonga Swetso, the Aunties had been very pleased to tell Gigs, was the four-year-old Frankie's phrase for "goody." He'd made up lots of words and phrases when he was that age, the Aunties said, but Bonga Swetso had been everyone's favorite. The best by far. They couldn't think how they'd failed to tell Gigs this before.

How indeed? Frankie had thought, knowing instantly that Gigs would seize Bonga Swetso and run with it.

They stopped together at Ronald's corner and crouched down, but the dachshund wasn't there.

"Down at the river," said Gigs. They peered through the fence slats at the trim lawn and carefully pruned shrubs in Ronald's section. On extremely hot days, Ronald's naturally bad personality tipped over into real malevolence and his owners took him to the river for a dip in a vain effort to improve his mood.

"Bonga Swetso!" said Gigs, standing up. "Swim. Then we'll get an ice cream. Then I'll do some practice and come up to your place. What's Louie's cake?"

"Black Forest cherry," said Frankie. He'd put the cherries to soak in the Kirsch this morning, under Ma's watchful eye.

"With chocolate curls?" said Gigs.

"Of course."

"And we haven't tested Louie," said Gigs. "I'll bring the sphyg. That'll be everyone, then. We can start pasting everything onto the cardboard. Bonga Swetso!" He banged shut Mrs. Da Prini's letter box and smacked his hands together in satisfaction.

Gigs was in one of his bossier moods, but Frankie rather enjoyed a bossy Gigs. It was certainly infinitely preferable to the sulking version. After school on Sydney's first day, they had climbed the Zig Zag in almost complete silence. Gigs had trudged past Ronald and ignored Marmalade; Frankie had closed Mrs. Da Prini's letter box with almost furtive care.

It was the Aunties and Bonga Swetso that had saved the day. Gigs had come up with the sphygmomanometer after dinner to do the stress test. It was as if he was swathed in an invisible black cloud. He'd eaten three brandy snaps without cracking a smile. And then Frankie had fixed the sphygmomanometer cuff to Alma's hambone arm and everyone, including Gigs, had started laughing.

It was the next day, when Sydney had joined lunchtime cricket, that really sealed the deal, though. Frankie had been thinking about that with great pleasure every day for the last two weeks.

"Bonga Swetso!" he said with a laugh, as they turned the corner for the top.

Frankie opened the back door to the smell of warm honey and toasted walnuts. *Baklava.* He was expert at figuring the different cakes under construction, usually just from the smell (for which he awarded himself an A+) or sometimes from the bowls and ingredients on the bench (B+).

Ma was brushing the filo pastry sheets with melted butter, a steady painting motion. Frankie stood for a moment watching the white pastry become transparent. It looked like wet, brown paper, brittle and eminently breakable, but Ma could wield the ghostly sheets with no difficulty at all.

Frankie liked to watch Ma while she baked. She was like a practiced conjuror, her movements sure and splendid. Ma did everything in the kitchen with great calm. No matter how many cakes were in process, no matter how many different tasks needed to be completed in short order — creaming butter, toasting nuts, melting chocolate, greasing pans — she never rushed or panicked. And, as if in response to her unruffled presence, the ingredients seemed always to play their part; they almost never burned or curdled or spilled.

When Gordana baked, it was another story. Frankie believed the utensils and ingredients became instantly anxious when Gordana entered the kitchen. The beater stalled and coughed and sprayed the walls; bowls shattered inexplicably; eggs imploded; a burning odor prevailed. Gordana banged and crashed a great deal while she was baking. She slammed pans and cupboard doors. She stomped about in a cloud of flour and sugar and baking soda. She swore at biscuit mix when it stuck to her fingers. It was no wonder, Frankie thought, that her afghans and peanut cookies had a shrunken look about them. They were born frightened, and they never recovered.

He figured his own baking style was somewhere between Ma's and Gordana's. The kitchen wasn't a train wreck or anything, but he did seem to walk an agitated tightrope, darting between bowls, checking and rechecking the recipe nervously, remembering things at the last minute. These days, he could do a decent carrot cake and Anzac biscuits, but only if all the planets were in alignment.

Frankie pinched a spoonful of chopped walnuts from one of the china bowls lined up in front of Ma.

She moved the bowl away from him. "School okay?" She kissed his cheek.

"Not bad," said Frankie. "Started new book project. New partners. New girl and me. New cricket practice time." He usually gave Ma the day in shorthand. It was simpler.

"Sydney, the new girl?"

"And her sisters are called Galway and Calcutta. Can you believe that? What's for dinner?" There was a competing savory smell in the kitchen but he couldn't pin it down.

"Chicken pie," said Ma. She sprinkled walnuts on the filo. "Galway and Calcutta!"

"They were born there," said Frankie. "Like Sydney was born in Sydney. Can we have mashed potatoes? Louie's favorite. And he prefers canned peas." Conveniently, this was also what Frankie preferred with his chicken pie.

He began assembling the ingredients for a massive banana smoothie and thought back yet again to Wednesday a fortnight ago. Just now, it was his favorite default memory.

"Your mate's in a pet," Sydney had said at lunchtime. She was following Frankie to the canteen, though he hadn't asked her.

"A pet?" said Frankie.

"A big fat sulk," said Sydney. She bought a bagel with cream cheese and jam and waited while Frankie got an apple juice. "He doesn't like me," she said. Since this was obviously true, Frankie said nothing. The puzzle was *why*. Sydney was certainly different, but that was a good thing, surely? Apart from Vienna, who Frankie had known forever because her father was a friend of Uncle George's, and maybe Renee, the other newish girl who seemed passable, the rest of the girls in the class, if not the entire school, were exceptionally silly.

They were always feuding or having hysterics about project deadlines. Or they were trying to match each other up with different boys in Year Eight. Frankie had spent weeks last year worrying about what to do every time a girl rang him up. He hadn't wanted to be rude, but he also strenuously had not wanted to go to the movies or The Mall with them. That was the other thing: all the girls in his class ever did was go to The Mall. He and Gigs had had many a conversation about the crucifying boringness of The Mall and the complete tedium of having to go there with any of the girls from their class. They'd rather score an own goal, they decided, than go to The Mall.

Frankie poured milk into the blender and broke two eggs into the liquid from a great height. He enjoyed the wet sucking sound that it produced. He peeled two bananas, sliced them carefully down the middle, and chopped them into thirds.

Sydney, he thought, was very much *not* a Mall girl. For a start, she wore very un-Mall-like clothes. Plus, her hair was dreaded and this had already caused a minor sensation in room 11. Most of the girls in room 11 stuck to a narrow range of hairstyles, strictly no dreads. Apparently there was a rule somewhere — probably in Bronwyn Baxter's head — which decreed a girl couldn't get dreads till she was in high school.

Sydney seemed oblivious to rules of the Bronwyn Baxter sort. She marched to a different drum, as Uncle George liked to say about people. She was an independent operator (another Uncle George-ism). Independent operations, Sydney-style, apparently meant making friends with a boy in the class rather than all the other girls. This really was very interesting, Frankie thought. He'd never seen it before. When a new girl arrived, she was usually swallowed up by the phalanx of room 11 girls, just as a new boy was somehow magnetically pulled toward the cricket game at lunchtime, or the clusters of other boys wandering around the grounds, chucking balls or wrestling one another to the ground.

Not Sydney. She'd ignored most of the girls and they'd ignored her right back. At lunchtime on her second day she'd followed Frankie over to the cricket pitch. He really didn't know how to tell her that no *girl* ever played cricket at lunchtime; it was strictly boy territory. But, no problem. Gigs did that for him, anyway.

"I can bowl, you know," said Sydney.

"Yeah," said Gigs derisively. He was tossing the ball high, over and over, and catching it with increasingly wristy flourish. Frankie felt small prickles of tension starting on his arms.

"I was strike bowler for my school team in Australia," said Sydney.

"You lived in Australia?" said Frankie, blushing at the question as soon as he'd uttered it, since she'd just said so. But diversionary tactics seemed necessary.

"Girls can't bowl," said Gigs. "They've got stupid elbows." Frankie and Gigs had privately concluded this some time ago, but Frankie wished now it wasn't so.

"My sister can bowl," said David Robinson. "And she's fast." Frankie and Gigs had also privately admitted that David Robinson's sister, Julie, was the exception to the otherwise iron-clad girls-can't-bowl law. But Gigs rightly said this was because Julie Robinson was practically a man; she was big and fierce and had a six-pack where other girls had breasts.

"I'm fast, too," said Sydney, at which moment she darted sideways and upward and expertly intercepted Gigs's ball on its downward trajectory. She ran to the other end of the pitch and proceeded to send down a ball of excellent line and length. Seventy ks, Frankie reckoned, giving it a practiced assessment.

"Boy!" he said, stealing a look at Gigs.

Frankie particularly enjoyed reliving that ball of Sydney's. He dug deep now into the vanilla ice cream and added two scoops to the blender. He considered the height of the mixture for a moment, then added a third scoop.

"Hey!" said Ma.

"It's a three-scoop kind of day," said Frankie. He stabbed the blender button and watched the banana, milk, eggs, and ice cream bump and bounce and transform themselves into his smoothie.

Gigs certainly had his blind spots, Frankie thought—his little brothers and sister being three of them. But the good thing about him was his basically fair-minded nature. He always gave skill its due. And cricket skill was particularly high on Gigs's priority list for a perfect human being.

After Sydney had bowled that ball and David Robinson had fielded it and the guys had gathered around, all grinning, Sydney had stood, hands on hips, bulging her eyes at Gigs, and Gigs had stared back and Frankie had held his breath for what seemed an entire historic era.

"Not bad," said Gigs, finally. "Can you bat, too?"

Frankie had felt like bursting into song.

Right now, he decided to drink straight from the blender. No point in making extra dishes. He took two straws from the cupboard and headed for the stairs.

"We're going to Upham's. I can get anything you need," he called to Ma.

"More honey. And lemons. I need to do the mint and honey cake later tonight." Ma often baked late. It was an occupational hazard, she said. If there were early-morning orders, late-night baking was unavoidable. She put the cakes in the oven and went to bed with the timer. She said it was like getting up to feed a new baby.

"And cream for Louie's cake!" she called.

"Make a list!" Frankie shouted. After-school shopping always fell to him. Gordana was never around to do errands. She was either at work or the gym. Apparently, earning money or getting fit relieved you of all household tasks. Frankie wondered if he should get a paper route. Or take up boxing.

The smoothie was very good. Frankie sat on his bed with the blender balanced on his raised knees and sucked hard. It was enjoyable being disgusting. When he was full, he was going to lie down and listen to some music, an even more disgusting undertaking because, apparently, you weren't supposed to lie down on a full stomach. Too bad.

Then he'd go to Upham's with Gigs, then the supermarket. He'd go to Pak'nSave because it was nearest to Upham's, even though, as far as he knew, Pak'nSave still had a ban on Louie for shoplifting in Year Ten. Louie's name was somewhere on a list of Bad Boys, and for years, Frankie had boycotted Pak'nSave out of brotherly loyalty — also a lurking fear that the checkout girls had him marked as a potential delinquent. Louie had eaten a piece of Belgian slice from the in-store deli while he was pushing the trolley around the aisles, and technically this was stealing.

"Damn right, it's stealing," Uncle George had repeated every few minutes to Louie. The school counselor had given Uncle George strict instructions not to minimize the eating of in-store Belgian slice in the supermarket aisles. Frankie had heard Uncle George explaining it to Ma. Ma had been upset with Louie, too, but mostly, it seemed to Frankie, for eating supermarket Belgian slice when it was so inferior to her own. Louie had sworn black and blue he'd just forgotten to pay, but Frankie doubted it. Personally, he'd always thought it was Louie's cunning way of permanently avoiding shopping duty.

That was four years ago. Louie was nineteen now — today! — and a responsible citizen, apparently. He worked for De Souza's Document Destruction, collecting bins of print material for shredding. It was the perfect job for Louie. He got to drive around the city in a white truck with a car phone and a CD player; he got to take his beagle, Ray Davies, with him; he got to chat up dozens of girls in dozens of offices.

Louie was a big fan of girls. Once Louie had been like Gigs, devoted to soccer and cricket statistics, and roundly contemptuous of all females and female pursuits. Then suddenly, in Year Ten, seemingly overnight in Frankie's memory, he'd begun talking to girls on the phone for whole evenings at a time. Shortly after that, he'd started going out with Honey Johnson. Honey Johnson was the Bronwyn Baxter of Louie's year. Her name really was Honey, a fact Frankie had always been rather fond of; she was a know-it-all with a pert blond ponytail and surf shop clothes, and she was very pretty. An alpha girl, Uncle George had said, then sighed. Everyone had his Honey Johnson moment, said Uncle George, and there was no going back after that.

A thought struck Frankie with sudden force. He slid off his bed and changed into his swim trunks. Last week, Gigs had asked Bronwyn Baxter to be his book project partner. Frankie had experienced a moment of terrible disorientation when Gigs had done this. If there was one immutable fact in their lives, it was that Bronwyn Baxter was sillier than a headless gnu. So they *had* to choose new partners, but there were plenty of other people Gigs would have been happy to work with. Solly, for example. Or David Robinson; he was a good guy. Or Vienna. She was fun, even if Gigs didn't have any time for girls.

But perhaps he did have time for girls now and Frankie hadn't noticed. Perhaps this was his Honey Johnson moment. Could that be possible? Frankie walked up the stairs slowly and opened the hall cupboard. He stared into it, briefly unseeing. Gigs wouldn't be thirteen until June. Surely he wasn't old enough to have a Honey Johnson moment? But then, Seamus Kearney must have had his when he was about five and a half. As long as

Frankie could remember he'd been going on about girls in what Mr. A liked to call "a malodorous way."

Frankie took the shopping bag from the hall cupboard. It was sturdy burlap with a wide reinforced strap that made it perfect for hefting groceries. Gordana had made the bag years ago. She'd dyed it purple and embroidered Ma's name on it, though of course Ma never took it anywhere. Frankie had admired the bag enormously at the time. He thought Gordana's embroidered rolling pin and eggbeater were quite brilliant. He thought the way she'd decorated the letters of Ma's name— F R A N C I E —with wooden spoons and measuring cups and cookie cutters was especially nifty.

It was a pity Gordana didn't do that sort of thing anymore, Frankie thought. She'd done a lot of sewing and artwork back then. She'd been full of good ideas. She'd planned to be a clothes designer. Frankie didn't know what Gordana was planning these days. Probably a job in reception; she spent enough time on the phone.

Gigs was turning in the gate, chewing his way down a Killer Python. Frankie was halfway down the path when Ma called out to him from the front door.

"One more thing!" she said. "Some oranges! For zest!" Frankie turned and waved to show he'd heard. Ma stood well back from the open door, her face in the shadow.

"Hey, Francie!" Gigs called.

"Hey, Gigs!" came Ma's voice. "You coming back for cake?"

"Definitely!"

Frankie checked the letter box. He'd forgotten to do it on the way in from school. The mail was still there. Gigs handed him the Killer Python and he bit off the blue section. That was their arrangement. Frankie always ate the blue and green sections if it was Gigs's Python; they reversed the practice if Frankie had bought the Python. Neither of them much liked the blue and green flavors, but they did not like to waste a particle of any candy. Frankie couldn't remember the two of them ever having discussed this; they'd just always done it. There was a lot you didn't need to discuss with Gigs.

"First one to the library," said Gigs, punching him on the arm. But Frankie could hit *presto* from a standing start and he pulled ahead of Gigs immediately. Gigs always proposed their races, though he never won any. Frankie was the runner, they both knew that. Just as Gigs was the better batsman.

Frankie pushed through the sticky westerly heat and down the hill, the dust pricking his nose, the supermarket bag flapping like a hefty wing. Behind him Gigs did his bloodcurdling downhill holler.

He didn't seem like a guy who'd had his Honey Johnson moment. Frankie really hoped not. He didn't want anything to change.

Frankie gave Louie a Kinks LP for his birthday. Louie had a large vinyl collection at his flat, and an ancient turntable; Uncle George had given it to him as a leaving home gift. Uncle George said that all self-respecting lovers of rock music still owned a turntable, despite the digital revolution. Uncle George's own turntable was, apparently, a contemporary work of art, a modular triumph, sleek high-end industrial design, unsurpassed during the hi-fi revolution.

"So how come it only plays crap music?" Gordana asked. Gordana was no fan of Uncle George and Louie's music, and she especially hated their Wall of Sound evenings. These were kind of earsplitting tournaments, with LPs as weapons. Uncle George played something loud (say, an old Black Sabbath record) and Louie responded with something *very* loud (say, a pre-digital Metallica album); then Uncle George played something even louder (King Crimson) and Louie, etc., etc.

Sometimes Gordana began actually screaming at this point, an enraged ascending scale that climbed the stairs, too, and penetrated the Wall of Sound. Uncle George and Louie often had bets as to how quickly they could force a Gordana protest.

"One and a half sides!" Louie would say. "You win, old man."

"Two whole octaves," Uncle George would say. "And rising. What a vocal range. That girl should go on the stage."

Once, Gordana had burst into the living room with Louie's old Super Soaker and begun spraying Uncle George and Louie, both of them sprawling on the couches but doing the horizontal semi-dance spasms that always accompanied their listening.

Frankie had been sunk deep in the fluorescent green beanbag with Ray Davies—a puppy at the time—asleep in his lap. Ray Davies always slept through Wall of Sound evenings, leaving Frankie a quiet audience of one. Frankie loved watching Uncle George and Louie, wildly competitive, gesticulating, singing, shouting out over the cacophony miscellaneous facts about bands that they both already knew. He loved the music, too—the guitar pyrotechnics, the chord layers, the buzz-saw sound of the feedback. He loved the opulent cushioning of the beanbag, the heat of Ray Davies's bony bundled-up form, the sweet dusty smell of his coat combined with the cake aromas from the kitchen. He loved the *predictability* of it all, even Gordana's banshee outbursts.

The Super Soaker attack hadn't been quite so predictable, of course, and that evening had gotten a little out of hand—Ray Davies had woken up in fright and agitatedly eaten a book. Louie had howled, enraged, and slipped on the wet floor when rising to go after Gordana. Uncle George stood, a hulking human canopy over the turntable and LPs, stretching out his jersey, trying to protect his treasures from the water.

"Stop it, you lunatic child!" he'd yelled at Gordana. "Stop it! Francie! Stop the kid. She's gone insane!"

There was no insanity tonight, Louie's birthday — if you didn't count the Aunties, who always had a distinct aura of the wacky about them. Louie played his Kinks record — not loudly — and told them all (again) about the real Ray Davies suing the Doors for stealing a Kinks song, and winning.

Louie was a big fan of suing. "We should sue!" had been his refrain for years — when his eleventh-birthday roller blades broke at his party; when the fish and chip order was one fish short; when a business proposal of Uncle G's was undercut by a competing client; when the washing machine malfunctioned; when bread went moldy. In Year Ten he'd wanted to sue his French teacher, Mr. Beaumarchais, for being unintelligible.

Next to thinking about suing, Louie's favorite pastime was dreaming up ways to make money. At the moment, he was buying and selling secondhand sneakers on the Internet. Last year, he'd designed badges and sold them at the River Market on Saturdays. The badges bore skulls and machine guns and filthy sayings, and they sold like hotcakes. Louie had wanted Gordana to design a line for girls, but Gordana said she'd rather be voluntarily bald and have false teeth than ever be in business with Louie.

The Aunties, on the other hand, loved Louie's business schemes.

"What's new in the world of commerce?" said Alma now. She was leaning back on the couch, resting a plate of Black Forest cherry cake on her vast bosom.

"Window cleaning," said Louie. "Elvis wants to sell his business. You wanna lend me five K?"

"Could do," said Alma, tipping the cake plate toward her mouth. Frankie wondered if Alma was going to *drink* the cake. It was her third piece. Gigs was on his third, too. The rest of them lay around in various post-dinner positions, very full, defeated by Ma's cooking.

"When would you have time for window cleaning?" said Gordana. "You already work all day Saturday."

"*I* won't be doing the windows," said Louie. He was standing beside the stereo, preparing to flip the record. "The secret to making money is getting *other* people to work for you. . . ."

"Oh, yeah, I forgot," said Gordana. "That's why you subcontracted Ma's cakes to the Watson boys."

"Ha, ha," said Louie.

"No bickering, please," said Ma.

"Let's *not* rake up the unsavory past," said Uncle George.

"Ooooh, the Watson boys' debacle," said Nellie. "That really wasn't your finest moment, Louie."

Louie let the stylus down gently on the other side of *The Kinks: 18 Original Golden Greats* and held his arm high, waiting one, two, three, four seconds and then giving the downbeat for the first guitar chords of "Lola." They all laughed. You had to give it to Louie, Frankie thought. He was very funny. Even his disasters were funny.

Take the Watson boys' debacle, as Nellie styled it. Louie had convinced Ma that he could organize the delivery of her cakes to her various clients around the city. He had his van! He could do it cheaper than her current courier service! He was reliable and efficient!

You really couldn't argue with that, Ma said later. But it paid to remember that Louie's vision nearly always outstretched his capacity to realize it. It was true Ma paid him a good rate. But, privately, Louie calculated he could make even more if he subcontracted the cake delivery and took a second job. Subcontracting to the Watson boys was, he reckoned, his master stroke. The Watson boys were gearheads who would work for small potatoes as long as they could drive a car, any car, any old beater with four wheels.

So, Louie packed Ma's cakes in the van, drove around to the Watsons, gave them the list of deliveries, then had them drop him at Vander's Deli, where he made peanut sauce, hummus, taramasalata, and various other dips for three hours. (He'd learned these all from Ma; Louie was an excellent cook.) The Watsons picked him up after they'd had a hard-and-fast out the back of the airport. At the end of a working day, Louie had a wage and a half.

Of course, Louie never told Ma about this happy arrangement, because the Watsons were famous idiots who'd been fired from every after-school job in the suburb and couldn't be relied on to deliver a note to the teacher, let alone a dozen exotic — and expensive — cakes to restaurants and cafés around town. It wasn't until the Summit Restaurant had phoned Ma to inquire after their Dunkel Mandeltorte that Louie got caught.

The Dunkel Mandeltorte was no longer recognizable; it was completely crushed along with two Sacher tortes, a three-layer lemon ricotta, a vegan chocolate cake, a hummingbird cake, four boxes of petits fours, and two trays of baklava. The great sticky mess was down a steep gully in Mount Pleasant, which was where Zevon Watson had plunged the van after misjudging a sharp bend.

Miraculously the Watson boys were unharmed, but Louie's van was a write-off and Louie himself was grounded for a month. For sheer *greediness,* Uncle George said.

"What about my sheer *enterprise?*" Louie had shouted.

"Avarice!" Uncle George shouted back.

"Don't bicker," Ma had begun.

"This isn't bickering," Uncle George yelled. "It's *war!*"

Frankie had looked up *avarice* in the dictionary: *an unreasonably strong desire to obtain and keep money.* Louie certainly had a strong desire for money, but Frankie couldn't decide if it was unreasonable.

"The best way to make money *is* to get other people to work for you," said Teen now. Teen had owned a lot of shops in her time and was moderately rich.

"But the *funnest* way to make money is gambling," said Alma firmly. "And I have unmarked bills burning a hole in my pocket." She heaved herself off the couch. "C'mon, Gordana. I haven't taken money off you in months."

"Homework," said Gordana. "Big assignment. Art History. Due Friday." She stayed right where she was, hunched over a magnifying mirror and plucking her eyebrows. Frankie rolled his eyes at Gigs. He hadn't seen Gordana near a textbook in the last year. Gigs's theory was that Gordana didn't actually go to school, though she walked down the hill every day in her St. Agatha's uniform. He reckoned she changed at the library, then went off to a secret job. Frankie and Gigs had spent much satisfactory time speculating about Gordana's possible other life.

"I'm in the kitchen," said Ma.

"I'll help," said Nellie. "I'll grate and chop."

"Frankie? Gigs?" said Alma. "You and me against George and Louie and Teen."

"Bonga Swetso!" said Gigs, ducking away from Frankie's punch. It *was* best playing with Alma, Frankie agreed; she was practically unbeatable. Louie and Uncle George were sharps, too, and Gigs held his own. Frankie was the liability, if the truth be told. He had a tendency to lose focus, his mind wandered, and sometimes he forgot what was trumps.

Alma had taken Frankie aside one Tuesday evening when he

was nine years old. They had been playing four-handed euchre and Frankie had been quietly worrying about a small spider colony in the right top corner of his bedroom, above the closet; he was certain they were white-tails. He'd read in the paper about a North Island man whose hand had become gangrenous after a white-tail bite he'd sustained *while sleeping.* It was still unclear, apparently, whether the gangrenous hand would have to be amputated. Frankie was thinking so hard about the awfulness of a one-handed life that he played a two of spades on a heart lead, thinking that spades was trumps.

"Frankie," Alma had said solemnly. They stood in the hallway, her arm around his shoulders, heavy as a slumped body. "You know I don't dispense advice. It's not my style. Everyone must work the world out for himself, I say. And, really, I don't have any advice to give. I don't have a store of maxims or shibboleths—"

"What's a shibboleth?" Frankie said.

"Never mind," said Alma. "That is, I haven't *until this moment* ever had a foolproof piece of advice to offer anyone. But it's come to me tonight—a Rule to Live By, an Unshakeable Truth— Frankie." Alma had leaned into Frankie. He smelled her cheroot and face powder and Knight's Castile scent. He watched the soft froggy swelling of her triple chin. "Frankie, my darling boy, *always remember what is trumps.*

"There you are," said Alma, straightening up, pulling the voluminous red cardigan over her swollen middle. "That is it. My Benedictine Rule. All you need for navigating life's tortuous road. Remember what trumps is! Okay? Good boy." She'd bent over and planted a kiss on his cheek and pushed him back through the door, to the card table.

Frankie had done his best when playing cards ever since, but it wasn't easy. It depended so much on his catalog of preoccupations. And the sad truth was, he really didn't care enough about cards, trumps or otherwise. He just didn't care about winning. Gigs and Louie loved to win; they especially loved trying to beat Alma. They sat upright; they arranged their cards swiftly; they concentrated all their wits on the progress of play.

Whereas Frankie found his attention fatally wandering to other matters. Tonight his thoughts were diving backward through the day, back to the morning at school, to the book project, which he was greatly enjoying. To Sydney's suggestion that she come around to his house to work on the project, which he'd found alarming. To Mr. A's color-coded handouts on camp, which were now burning a hole in his backpack. To the whole problem of camp, now less than a month away. To the fact that Ma hadn't even collected the *mail* once in the last fortnight —

"Frankie?" said Louie. "Your bid."

And see? Already he'd failed to hear what everyone had bid in the first round. He thought quickly. It was five hundred. Alma always bid high in five hundred. So did Louie and Uncle George. They never liked to give away the lead.

"Pass," said Frankie. He nearly always passed. He was drearily cautious.

"I go *eight* diamonds!" said Gigs. He beamed around the table.

"Living dangerously, Gigs, my man," said Uncle George, knocking the table to signify a pass.

"In his dreams," said Gordana. She had finished plucking and was leaning on Uncle George now, scanning his cards. Ray Davies nudged hopefully at her heels. He wanted to play rough-and-tumble; he hadn't had as much dinner as everyone else.

"What's trumps?" asked Gordana.

"Ask Frankie," said Louie.

"Diamonds," said Frankie virtuously.

"Good boy," said Teen.

Gordana moved on to Louie. "Which one's the left bower and tell me again *why* it's called the left bower?"

"Bugger off!" said Louie, batting her with his cards.

"Keep your hair on," said Gordana. She flicked his head with her hand and Ray Davies began yapping with protective fierceness.

"Come here, boyo," said Louie, playing a card. He leaned back in his chair and let Ray Davies up onto his lap. Ray Davies rested his nose on the table and stared longingly at the remains of the Black Forest cherry cake.

"You know how I feel about canines at card games," said Alma. "Mine, I believe." She swept the cards in, led her next card, and signaled Gordana to pour a whiskey, all in one fluid movement.

"Damn," said Gigs, frowning.

"Oh, good *God,* Angelo, will you ever learn?" said Gordana, slopping the whiskey as she poured it into Uncle George's glass.

"*Watch* it!" growled Uncle George.

"Good *God,*" said Gordana, bringing her face down to Uncle George's. "Your nose needs a serious plucking. How could you let it get this bad?"

"Go *away!*" yelled Uncle George, Louie, and Alma all at the same time.

The phone rang.

"I'LL GET IT!" said Gordana. She skidded across the floor, in her socks, like a boisterous ice dancer. Ray Davies leaped off Louie's lap, anticipating a bit of action.

"Frankie?" said Teen. She nodded at the table. Frankie looked at the played cards and back at his own hand. He couldn't remember if all the clubs had been played. He leaned over to Gigs.

"No table talk!" said Uncle George.

"Good *God!*" said Gordana, doing a hefty glissade back to the table with the phone. Ray Davies clattered in her wake.

"This is really *not* the way I like to play," said Alma, taking a big gulp of whiskey.

"Pffffphone for Pffffphrankie," said Gordana, loudly. "Some tottie with a deep voice."

"Grabotsky frigintalius, Yendysalia!" said Gigs, waggling his eyebrows.

Frankie felt his face go very hot.

"The rest are mine, I rather think," said Alma, putting down a splayed hand.

"Are you going to take it, or what?" demanded Gordana.

"Sanquito definatus miribilius deswenko," said Gigs.

"Has my little brother got a girlfren?" said Louie, shuffling the deck.

Frankie pushed back his chair and grabbed the phone from Gordana.

"Leave the poor lad alone," said Teen. "More cake, anyone?"

"Gordana, take his hand," ordered Alma. "Let's get this game *going,* for heaven's sake."

"Seriously, has he?" said Louie.

"Don't be ridiculous," said Gordana, thumping down in Frankie's chair. "He hasn't even got underarm hair."

Frankie turned his back, hating them all. He stood in the recess between the bookcase and the television, staring vacantly at the cover of the book on the end of the shelf, *Animal Farm*.

"Hello," he said.

Behind him, the card game seemed to have gone rather quiet.

"It's Sydney!" said the phone.

50 :

"Hi," said Frankie with great nonchalance. He pulled *Animal Farm* off the bookcase and sniffed it absently. Uncle George had read him *Animal Farm* during the winter he was nine. He could remember it so clearly; the smell of the book brought it all back — Uncle George's bass voice, the soft brush of the flannelette sheet on his cheek, the dawning realization that Boxer was going to die, his own fingers picking anxiously at the stitching on his Buzz Lightyear duvet.

"Sounds like a circus at your house."

"It's my brother's birthday."

"The one with the beagle?"

"Seven hearts!" said Teen.

"Eight spades!" said Uncle George.

"Don't be ridiculous," said Gordana. "You can't do *eight* spades. I've got about five."

"Yeah," said Frankie.

"So," said Sydney. "About tomorrow. I can come. My mother says it's okay, but I have to be home before it's dark. So, shall I just come home on the bus with you? I've already got the story plan. You'll really like it."

Frankie felt suddenly weak.

". . . Vickerman," he heard Gigs say. What a traitorous weasel.

"Tomorrow," said Frankie, stalling.

"Yeah, Wednesday," said Sydney. "Thursday's no good because I have to look after the little ones while my mother's reading to the blind."

"The blind," said Frankie dumbly. He had a sudden and most absurd vision of a woman sitting in front of a blind — a Venetian blind — reading aloud from a book.

" . . . opening our bowling," Gigs was saying.

"Is she cute?" said Louie.

"No," said Gigs. "But she's even faster than David Robinson's sister." That settled one thing, then—Gigs was certainly not having his Honey Johnson moment. A small part of Frankie's brain registered mild intrigue at his ability to hear and think and feel about five things at once, even in the middle of great stress.

"Yeah, *the blind,* you egg," Sydney said. "People who can't *see.*"

"See," repeated Frankie. He seemed to have turned into a witless echo machine. He put down *Animal Farm* and began fiddling with the latch on the window beside the bookcase. He could see the Fat Controller outside on the garden bench, poised and still, watching the house balefully. The Fat Controller was allergic to Ray Davies and had to repair to the garden whenever Louie came around.

"Yes, *see!*" said Sydney.

". . . changes schools heaps," said Gigs. "And *countries.* Probably won't be on the team next summer, so we may as well go for it."

"See, see" said Frankie. "Si, si." He wanted to laugh hysterically, relieved at his sudden genius, but he leaned out the window instead, lapping up the cooler evening air. "Si, si, yes, yes. Tomorrow's okay. Hey, what's the time?"

"Forty-five past eight," said Sydney. He'd noticed she always said the time this way. "Why?"

"Hey, Frankie, don't fall out the window," called Louie.

"Hey, Frankie, don't fall in love," sang Gordana.

They all laughed like idiots.

Oh, bite me, thought Frankie. He decided to throw all caution to the winds.

"It's not even dark yet," said Frankie. "You can stay for dinner, too, if you want. My ma's a mean cook."

* * *

"Are you asleep yet?" whispered Frankie, walking around to Ma's side of the bed.

The light was still on, but Ma's eyes were closed and the book had fallen out of her hands. She sometimes fell asleep like that. Uncle George would put her book away and turn off the light when he came to bed.

"Nearly," said Ma, keeping her eyes closed. "How're you doing?"

"Fine," said Frankie, sitting on the chair beside the bed. He picked up Ma's book and examined it. Eugene Onegin *by Pushkin. Another Russian. Ma had a thing for the Russians. Uncle George said if she ever met anyone called Vladimir, she'd be off.*

"You right?" said Ma. She opened her eyes.

"Yeah," said Frankie. He turned to the last page of Eugene Onegin *and read the final lines.* Fate has taken so much: good friends who've not remained at life's great feast, who have not drained their cups . . .

"But," said Frankie. He kept reading. . . . Who have by now forsaken life's narrative . . . "I was wondering . . . how long does food poisoning take?"

"Frankie," said Ma. "Why would you have food poisoning?"

"I think my chicken sandwich was past the use-by date. I'm pretty sure it was off." As you have seen me leave my cherished friend . . .

"When did you eat it?" said Ma. She closed her eyes again.

"This morning."

"What's the time now?"

"Ten p.m., of course," said Frankie, and they both laughed.

"You're fine," said Ma. "Food poisoning only takes eight hours."

"You sure?" said Frankie.

"Yes," said Ma.

"Completely *sure?*" said Frankie

"Promise," said Ma.

"Bonga Swetso," said Frankie. "'Night."

THREE

Tuesday, March 14

It was two weeks since Sydney had first come over to Frankie's house, and now they were walking casually down the hill to the village, as if it were a regular occurrence. It practically *was* a regular occurrence. Three times in the last week they'd taken a walk down the hill for one reason or another — to the library for Ma, to the dairy for chocolate raisins, to Upham's to cool off.

They were taking it slowly today and playing Knob-Shine as they went, tossing the cricket ball back and forth, trying to catch each other out. Frankie was already a KNO but Sydney hadn't dropped the ball once. She was a pistol with that ball.

Knob-Shine was a Gigs invention (it was a variation on PIG and DONKEY, which they'd learned in Year Two; now they were older, Gigs said, there was more incentive to win if you were going to end up a knob-shine). Gigs had introduced Knob-Shine to Sydney the second time she'd come over to Frankie's, and Frankie had noted this moment for the milestone it was. Gigs's acceptance of Sydney was complete now. Frankie thought he could probably let Sydney in on Chilun. She'd pick it up in a flash, for sure.

Gigs had band practice but would meet up with them soon. It was the final day at Upham's before it closed for the winter. Usually the pool was open much later and Frankie and Gigs did their spear-diving amid autumn leaves falling steadily from the elms and sycamores around the pool complex. But this year, Upham's was closing early, for refurbishment. The Council was building new changing sheds and sinking a pool for the over sixty-fives.

(The Aunties were very pleased about this development; they didn't like the aqua-aerobics group at their local pool. Frankie had never seen the Aunties in their bathing suits and flotation belts, but he could only imagine it was an alarming sight since he *had* seen the actual bathing suits. He planned to keep on never catching that sight for the rest of his life, which would mean giving Upham's a wide berth at least one day a week next summer.)

The early closing of Upham's made it seem as if summer had been brought to an abrupt and premature close. Frankie experienced a twinge of pre-winter melancholy. But it was only a twinge, because the weather was still so balmy. True, the maples were on the turn, from green to red, which, according to Uncle George, marked the end of the golden weather and the beginning of winter Sturm und Drang. (Uncle George hated winter. It made him cabin-feverish and itchy and more unpredictable than usual. Frankie had looked up *Sturm und Drang* in the dictionary, which said it is *a state of violent emotional upheaval.* As usual, Uncle George was exaggerating.)

The days were shorter, too, and the mornings cooler, and the last cricket game of the season was only two weeks away. Normally Frankie would have felt great regret about it all, even as he felt a competing surge of optimism, knowing soccer was about to begin. But this year everything seemed subtly different.

It was Sydney, he was sure. It was somehow difficult to

feel melancholy around Sydney—even with a vast list of worries, including the intractable problem of camp, and strangely, Frankie didn't feel his usual excitement about soccer. He didn't *think* he was having his Honey Johnson moment, but there was something about Sydney, nevertheless. He wasn't sure how to describe it. She was lit up, humming, maybe—not literally humming, of course, just seeming to have a hum about her. It was as if she were wired, electrically charged. Frankie felt extra alert when he was with her, as if he were passing through some rogue force field. She certainly *alarmed* him occasionally; he never quite knew what she would say or do next.

"Question," said Sydney. And here, in fact, was a perfect example. "Question" was a typical Sydney opening salvo, a shot over the bow, as Uncle G would say—*and* promising choppy waters ahead.

Sydney was an insatiable questioner; a steady stream issued from her mouth the entire time Frankie was with her. She had a bottomless bag of queries about everything, and everyone—Frankie, Gigs, Ma, Uncle George, the cat, the dog, the people next door . . . She was *indecently* curious. She seemed quite unrestrained in the way other people were, by delicacy or a sense of personal privacy, or the idea that it was perhaps none of her business. Apparently most things were her business.

You never knew what was coming. Frankie found it strangely exhilarating and sometimes terrifying. Any day now, any *moment* now, he just knew, Sydney was going to ask a couple of questions he really wouldn't want to answer, but he couldn't for the life of him think how to avoid this looming occasion.

"What?" said Frankie. He threw the ball at her, very fast, a feeble attempt at distraction. She caught it skillfully and returned it just as fast.

"K-N-O-*B*," said Sydney. "How come Gigs doesn't like his brothers and sister?"

An easy one.

"They're noisy. They're messy. They get in his way. They take his things. And they take all Chris's attention. It was much better before they came. He says."

"But he likes his stepmother?" said Sydney.

"Of course," said Frankie. He threw the ball trickily from behind his back.

"Not of course," said Sydney, fluffing the catch.

"A*ha*! *K!*" Frankie permitted himself a small hop of triumph. He retrieved the ball from the gutter.

"I didn't like my stepfather," said Sydney. "I *despised* him. He was a big fat weasel. It was Christmas in Paris when we left him. But I like my sisters. Why do you call your father Uncle George?"

See. That was her style. She lobbed tougher questions hard on the heels of a dolly. It was exactly like her bowling.

"He's always been called that," said Frankie. "When he was born, he was already an uncle, so they called him Uncle George. The rest of his family is much older. Half of his nieces and nephews are older than him. One of them is *retired*."

"I thought he mustn't be your father," said Sydney.

That was perfectly understandable, Frankie conceded privately, since, once upon a time, he had thought precisely the same thing.

It was after he'd been at school awhile, a time when his family began to appear unsettlingly different from other kids' families. The food they ate, for instance. Normal people, Solly Napier instructed him, had quite different things in their lunch boxes; normal people ate dinner earlier; normal people didn't have carpet in their dining rooms; normal people *always* drank milk with their dinner.

It had taken Frankie some time to figure out that by "normal people" Solly merely meant the Napiers, but for a while, he asked Ma for packets of chips and muesli bars and earlier dinners; for a while he ostentatiously poured himself large glasses of milk to have with dinner. He didn't even like plain milk.

But it did seem that most people, not just the Napiers, called their fathers Dad or Pop or Pa or Papa or—in the case of the Aunties, who often talked about the long-dead head of their family—Pater. Lily Bunz called her father Vati, but that was German for Daddy. True, Uncle George mostly called his deceased father the HOD, which meant Head of Department, but even he occasionally referred to him as "my old dad."

Ma had assured Frankie that Uncle George was indeed his dad, and Uncle George had proved it by demonstrating that the hammerhead second toe on Frankie's left foot was identical to the hammerhead second toe on *Uncle George's* left foot. It was a small but very fetching genetic malformation, Uncle George said. It was a family heirloom, and possibly the only kind Frankie would inherit (not counting the HOD's frying pan from the Western Desert, which Uncle George was thinking of leaving to Frankie since Louie would probably sell it to the highest bidder on Trade Me).

"He's definitely my father." Frankie threw a high leisurely ball and Sydney caught it with exaggerated grace. "And Louie's, and Gordana's. No doubt about it. We've all tried to call him Dad, but it doesn't work. *Everyone* calls him Uncle George, even Ma."

They came to a stop at the bottom of the hill road, outside the Boys' and Girls' Gymnasium, where Gigs was meeting them. Frankie had gone to the B&GG for trampoline classes when he was younger. Louie had walked him down the hill every Friday, talking, talking, all the way. Louie had done tramp in his time, too; he'd reached intermediate level and had even won a trophy at the trampoline regionals. Then he'd fallen out of a first-story window at school and broken his leg in three places, and that was the end of his tramp career. (Though it seemed to mark the beginning of his semi-delinquent career.)

Frankie had been good at tramp, too, when he wasn't worrying that his neck would accidentally snap during backdrops and half twists. He'd heard once about a man who'd become paraplegic after a freak trampoline accident and it preyed constantly on his mind, though Ma assured him over and over that safety measures were very carefully observed at the B&GG.

The best part about tramp had been Gino, the young instructor with curly black hair like a King Charles spaniel's. Gino was poetry in motion, Louie said, and Frankie believed it. Gino could cody and rudy and barani and execute a Miller Plus that made your stomach plunge to your knees as you watched. But Gino had gone to Italy to join a circus and Frankie had given up tramp soon after. It just hadn't been the same.

Frankie stared up at the high windows of the B&GG. Probably there were kids in there now, practicing their tucks and pikes. He could almost hear the springs of the trampolines, straining and singing. He could almost smell the cold of the concrete walls.

"So," said Sydney. "You have to tell me more about the Aunties. When can we go there?" She rubbed the cricket ball vigorously on the side of her skirt.

It was a nifty skirt, Frankie thought, wide and circular and bright orange, and decorated with ragged black triangles. Sydney made her own clothes. She had told him this on her first day at school, and now he noticed whatever she was wearing. He had never noticed girls' clothes in his life before now — apart from a dress Gordana had worn last year to the St. Agatha's Ball.

Uncle George had said it was a virtual dress because it was hardly there. The dress was pink and silky and apparently designed to reveal as much of Gordana's skin as possible. Frankie was used to seeing wide expanses of Gordana's flesh because all her clothes were skimpy, but he'd never seen as much of her breasts before. They were so abundant and startling that Frankie and Gigs had been forced to repair to the hallway and goggle wordlessly at each other for minutes at a time.

Sydney's clothes weren't revealing, but they were conspicuous, nevertheless—loudly colored, painted with crazed brush strokes, or adorned with geometric patches. She seemed to have a thing for triangles, Frankie noticed. Also, for T-shirts with lettering. Today she was wearing a white shirt printed with a joke Frankie had been puzzling over for some hours: . . .*why, wye, wai, Delilah* . . .

"Why do you want to know more about the Aunties? Why would you want to go there?" Frankie said, backing away to receive the ball.

"Because I don't have any aunties," said Sydney.

"They're *great*-aunts, anyway," said Frankie.

"I know," said Sydney. "But they're so funny. And so *fat*. It must be so satisfying *looking* at them."

Well, *no*, thought Frankie, *satisfying* was not the word that sprang to mind. But Sydney was right, the Aunties were certainly fat—they were enormous; they were *obese*—but he was used to it. It was somehow typical of Sydney to think that their size was interesting. He knew she wasn't being rude.

Sydney had met the Aunties on her third visit. She and Frankie and Gigs had been walking up the hill from the pool, practicing Knob-Shine. There was a loud horn blast behind them and the Aunties pulled over in Alma's black Morris Oxford.

It was a Thursday, so Frankie knew the Aunties were returning from a movie and shopping. Their weekly timetable was set in concrete. Frankie knew it as well as his own routines because he'd stayed with the Aunties for long periods when he was younger. He knew their peculiar habits like the back of his hand. He knew that the trunk of the Morris Oxford would be stuffed with groceries and wine bottles. There would be sweet treats and library books and a new gadget for Nellie from the Hardware SuperStore.

Frankie knew exactly the contents of the grocery cartons and the types of sweets (chocolate ginger, Liquorice Allsorts, Curiously Strong Peppermints). He knew that the library books would divide pretty much into three categories—romance novels for Nellie, biographies for Teen, thrillers for Alma—and that there would be a pile of magazines, including *Majesty* because all the Aunties followed the doings of the British Royal Family.

On Thursday they usually dropped off groceries at Frankie's house, but they didn't stop for tea or cake because Thursday was the night they had their old friend Maurice Pugh for curry and cards. Maurice Pugh was a curry addict and a recovering gambler. He could still eat as much curry as he liked, but he could only play cards as long as he didn't bet on the result. Maurice had told Frankie once that this had robbed card playing—and life—of much of its excitement, but the upside was that now he had enough money to buy food. Maurice Pugh had, apparently, once lived for an entire year on donated fruitcakes.

The Aunties had been to a film at the black-and-white festival. They leaned out the windows of the Morris Oxford, telling Frankie and Gigs and Sydney all about it. An oldie but a goodie, they said. A classic. Nellie had gotten hiccups from crying. (Nellie nearly always cried, especially when the music swelled. Film music was better back then, they all said—something Frankie had heard them assert about a million times.)

Of course, once the Morris Oxford roared away, Sydney

poured forth a torrent of questions. What were their *names* again? How come they all lived together? Hadn't they ever had husbands? What was their house like? Did they dye their hair? Where did they get their clothes? How come they were so *fat*?

"It's because they *eat* so much," said Gigs. "Their dinners are *massive. Feasts.* It's like the Romans. Awesome." Sydney said she was going the next time they visited. Definitely.

Sydney didn't wait for invitations anywhere, Frankie noticed. She just invited herself. And why not take her to the Aunties? As Uncle George said often enough, they were more entertaining than two weeks at the circus. Might as well share it.

But since then, the book project had taken up most of their time after school and on the weekends. Sydney had been over five times now. Not that Frankie was counting. Gordana was counting, though — he could tell. Gordana was practically expiring with curiosity about it all, though miraculously she'd restrained herself so far and said nothing. Any day now she'd blow a valve — Frankie just knew it. She'd start in with some casual, smart, *throwaway* remark and Frankie would want to kill her with his cricket bat.

"Is it like having three grandmothers, then?" said Sydney. She stood still, not throwing the ball, squinting at him.

"S'pose," said Frankie. "Sort of." He pictured the Aunties briefly. "Nah, not really. My real grandmother wasn't a bit like them."

Uncle George's mom had been small and white haired and gentle, a storybook grandma. She'd lived a very quiet life in a small brick house, just Gran and her old tomcat, Patrick. Frankie had never understood how someone like Gran had produced someone like Uncle George, who always seemed too big and hectic and loud for a tidy brick house with neat squares of lawn and orderly flower beds.

Gran was dead now. Her ashes were in a blue ginger jar on

the table in Uncle George's home office. Uncle George was supposed to be taking them down south to scatter them from a cliff, on behalf of his elderly sisters and brothers, but, of course, he never quite got around to it. Too busy down the salt mines, he said. (Louie said if he waited just a bit longer, he'd be able to take his brothers' and sisters' ashes, too. Louie didn't like that side of the family. He firmly believed Uncle George was a foundling, left on the doorstep by a wayward woman.)

Occasionally, Frankie went into Uncle George's office and stared at the blue ginger jar, trying to get his head around this version of Gran: a pile of sandy particles, waiting with characteristic patience it seemed, *stored* in the office, like manila folders and paper clips. Uncle George's dad, who'd died before Frankie was born, was buried at the Northgate Cemetery, which was a little more regular. Granddad Parsons had a fake-marble headstone with a photo inset of him in Eighth Army battle dress. Frankie had stared at that photo a few times, too, trying—and failing—to feel *related* to it. It was all very puzzling.

He couldn't imagine the Aunties dead—buried or cremated. It seemed impossible. They were too vivid, too decidedly solid and *in* the world, like decorated historic buildings or geological formations. They were like the Bridge of Remembrance hung with bunting, or the Southern Alps, snow-covered and brilliant on a sunny winter morning.

"I stayed with them a lot when I was young," he told Sydney. "It was mad. Mad as *mad.*"

"Tell me," demanded Sydney. She leaned her back against the side of the B&GG building and slid to a sitting position on the footpath. Frankie followed suit.

"Well," he said, recalling it all with the usual mix of feelings— a prevailing hilarity and excitement shot through with worry, like an exhilarating speedboat ride, seasickness hovering.

"Mostly I went to school, but sometimes they said not to bother—it was when I was in primary school. They only half believe in school. They think you can learn math from card games, and gardening teaches you botany, and having pets and insects teaches you zoology, and going to church teaches you singing, and driving all over town teaches you geography, that sort of thing. They're really not like other people."

"Like my mother," said Sydney. "She says she's a living example of the unnecessity of school. But she can't add."

"Plus, I don't think *unnecessity*'s a word," said Frankie.

"See?" said Sydney. "What did you do when you didn't go to school?"

"Just did what they did. They have *very* full days," said Frankie. "I know their routines by heart. For instance, they never get up before nine a.m., except on Tuesday mornings, when they do tai chi at War Memorial Park with other old ladies."

"Tai chi?"

"It's good for arthritis," said Frankie. He was sure he had an unnatural amount of knowledge about elderly peoples' health issues.

"Did you go, too? Are they the fattest people at tai chi?"

"Of course," said Frankie. "They're the fattest people everywhere. But they're surprisingly nimble." This was a direct quote from Uncle George. "You're obsessed with their fatness."

"No, I'm not," said Sydney. "I'm *intrigued* by it."

"For breakfast," Frankie continued, enjoying himself now, "they have porridge—organic oats—with cream and golden syrup, of course, and piles of toast and jam, and about seventy pots of tea while they do the cryptic crossword. Teen is the best at that, though Alma thinks *she* is. Except on Tuesdays, when they go to Number 17 after tai chi, and have pancakes and coffee—*a lot* of pancakes, with ice cream. They know the owner, Johnny Mac. He's an old card-playing mate and he was the first person ever in the city to have a commercial espresso machine. I know *all* the stories about *all* their mates."

He was sounding about a hundred and five, Frankie thought, and heavy with the weight of memory and experience.

"Keep going, keep going," said Sydney. She had found an old nail and was scratching primitive figures into the footpath. Three dumpling figures standing on tiptoe.

"In the mornings Teen gardens. They've got a big garden, all ugly old-fashioned flowers, you know, gladioli and dahlias and chrysanthemums. She can actually bend over to weed, but Nellie and Alma are too fat, so they write letters to the editor and to friends everywhere. Uncle George says they're single-handedly keeping stamps viable."

Sydney was scratching flowers now. Frankie grabbed the nail and drew Teen lying on her back amid the blooms, cast like a stray sheep.

"Sometimes I helped Teen in the garden, and sometimes Alma made me write letters. She thinks writing letters teaches you how to tell a story and how to spell. Nellie bakes on Mondays and Fridays; they always have full tins of biscuits and cakes—that's where Ma learned to bake—" Frankie stopped for a breath and immediately regretted it because it gave Sydney the opportunity to ask a question. He had a good idea what the question might be.

"Where's *Gigs*?" he said, standing abruptly and scanning the hill road. There was no sign of Gigs. No *sound* of him, either. Gigs never just walked silently down the hill. "He must be dropping his trombone off. I'm hungry. You hungry? We could get some—"

"Imagine living with your sisters *all* your life," said Sydney. She was standing now, tossing the ball again.

The prospect of living with Gordana all his life seemed to Frankie more remote than the prospect of growing an extra leg.

"Imagine living in the same *house* all your life."

"I have," said Frankie.

"I've lived in twenty-two," said Sydney. "That's not counting caravans or tents. And you haven't. You've lived at your Aunties', too."

"Not *lived*," said Frankie. "Just stayed." He could feel that question approaching again. He could almost see the outline of the ghostly words solidifying in the air between them. He could *hear* them, faint whispers, gaining volume by the second. He began jumping on the spot, his hands in the air.

"C'mon, throw it, *throw* it. I may as well get the shine on the end of my knob."

Was it possible he had just said such a thing? And to a girl? He could hardly believe himself. And he wasn't even blushing. He was sweating and babbling instead, jumping around, catching the ball, throwing it again, and pouring out the rest of the Aunties' week like some hard-wound talking toy.

"So, so, they play bridge three afternoons a week. In the summer they do aqua-aerobics. Every second Tuesday they come to us for dinner, of course. Every Thursday they shop and cook for Maurice and see a movie; they're crazy about movies. Once a week Nellie goes and cooks for the priests; she's crazy about priests. . . ." He dispatched balls, back and forth, with admirable force and accuracy, losing no letters, while Sydney, distracted by the gush of information, advanced to KNO.

Frankie began on the Aunties' activities outside the house.

"They do all these classes and go to all these clubs. Nellie and Teen do china painting and mosaics on Mondays, and Alma goes to lectures at the university. She goes to whatever's on; she doesn't care what the subject is as long as it's on a Monday. So far she's done Linguistics, the History of Western Philosophy, China in the Twentieth Century—"

Frankie stopped jumping momentarily to think, wanting to get this right. He enjoyed Alma's university education. It was as eccentric as she was. It meant she had bizarre but interesting pockets of knowledge. She said it was handy for crosswords and Trivial Pursuit.

"She's done Crime and Torts and Math and Japanese. This year she's doing Art History: The Portrait.

"And they all belong to the Richard the Third Society, some weird club. They go there once a month to hear lectures about him—he was a king—and every December they have a big feast on the day he died."

He caught the ball and stopped.

"He died at the Battle of Bosworth," said Frankie, as if he were saying amen. He flung himself down on the grass verge, his heart racing. He'd had it; he was swimming in sweat.

Sydney stood, hands on her hips, staring at him. She had been rendered momentarily speechless, it seemed, by this litany of activities.

"*Why* is there a society for Richard the Third?" she said. "Who was he, even?"

"A much maligned monarch," said Frankie, quoting Alma. "A king. He did things. Or he did not do things. He did *not* kill his nephews. Or something." He lay back and closed his eyes briefly. Where was Gigs? He needed a swim.

"Oh, and," he said wearily, "Teen and Nellie go to church on Sundays; Teen plays the organ. Alma stays at home, because she's an atheist. On Sunday afternoons, they go sightseeing in the Morris Oxford. Alma always drives and Teen always sits in the passenger seat and Nellie always sits in the back. It's according to the order of their ages.

"Oh, and"—Frankie wondered if you could fall asleep while actually talking—"they belong to a choir—the Fat Ladies' Choir. It's got another name, but everyone in it seems to be fat, so Louie calls it the Fat Ladies. Uncle George banned him from their concerts because he just got the giggles. And that's all I can think of right now."

At that moment, the roar of the Gigs downhill special reached their ears. Frankie sat up groggily, and they watched him, running so fast he seemed almost to be flying. He arrived breathless, red-faced, and grinning, little streams of sweat running down his bare chest and belly. He was wearing his man-eating-shark trunks and carrying three ice blocks.

"Ran all the way," he said. "Quick, they're melting. Man, I need that swim."

You and me both, thought Frankie, very, very pleased to see him.

"He's a KNOB and I'm a KNO," said Sydney. She held the ice block against her forehead.

"Bonga Swetso!" said Gigs.

"Question," said Sydney, as they turned the corner for Upham's.

"What?" said Frankie, holding his breath.

"*When,* but *when* is the next Fat Ladies' concert?"

Frankie lay on his bed. The Fat Controller lay on the bed, too, or more precisely on Frankie's toes. She often settled herself there, so that it looked as if Frankie had a pair of extremely fluffy slippers on his feet.

He was tired again after the long swim, and stuffed full of Ma's salade Niçoise. Sydney, it turned out, had once eaten salade

Niçoise in actual Nice. She stayed with her father in Amsterdam every year, and quite often, she told them at dinner, they drove to other countries for the weekend.

Frankie found the idea of driving to another country quite incredible. He found the idea of merely *being* in another country difficult to comprehend. Louie and Gordana had been to Australia, and Gordana had been to Tahiti, and even now Louie was salting away money for a motorcycle trip in South America. Gigs had been to Australia *and* America *and* England. But Frankie hadn't been anywhere, except to the North Island with Alma when he was nine and, according to Gordana, that certainly did not count.

Frankie and Alma had stayed with the Aunties' second cousin Henry Ward, a very rich bachelor with a very big house, a very big swimming pool, and a minuscule private plane. Henry Ward had offered to take Frankie for a ride in the plane but Frankie had politely declined. The plane looked freakishly tiny to him. He found large planes difficult enough.

Frankie had spent many hours worrying about traveling on the plane to the North Island. Every night for weeks, he'd hovered by Ma's side of the bed, shamefacedly blurting the catalog of disasters he felt certain awaited him.

"They're very careful about plane parts," Ma had said. "They have dozens of engineers. They check things every few hours."

"But the pilots," said Frankie. "What if they had a heart attack or food poisoning? What if they were drunk?"

They had constant health checks, Ma said. And anyway, it was really the computers that flew the plane. Frankie hadn't found this at all reassuring. Everyone knew computers broke down.

He had lain in bed visualizing the wings of the plane softening inexplicably, drooping slowly like dampening paper, and falling off the plane in midair. He imagined little licks of flame,

unnoticed in the cockpit, snaking down the aisle and engulf-
ing them in a fireball. He imagined terrorists disguised as stew-
ards, producing guns instead of sweets. He imagined unchecked
bottles exploding in the baggage department. He imagined flailing around in the Pacific Ocean, dodging sharks, watching Alma
float farther and farther away from him.

Eventually Ma said that perhaps he shouldn't go, but Uncle
George had unexpectedly put his foot down. This was such a
rare event that everyone had been startled. Uncle George almost
never gave his children instructions; he rarely disciplined them.
He said that it wasn't in him to act the paterfamilias. He was
happy for everyone to go their own way, as long as they didn't
disturb his peace or break the law. (He'd been obliged to be stern
with Louie during his semi-delinquent period, but it was perfectly
obvious that his heart wasn't in it. Uncle G roared at Louie and
repeated the counselor's words, but no one was convinced.)

So, when Uncle George said that Frankie was getting on that
plane or his name wasn't George Llewellyn Parsons, it was so
surprising that neither Frankie nor Ma had argued. Gordana,
who had been loudly derisive of Frankie's plane phobia but who
could also be contrary at a moment's notice, demanded to know
why Frankie should have to fly if he didn't want to.

"Because it's important," said Uncle George.

"Why?" said Gordana.

"Because then he'll have proof that none of those things
happened."

But they might, they might, said the rodent voice that colonized
Frankie's head at these times. The rodent voice was thin and
whining and the perpetual bearer of unpalatable facts. When the
rodent voice was in the ascendant, nothing Frankie tried would
shut it up.

But none of those things *did* happen, and Frankie had a

glorious time in Henry Ward's swimming pool, where there were no errant Band-Aids nor the slightest suspicion of snot. Henry Ward had taken Frankie to visit a bird sanctuary, too. He'd taken him to the Botanic Gardens to check out an albino duck. He'd lent Frankie his binoculars to watch the shags and skuas at low tide.

Still, Frankie hadn't been in a hurry to get on a plane since then. Of course there was the big Queensland vacation after his thirteenth birthday, when, according to family tradition, Uncle George would take him to visit his favorite cousin, Colette, who ran a bed-and-breakfast in the Glass Mountains. Gordana and Louie still talked about their thirteenth-birthday trips, and Frankie often thought about those mysterious mountains glinting in the Australian sun. All the same, he was counting on Uncle George being too busy to take the vacation.

Meanwhile, he had other more immediate concerns.

Frankie sighed heavily and stared up at the ceiling. Robert Plant stared moodily back down at him.

Robert Plant was a golden god. Or so he'd once claimed. Frankie didn't doubt it; Robert Plant looked exactly like his idea of a Classical god, golden or otherwise. He was tall and lithe, with perfect chiseled features and a great mass of blond, cork-screwed hair. He was impossibly handsome, and he sang pretty well, too.

Louie had introduced Frankie to the music of Led Zeppelin, Robert Plant's band, and had given him the poster. Sometimes when Louie came over for dinner and laundry, he and Frankie and Uncle George watched old Zeppelin concerts on DVD. Uncle George liked Robert Plant, too, because Robert Plant had been a golden rock god back when Uncle George was Frankie's age, which meant — Frankie couldn't believe how long it had taken him to realize this — that Robert Plant was now a fat, grizzled old has-been. Louie advised him not to dwell on this.

It had been a bad day, Louie said, when he'd seen *sixty-year-old* Robert Plant on TV.

All the same, in his secret mental notebook of improbable dreams, Frankie wished he could somehow be magically transformed into a Robert Plant look-alike. The Robert Plant of forty years ago, that is. It was probably genetically impossible. Ma was short and dark and so were all her relatives. At least, he *supposed* the Aunties were dark. It was hard to be sure, because they dyed their hair such odd shades. They were certainly short. And extremely wide. They were practically the same sideways as up.

Uncle George was dark, too—olive-skinned and almost black-haired. The silver in his hair was nature's makeover, he said. He wasn't particularly tall, nor was his body godlike in its proportions. It was large and comfortable, like a friendly Kodiak bear. He'd always "locked the rugby scrum," Uncle George said, whereas Frankie was more your nippy halfback. Or a rowing cox.

Or a jockey, Frankie thought gloomily. He was doing his best to fill out and grow up by way of two-egg, three-scoop smoothies, but so far, so hopeless. He seemed to have stalled on four feet and his black hair stayed determinedly straight and uninteresting.

Frankie slowly moved his feet out from under the Fat Controller. He heaved himself from the bed and investigated his face in the mirror. No change since this morning. Still the same delicate girlish features and soft skin. His eyelashes were an embarrassment, thicker and curlier than a china doll's, and his eyebrows were much too shapely. When Gordana was in a friendly mood, she said he was cute. When she was feeling savage, she said she was almost certain he had a surplus of female hormones.

No one could ever have accused Robert Plant of excessive female hormones. He had a healthy five o'clock shadow and an incipient mono brow. Once in the night, when the thought of galloping girlishness became too much for him, Frankie had thrown himself on Ma's bed and asked her to tell him straight up if he had a secret feminizing condition and if it could be fixed by drugs.

Naturally, she'd insisted he was perfectly normal; she always did. She said it was just a matter of time before he filled out. No mention of his face. Frankie remembered distinctly that Louie had been having thrilling adventures with Uncle George's electric shaver by the time he was thirteen. And his legs had been thick and solid as a tree trunk. Frankie's thirteenth birthday was only six months away and his skin was as smooth as a baby's bottom. And his legs were not at all promising. He pulled up his jeans for a hopeful check. Just as he'd expected — slender and hairless as a ballerina's.

Since he was doing a general inspection, he decided to risk an assessment of his chest rash. He'd been very determinedly not looking at it lately. But had it spread a little more? It was hard to tell. Frankie decided he would measure it. He rifled through his desk drawer for the wooden ruler he kept precisely for the purposes of private medical checks. It was a nice old ruler. Gordana had given it to him for his tenth birthday. She'd been much kinder to him back then. She'd seen the ruler in a junk shop and knew he'd like it because it was decorated with faded pictures of native birds.

That had been during an earlier bird phase, when he'd spent whole weekends wandering up the bush, spotting kereru and gray warblers and bellbirds. Frankie would have liked a pair of South American lovebirds like Solly Napier's, but he'd given up the idea of having any as pets. It would be cruel and unusual punishment keeping a bird while the Fat Controller was around. The Fat Controller, though mightily proportioned, was — like the

Aunties — very nimble on her paws. She was one of the cat world's great hunters. No bird was safe around her. So Frankie satisfied himself with drawing undiscovered rare birds and giving them names.

The ruler was so old it measured in imperial. His chest rash was shaped like a slightly disfigured kidney bean and was approximately two inches by three, with a small jutting part on the top left. He wrote this down in the back of his sketchbook and resolved to measure again tomorrow night. It was always better to be armed with the facts when he reported an ailment to Ma or Uncle George.

This rash is metastasizing daily, he could say. *We should go to the doctor immediately. Metastasize* was a good word, he thought, though it made his stomach dance with fear. It had been one of his dictionary-game words last year. He'd done as usual and let his *Concise Oxford* fall open randomly, then stabbed his finger at the page. *To spread in the body from the site of the original tumor.* The sight of the word *tumor* always produced a white noise in Frankie's head. So, maybe a rash wasn't a tumor. But it could be. Underneath. Frankie shoved the ruler back in the drawer and slammed it shut.

He sighed even more heavily and began tidying his desktop, which was in some disarray after Sydney's visit. Frankie had brought another chair into his bedroom, and he and Sydney sat side by side when they worked on the book project: Sydney writing in her thick sloping script, Frankie sketching ideas to accompany the story. It was very companionable.

They'd developed the story together — more or less equally, Frankie thought, though Sydney seemed to have twice as many ideas as he did. She was very good at plot. She said it was because her life had been full of plot from the moment she was born. But Frankie had come up with the title, *The Valiant Ranger,* which he considered a good joke since that car wasn't anywhere in the story. It was all birds. The valiant ranger was a Department of Conservation worker trying to save a rare bird. Saving the rare bird meant fighting international rare-bird smugglers and falling down the occasional ravine. The best part—as far as Frankie was concerned—was that he got to invent a species of rare bird. It was small, as small as a budgie, and delicate, and a crucial cog in the ecosystem.

Sydney liked to spread out as she worked. She wrote fast, covering sheet after sheet of paper. When she was displeased with something she'd written—which was often—she scored thick lines through the sentences and shoved the paper aside or screwed it into a tight ball. If she was satisfied, she slid it Frankie's way. They'd developed a very smooth operation in just a month, which still surprised Frankie. It was quite different from the way he and Gigs worked. For a start, *they* almost never sat down.

Occasionally he felt a little disloyal to Gigs—especially when Gigs regaled him bitterly with stories of Bronwyn Baxter's uncooperativeness—but mostly he just enjoyed the project. And Sydney. She was funny. She had good ideas. He liked her eye-bulging and her funny gruff voice and the sound of her bangles rattling. He liked that she was interested in his life—mostly. He liked *telling* her about his life—mostly. Sometimes, it was as if he was seeing and hearing it all for the first time himself.

Frankie shuffled the papers into a tidy stack and weighted them with his block of hacked-out kauri gum. He liked to keep his desk, his entire room (his whole life really) very neat. Sydney had immediately remarked on this.

"If my mother saw this, she'd bet you were a Virgo."

"I *am* a Virgo," said Frankie.

"That's what's so annoying about my mother," said Sydney.

"What do Virgos do?" asked Frankie.

"They're obsessively neat and tidy. Everything has to be in its place. They're nuts."

Frankie blushed, feeling as if he'd been caught naked. It was the truth.

Take his desk — it was ridiculously symmetrical. The South Park Club Cricket cup sat in the top left corner, holding all his sharpened pencils. Top right was the soapstone box with his collection of birds' feathers. His one- and two- and five-cent coin towers were lined up along the top center.

Ma's old music box with the one-armed ballerina was positioned just near his left hand so he could lift the lid and play it when he was drawing. Louie had fiddled with the mechanism so the box played "Lara's Theme" backward. The new tune was very peculiar, yet familiar, and it always made Frankie smile.

His old bear, Kidder, grubby with age, the stuffing sprouting from his neck, sat on the right of the desk, leaning against the windowsill, and between Kidder's stumpy legs stood Maxwell Smart and Agent 99, the Fimo figures Gigs had made him for Christmas. The trio was a static audience regarding him blankly as he did his homework.

In front of them was the framed photo of Ma and Uncle George on their wedding day, posing outside the stone church with Gran and Grandad Parsons and the three Aunties — Uncle George, dashing in a straw boater and Ma, doubled up, helpless with laughter at something Uncle George had said.

Finally, dead center, in pride of place, was Morrie, the plastic skull Louie had found at a garage sale. Frankie had decorated Morrie to soften his hideous aspect, draping his silver cricket bat chain across Morrie's cranium. A kereru-bird feather sprouted from his empty brain, and dried rosebuds filled his eye sockets.

Sydney had picked up and inspected everything on Frankie's desk.

"Are you sure he's imitation?" she said, cradling Morrie in her hands. She rotated him gently, counted his teeth.

"He couldn't be real, could he? It'd be illegal," said Frankie. He didn't know this for sure, but he felt it should be the case.

"Why is he called Morrie?"

"Louie. He gave him to me when he moved out."

A skull was a very Louie kind of present, and Morrie was spooky, no doubt about it, especially on nights with a full moon. On those nights, Morrie's creamy head seemed to glow in the moonlight. Frankie had to turn over in bed, away from his rose-bud gaze. Sometimes he buried his ears in his pillow, afraid that Morrie might suddenly begin speaking, like some cartoon skull.

On the other hand, occasionally Frankie spoke to Morrie — and Robert Plant. Of course, he would rather be devoured by a colony of bull ants than ever confess this, but the truth was, sometimes — almost without noticing it — he blurted things out to both of them. He figured it wasn't a problem unless either of them ever answered back.

"So, you two," said Frankie now, picking up the sheaf of colored papers that had been persecuting him silently for days. He waved the papers under Morrie's bony nose. "*What* am I supposed to do about camp? Eh? *Eh?*"

Camp. *Camp. Campcampcampcampcampcampcampcamp* . . . It wasn't so much an odious word now as a chant, haunting his head morning and night. The chant had been gaining in force and volume since Mr. A had distributed the camp papers two weeks ago. On Friday the forms were due back at school.

The papers were color-coded in Mr. A's usual way. Orange, yellow, green, blue — what Mr. A called "the bureaucratic rainbow." The bureaucratic rainbow was, he said, a hangover from his probation days, when he had nearly drowned in color-coded forms. Gigs had raised his hand and said that this meant Mr. A had been burned-out *and* wet back in his probation days, and could those two things actually happen at the same time?

"In the world of corrections,"—Mr. A fixed Gigs with a gimlet eye —"*anything* can happen. Listen up, please . . . *One*—the *orange* sheet is a permission slip for your parents or guardians to sign."

He held up the yellow sheet. "*Two*—this is a list of costs. *Three*—the *blue* sheet is a list of gear you will need for camp. Note that it *excludes* listening devices of *all kinds*. This means Walkmen, Discmen, MP3s, iPods, iPod Nanos, iPod Shuffles, mobiles, two-way radios, field telephones, car phones, tin cans joined with a string . . . Is this crystal clear to even the most obdurately cloth-eared among you?"

"What's obdurate, Mr. A? What's cloth-eared?" said Bronwyn Baxter.

"*Four*—the *green* sheet"—Mr. A ignored her —"is a note enticing your parents to accompany us, one day, two days, three, a morning, an afternoon, half an hour, twenty-seven seconds, whatever they can manage. . . . Bring all these back read and signed by your parents or guardians, two Fridays from now. No questions! Dictionaries out!"

Frankie, trying not to think about camp and its implications, had noted automatically that Mr. A had had a haircut. About two inches, Frankie figured, assessing the newly neat halo of silver hair. He'd had an eyebrow trim, too. His eyebrows looked like eyebrows now instead of shaggy hay bales. Gigs and Frankie were convinced that Mr. A was bossier and more officious in the days immediately following his haircuts.

Frankie had stared vacantly at the colored sheets for some time in class, then stowed them in his backpack. At home he had transferred them from his backpack to his desk, where he regularly stared at them, since they had continued to lie there, unread and unsigned, for the last fortnight.

It was hearing about the Year Eight Notts camp five years ago that had made Frankie wish fervently to transfer, along with Gigs, to the school. Gigs had told him all about it; his cousin Vivi had told *him*. It was *amazing*, Gigs had said. *Eight days* more or less in the bush, horseback riding, bird-watching, kayaking, rock climbing, a mini drama production with the band, a dance competition . . . The camp was the high point of the Notts experience. No other school had anything like it, blah, blah, blah . . .

Frankie wound up the old music box and watched the one-armed ballerina perform her jerky pirouette. He thought of the ballerina as Lara, though she didn't look anything like the Lara in *Doctor Zhivago,* which was the film that "Lara's Theme" came from. *Doctor Zhivago* was Ma's favorite film; naturally it was set in Russia. Frankie had watched the film often with Ma.

The film Lara was voluptuous and fair-haired, with pouting lips. She wore cloaks and fur and moved with grace. The music box ballerina was skinny and plastic, with only a few strands of black hair and no discernible lips. Her pink tulle skirt was tatty; her dance was bumpy and oddly fevered. It was because she was old, Frankie knew; the music box had been Ma's sixth-birthday present from her parents. It had also been her last birthday present from her parents because when she was six years and five days old, her parents had been killed in a car crash, and Ma had gone to live with the Aunties.

Frankie closed his eyes and listened to the mutated "Lara's Theme" slowing and slowing and finally stopping.

It was because of Ma that Frankie couldn't possibly go to camp. He could admit this to himself in the privacy of his bedroom, where only Robert Plant and Morrie were witness to his thoughts. It was not something he could discuss with Gigs or Louie or Gordana — with anyone else in the world.

The *problem* was, he just knew that those in charge — Uncle George and Ma herself — would not accept Ma as a reasonable excuse for Frankie staying at home. Which meant he would have to go. Except that he couldn't, because if he did, he would spend the week disabled by worry, the rodent voice taking up permanent, deafening residence in his head. He would feel nauseous with anxiety about Ma. (Who would do her errands? Who would keep her company? Who would chat to her at night when Uncle G was working and Gordana was doing as she pleased? Who would keep a constant and careful — though carefully nonchalant — eye on her? Who would hold her hand when she was feeling a little bit wobbly?)

But almost as bad, he, Frankie, would inevitably develop new and pressing worries, about himself and the world in general; he would lie awake in the camp bunk while everyone else was sleeping, obsessing about Chinese industrial pollution, about the ozone hole, about Peak Oil, about the diseases carried by horses and the perils of kayaking, about the possibility of campylobacter from camp food and septicemia from grazes and cuts. He would lie in his bunk while this catalog created a progressively more high-pitched white noise in his head and there would be no possibility of padding down the hall to Ma's room for reassurance.

Frankie banged the music box lid shut, and plastic Lara was confined once more to her horizontal position in the dark. He flung himself back on his bed, and the Fat Controller mewed halfheartedly at this rough treatment.

Frankie raised his eyes to Robert Plant and silently spoke his treacherous thought: *I'm tired of it.* He looked at Morrie and said the thought aloud: "I'm tired of it." He was tired, tired, *tired, so* tired of all the worry — worry about himself, worry about Ma, worry about the world. Then instantly he felt shabby and mean, disloyal to Ma, ashamed of himself.

He curled his fists so his nails dug into the skin of his palms. It was his way of being stern with himself, of pulling himself together. He clenched his teeth, then wobbled his jaw furiously so that it clicked and the sound rang in his head. He often did this to banish rodent thoughts before they took hold.

So, he was tired of it all, but what could he do? Nothing, that's what. It was just how it was.

There were worse things, of course there were. Floods in India. Earthquakes in Peru. Children with tuberculosis or kwashiorkor or polio. What was he complaining about? It was nothing, really, just an eternal inconvenience. But, so what?

He uncurled his fists and looked at the half-moon marks on his palms. He knew what he was going to do.

He would fake Uncle George's signature on the camp forms and tell Mr. A—with just the right amount of regret—that family circumstances meant he couldn't attend. Uncle George would never realize about camp because he was just too flat out these days to register anything, especially events on anyone's school calendar. And Ma would never know; Frankie was very practiced at protecting Ma from information that might upset her.

And good old Mr. A would be too sensitive and kind to ask awkward questions; he would just pat Frankie kindly on the back and suggest some books to read while they were away. Gigs wouldn't ask questions, either, because he never did. That was the good thing about Gigs.

Nor would his classmates say anything, because in five years they never had. Of course, Frankie hadn't told a single person about home, but he figured someone had—either Gigs, for kindly reasons, or that arch busybody, Bronwyn Baxter, because she loved to pass on gossip.

It was the best solution. In fact, it was the only solution. And if somehow—he couldn't think how and he'd canvassed all the possibilities—if somehow Uncle George and Ma found out later, after camp, it would be too late to do anything about it.

"So, that's that," he said to Morrie and Robert Plant. "All settled." He closed his eyes.

Or almost all settled. There was one remaining problem, of course. A three-foot-seven-inch problem with bulging eyes and rattling bangles, who could be guaranteed to do what everyone else obligingly did not—ask questions. There was no way out of that one—Frankie just knew.

He could hear Sydney's questions clearly. He'd been hearing them in his head for two weeks.

"Question," she would say in her raspy way. They might be anywhere, sitting at his desk, Sydney scribbling, Frankie shading the soft gray underbelly feathers of his rare bird. They might be sitting at the Pepys table doing their math or riding the bus to Frankie's place or walking down the hill to the shops on an errand for Ma. Sydney would be no respecter of place or time.

"How come," she would say with a bluntness that would make him flinch, "your mother *never* leaves the house?"

Frankie had spent a good deal of time thinking about how he would answer this. He had all manner of imaginary responses lined up.

"She has an allergy to sunlight," he would say.

Or, "She's actually clinically blind, but you can't really tell."

Or, "She has this incredibly rare foot condition. It stops you from walking any distance. Just easier to stay indoors."

Or, "She's in a witness protection program—she gave evidence in a big court case and now she has to stay more or less hidden in case any of them trace her whereabouts."

It was all crap, of course, but it didn't matter much what he said, because the other question would come hard on its heels, as predictably as frost on a winter morning.

"But how *long* has it been, how long since she went anywhere?" Sydney would fix him with those black bean eyes, her nose stud would seem to flash, and he would be stuck fast, a possum in the headlights, compelled to answer. Those eyes would pull the answer from him, draw it out slowly, like a syringe extracting blood.

"Hmmm," Frankie would say, strenuously casual, looking away, fixing his eye on something solid and ordinary: a tree, a parked car, the dictionary, the black-and-white hatching on his rare bird, the cricket cup and the sharpened pencils pointing to the ceiling like a circle of bayonets. "Hmmm," he might say again, so relaxed and unemotional he would seem practically comatose. "A while now, I guess."

Then he might pretend to recall just exactly how long. He might narrow his eyes, seem to be calculating the time, as if it were so unimportant, he'd never bothered to do it before. . . .

"Let's see," he might say eventually. "About nine years. Most of my life, really. It's normal for me. I hardly notice it. I honestly never really think about it. Really."

"Really," he would say again, ever so lightly.

"Did you know, the Russians had accidental daylight saving for sixty-one years and nobody noticed?" said Frankie. "It was Stalin's fault. He ordered the clocks put back in nineteen thirty-eight and then forgot to un-order them."

Frankie liked to pass on to Ma curious facts he picked up about Russia. He'd heard this one on a radio program about the history of daylight saving.

"I didn't," said Ma. "He was a terrible person."

"It's more terrible ending daylight saving," said Frankie. "Plunging us all into darkness."

"Don't you start," said Ma. She was lying with her hands tucked behind her head, listening to some piano music. Russian, of course. Some Dmitri or Sergei or Pytor. Frankie was looking at the yellow-haired woman in the painting, who somehow appeared more apprehensive than usual. Perhaps she hated the end of daylight saving, too. But no, they wouldn't have had it back then, when people wore billowing nightgowns and slept in four-poster beds. The radio said it had been invented in the nineteen twenties.

"Seamus and Eugene Kearney's brother might have hepatitis," said Frankie. He could never figure out the color of the woman's eyes. Hazel? Topaz? Ginger?

"Which one?" said Ma. Seamus and Eugene had six brothers; no one could really tell them apart— they were all big and baboon-like.

"Danny. He's turned yellow. His whole flat has turned yellow. It's incredibly contagious. Seamus and Eugene might have it."

"It's possible," said Ma. "Do you like this music?"

"It's okay," said Frankie. "I might have it," he said.

"Have what?" said Ma.

"Hepatitis," said Frankie. "I think my eyes have a yellow tinge."

"You don't have it. You never have anything to do with the Kearneys."

"But they're in my class. I could have touched things they've touched. Desks, door handles, dictionaries, cricket bats . . ."

Ma leaned over and turned down the music. "Do you wash your hands before you eat? Do you share food or bottles with the Kearneys? Do you always use soap?"

"Yes. No. Yes," said Frankie.

"I promise, you don't have it," said Ma. "You look too healthy. Tanned and clear-eyed. I think you've grown, too. The Aunties thought so."

"Symptoms don't show for two weeks and people can feel completely normal," said Frankie. Who cared about extra height when liver damage was almost certain?

"How's the book project going?" said Ma. "I like your title. Sydney told me. She's nice, Sydney."

"It's okay," said Frankie truculently. He wished she wouldn't try to distract him in this obvious way. It never worked.

"You reading anything good at the moment?"

"Articles on hepatitis."

"Frankie, please." Ma sat up in bed and took his hand in hers. "Listen to me. What type of hepatitis is it? A, B, or C?"

"C," said Frankie miserably. "And that's the worst kind."

"Aha!" said Ma. "It's also the kind that's passed on by blood."

They sat there in silence for a moment.

"Have you been sharing needles with any of the Kearney boys?"

"Ha, ha," said Frankie, but already he was feeling a tiny bit better.

They sat in further silence.

"Okay, then?" said Ma.

"Yes," said Frankie. He decided the woman in the painting had amber eyes. They were strangely transparent.

Ma turned up the music again.

"So, who wrote this?" Frankie asked.

"Shostakovich," said Ma. "Stalin was horrible to him."

"Wonder what he thought of daylight saving?" said Frankie, hauling himself off the bed and heading for the door.

"Only three months to the shortest day," said Ma.

"'Night," said Frankie.

FOUR

Tuesday, March 28

It was raining, a real downpour—you couldn't race between these raindrops. Frankie thought of Davy Crockett and the story Uncle George had once read him about Davy dodging between the raindrops and staying completely dry. Frankie had been impressed. He'd tried to do it himself until Louie told him it was physically and scientifically impossible. It really was a continual disappointment, thought Frankie, how all the little pieces of story magic were eventually crushed by the weight of reality.

He looked left and saw a stream of traffic bearing down, but ran across the street anyway, his new hoodie pulled tight. Even so, he was sodden by the other side. Perhaps Louie would have a spare sweater in his truck.

It was Year Eight work experience day, and Louie was picking Frankie up at 8:30 a.m. outside the city library so Frankie could spend the morning observing, and possibly helping him, "in the execution of his job."

"Execution of his job" was, of course, a Mr. A term.

"Why can't he just say, '*doing* his job'?" said Gigs irritably after Mr. A had given room 11 his famous Work Experience

Rave. Gigs was grumpy about work experience day because he would be spending the morning with his uncle Graham (a librarian) and the afternoon with his grandfather (a gardener at the Senior Center).

According to Gigs, these were the two dreariest possible jobs in the entire universe. And worse, Uncle Graham was a law librarian; all the books in his library were hefty, devoid of pictures, and deadly dull. Plus, Uncle Graham was very quiet and had absolutely no interest in cricket.

Gigs's grandfather could talk happily about cricket for hours at a time, but, unfortunately, gardening for the elderly really meant *weeding* for the elderly, and if there was one thing that made Gigs foam at the mouth, it was weeding.

"It's so *pointless*," he said. "You pull them out—if you *can*, because half the time the stupid root gets stuck and crap breaks off in your hand—and then, about one minute after you've pulled them out, they start growing again, practically in front of your eyes!"

Every spring and summer, Dr. Pete dragooned Gigs into the garden to help with the weeding, and every spring and summer, Frankie heard Gigs say the same things. He did *not* believe in gardens; they were a waste of space; he was *never* going to have one; he would have grass only in his backyard and a decent cricket pitch.

Gigs had wanted to go to the hospital with Dr. Pete so he could walk up and down the corridors in a white coat and stethoscope and make coffee with four spoons of sugar at the nurses' station. He wanted to check out the analog sphygmomanometers and the digital thermometers and the endoscopes. He wanted to watch all Dr. Pete's medical examinations. But these were mostly up people's bottoms, and observation was strictly confined to certified medical personnel.

Personally, Frankie found the idea of botty doctoring (as Gigs called it) entirely repulsive. He didn't know how Dr. Pete did it. Weeding seemed a very pleasant career by comparison.

"You would say that," said Gigs. "You get to tool around town in a truck with a dog! And eat kebabs!" Louie had promised Frankie takeout from the Istanbul. Gigs, on the other hand, was doomed to old-lady sandwiches and soft shortbread.

"Gravits plodney malet tarlick weasels," said Gigs, swiping fiercely at a patch of gravel with his bat. (They had been walking to Westside Park at the time, for the final school cricket match — another reason for Gigs's ill humor.)

"Dark curses on useless parents," said Frankie, translating for Sydney, who was walking with them. Or rather, part walking and part cartwheeling. She had recently mastered the cartwheel and practiced it at every opportunity. It didn't seem to bother her at all if she was wearing a skirt and so revealed thighs and knickers every time she turned an arc. Frankie felt obliged to avert his eyes, but Gigs had no such compunction. He had already told Sydney that today's knickers were *Bonga Swetso!*

"Quit moaning," said Sydney. "At least you've got uncles and grandparents. And at least they've got jobs. I've only got my mother and she doesn't believe in working."

"How can you not believe in it?" said Frankie. "You can't believe or not believe. It's a fact of life."

"Ask my mother," said Sydney, launching into a cartwheel. She was getting good, no doubt about it. Frankie could cartwheel very adequately himself but felt it undignified for someone almost thirteen. Sydney, who was six months older than Frankie, didn't seem to believe in the notion of undignified anything.

"My mother," said Sydney when she was upright again. "My mother thinks that some people are meant to have jobs and some aren't. She thinks that there are some people in the world who need to be supported by others. She thinks she's one of those people."

"But that's not *fair*," said Frankie.

"Who said anything about fair?" said Sydney.

"But how does she get money?" asked Gigs. "How do you live?"

"One step ahead of the creditors," said Sydney.

"Creditors?" said Frankie.

"The people you owe money to," said Sydney, raising her arms in preparation.

Frankie looked blankly at her.

"My mother doesn't pay her bills," said Sydney matter-of-factly, slipping sideways and down.

"But that's *absolutely* not fair," said Frankie to Sydney's bare legs. Her knickers were red and decorated with California thistles.

"Nah, it's not," said Sydney a moment later, brushing down her skirt and re-securing her dreads in their strange bulky pony-tail. From behind, it looked as if she had a knotty shrub growing out the back of her head.

"But the *point* is, because she doesn't work and because I don't have any relatives here, I've got nobody to do work experience day with. Which is why I need to borrow one of yours."

Standing now, shivering in front of the city library, Frankie could almost smile. It had been just a moment's work for Sydney to maneuver things so she could have the day at *his* house. With *his* mother. Baking.

Right now, Sydney was playing junior pastry chef. She'd be chopping nuts, creaming butter and sugar, separating eggs, any one of a dozen very pleasant tasks. She'd lick all the used bowls and sample the rough edges. Between cakes, she'd drink sweet tea, like Ma. She'd listen to Russian opera. She'd be *warm*. Even considering the Russian opera, which he hated, Gigs had been almost mute with envy.

Frankie hadn't been envious; he'd been very dismayed.

He didn't want Sydney alone with Ma. He didn't trust that situation at all. He'd lain in bed for three nights worrying excessively about it and then, at school, had pulled Sydney—literally—out of lunchtime cricket to have a very serious talk with her. As much as any talk with Sydney could be serious. He supposed it'd been semi-serious.

In any case, he'd put some rules in place. He was extremely stern about it. He'd decided to take a leaf out of Sydney's own book of wacko etiquette and, for once, talk straight and tough.

One, he said, she couldn't chatter on and on, because Ma liked it peaceful in the kitchen. Two, she wasn't allowed to ask *any* personal questions. Three, she definitely was *not* to mention camp.

"First," said Sydney, "I don't *chatter*. I *talk*. And I can be quiet when I have to. Second, what do you mean by personal?"

"You know what I mean," said Frankie. He didn't want to go into it.

She did know what he meant. He knew she knew. They absolutely did not need to go into it. Again. This had already happened when Frankie had said he wasn't going to camp and Sydney had finally blurted out the question that had been burning her up for weeks.

Frankie did not want to think about that.

He was looking out for Louie's truck and watching all the people in suits (the worker bees, Uncle George called them), crisscrossing at the intersection in front of the library, heading for their workplaces. Some had their heads down against the rain; some smoked last quick cigarettes; some held umbrellas and downed coffees as they walked. Some strode purposefully, and others moved at leisure, despite the rain, talking to their mates, laughing. They, Frankie supposed, were the keen ones.

According to Mr. A, people had very different attitudes toward their jobs. According to Mr. A, some people were as keen as mustard; they looked forward to work; they relished it; some people *lived* for their work. (Evidently Mr. A belonged in this category.) Others, said Mr. A, were less enthusiastic; they didn't *not* like their jobs—perhaps they mildly enjoyed them—but they worked principally because they needed to earn a living, as everyone must. (At this point Frankie had exchanged with Sydney what he was sure could be called *a wry smile.*) These were the people, said Mr. A, who worked to live.

Furthermore, according to Mr. A (you could write up all the "according to Mr. A-isms" and get quite a fat book out of it, Frankie thought) a surprising number of people knew next to nothing about what their nearest and dearest *did* at work. A lot of kids, said Mr. A, looking meaningfully around the classroom, had *no idea* what their parents' jobs involved. Or whether they liked them.

"Hence," said Mr. A, "*hence*—what does *hence* mean, Gigs?"

"*Forthisreason,*" Gigs intoned.

"*Hence*—work experience day! Where you will *experience,* insofar as it's possible—or at least *observe*—some of the particulars, or absorb the atmosphere of your parents', or guardians', or grandparents', or siblings' jobs!"

Hence, as happened annually, Year Eights were distributed about the city for the day, dogging the heels of their parents or other willing relatives as they went about a day's work. According to Mr. A, it had to be a close relative because his point was then best proved (*that a surprising number of kids, blah, blah, blah*). But failing blood relatives, you could hit up an obliging family friend or a friend's parent.

Hence, Solly Napier was at the offices of Napier Roofing for the day, standing beside his father as he supplied screws and seals and underlay and spouting, and watching his mother while she did the accounts. *Hence,* Vienna Gorman was down at the Bus Stop Theater for the morning, where her mother did lighting design, and in the afternoon with her father at the polytech, where he was a technician at the Jazz School.

Hence, Esther Barry was spending the morning with her grandmother at James Real Estate, where she was the administrator, and the afternoon with her grandfather in the Botanic Gardens, where he worked in the Begonia House. Esther's parents were both vets and she helped them on weekends, so she knew more than enough about their jobs; according to Mr. A this put her in the 27 percent minority.

Hence, Bronwyn Baxter was spending the morning with her mother, who was a district health nurse, and the afternoon with her father, who managed a cleaning company.

Hence, David Robinson was at Boys' College for the morning, where his auntie was a math teacher, and in a taxi all afternoon with his father, who was a driver. (David Robinson's mother was a counselor, but he couldn't observe her at work because her clients cried a lot.)

Hence, Frankie would be at Parsons Porritt Public Relations this afternoon, watching Uncle George "wrestle a recalcitrant rebranding to the ground." These were Uncle George's very words, and Frankie hadn't a clue what they meant, thus proving Mr. A's theory. (One of their tasks for the day was to make a list of all the specialist words and phrases their parents' jobs involved. Gigs observed with great regret that if he'd been with Dr. Pete, he could have legitimately put *arsehole* on his list.)

But *hence,* currently Frankie was standing in front of the city library, wet and cold, and possibly risking a chill, as he waited for his brother, who — very predictable, this — was late.

On any other day, Frankie loved the city library. Alma had enrolled him on his first birthday and he'd been coming pretty much weekly ever since. When he was little, he'd come with the Aunties and Gordana and Louie. Later, he'd come on the bus just with Gordana.

Louie had stopped reading books when he was ten, which was also the time he'd decided he wasn't, after all, going to be a zookeeper. Up until that moment, all the books he'd read had been about animals. He said he didn't see any point in reading unless it was about animals and he didn't want to read about animals now that he wasn't going to be a zookeeper. So he was giving up reading. Frankie still occasionally puzzled over this explanation.

Frankie liked reading, though not as much as Gordana. Gordana vacuumed up books; she devoured them. With a book in her hand, Gordana was deaf and dumb to the rest of the world. At the city library she fell into the nearest beanbag and chewed her way through book after book after book. Also — until a year ago — through all the fingernails on both hands. Until a year ago, when Gordana had started going out with Ben, her fingernails had been chewed to oblivion. But now they were fetching white half-moons and Gordana spent much time painting them black or scarlet or fluorescent blue. Gordana's nails were safe now, Gigs said, because she was too busy chewing Ben's face.

Frankie also worked his way through many books at the city library, but he did it at a leisurely pace, and he mostly chose picture books. He didn't care what anyone thought about this, nor did he imagine anyone took the slightest notice. That was the great thing about the library. It was both teeming with people and very private. Everyone was either busy selecting books or returning them. Or they were sprawled in a beanbag, lost in their own reading world.

Frankie missed those library visits with Gordana. She'd been just as bossy back then, of course, just as contrary and unpredictable, but going to the library made her temporarily affable. She played Lady with a Pram and other bus games with Frankie on the way into the city. They shared packets of Pebbles and Spaceman Candies and listened in on other passengers' conversations. Gordana didn't seem to mind Frankie bringing his beanbag right up beside hers once they got to the library; she was never scornful about his picture books.

It was always a Saturday when they went to the library, and afterward they lugged their bag of books to Pigeon Park. They sat on a bench there, eating hot chips, and Gordana didn't mind if Frankie sketched the pigeons. Gordana watched the passing parade and gave a steady commentary on people's odd behavior. She made Frankie laugh. But now Gordana worked at the Cupcake Café on Saturdays, and if Frankie and Gigs showed their faces, she said they had till the count of three to go to a galaxy far, far away.

Frankie began running gently on the spot. It was 8:45 according to the Victoria Clock Tower. He could go inside and warm up, but Louie had said it'd be strictly a drive-by and that Frankie must be ready and waiting outside. If he had a mobile phone, he could text Louie and say, *whr r u knob-shine?* but he wouldn't have a mobile until he turned thirteen. Uncle George said that the longer it was delayed, the better; it was sad enough having two children whose phones were extra body parts.

More like internal organs, Frankie thought. Once, when Louie had been suspended from school, Uncle George had confiscated his mobile for three days and it was as if invisible batteries inside

Louie had been near failure, or as if Louie were an indoor plant someone had forgotten to water. He'd been quite slowed down, limp and listless and strangely without purpose.

The rain was easing. Across the road Transistor Man and Skirt Man sat beneath the eaves of the old state services building, drinking takeout coffee. Transistor Man was developmentally disabled and listened all day to a large old-fashioned transistor radio held on his shoulder. Skirt Man was DD, too, and Chinese. He wore a little lacy blouse and a kilt that came to just above his tiny brown knees. The two of them lived on the city streets and sometimes at the Night Shelter. They were always together, except when they'd squabbled, which was relatively often. You always knew when they'd fallen out, because they cornered passersby and told them every detail.

Gordana said Transistor Man and Skirt Man were freaks; moreover they were freaks who smelled. But Frankie and Gigs liked the two men. They liked to chat to them; they shared lollies with them sometimes. Once, they'd pooled their money and bought Transistor Man new batteries for his radio. A lot of people did that. From time to time, people gave Skirt Man new blouses, too.

Louie said Transistor Man's name was really Douglas Golightly and Skirt Man was called Ping Song. Generally, Frankie took Louie at his word—he knew everything around town—but Douglas Golightly and Ping Song sounded suspiciously like the names of characters in a book. Ping *was* a character in a book. He was a duck in Louie's favorite book, *The Story of Ping*. Uncle George had often called Louie Ping when he was little; he said Louie was just like the yellow duck—a nosy little adventurer who secretly needed his family.

Louie had taken *The Story of Ping* when he moved out, which was fine, but he had also taken *Harold and the Purple Crayon* and that was Frankie's book, *his* favorite of all time. Louie said his need for *Harold* was greater; Frankie said he didn't think so. Louie said *Harold* was a necessary inspiration when you were making a new life. Frankie said *Harold* was a necessary inspiration in your old life, too. In the end, because Frankie could never win a negotiation with Louie, they'd agreed on six months each with *Harold*. Frankie was getting him back at Easter.

Frankie had first read *Harold* at this very city library when he was four. He could remember it quite clearly. Alma had plucked *Harold* from the shelf and Frankie had fallen instantly in love. It was Harold's genius with his purple crayon that thrilled him. Harold made things happen simply by drawing them. He solved problems with that crayon. He *drew* himself out of tight spots. The crayon took him out into the world and it brought him safely back home. It was magnificent. It was magical. Every time Frankie got to the end of the book and Harold drew—first his bedroom window with the little half-moon framed, and then his bed—Frankie would let out a long sigh of satisfaction. Then he would make Alma read the book all over again.

The Aunties had finally ordered him his own copy of *Harold and the Purple Crayon,* but Frankie insisted on borrowing the book from the library still. He liked having two Harolds sitting on the table beside his bed.

Frankie dated his own interest in drawing from around that time. Alma had bought him a sketchbook and his own packet of crayons—with several shades of purple—and he'd filled every corner of every page in the sketchbook with pictures. These days he drew in black and white. He could only dimly remember that madly colored world, the parade of figures and furniture and flowers, animals and birds and cars and buildings. The Aunties still had that sketchbook, along with others he'd filled. They were stacked on the bookcase in the spare bedroom, which was also known as Frankie's Room. One of these days he might get them down and have a look through them.

Now 8:53. The rain had stopped completely and the clouds were dispersing. The crowds of worker bees had thinned, too, just the late ones now, running, recklessly dodging traffic.

Frankie wondered how Sydney was doing with the grating and chopping. She didn't seem to him like someone who would be good in the kitchen. She was too wired; she was perpetually on tiptoe, as if ready any moment to run the one-hundred-meter dash.

"Your Ma's so *calm*," Sydney had said to Frankie. "She seems so in charge. She seems so *fine*."

"She *is* so fine," Frankie had said, ungrammatically and rather coldly, as if there could be no question at all about this. "She just doesn't leave the house. So what? That's her choice. It's the way she likes it."

"It's the way she likes it," he had repeated very firmly, to put an end to the conversation. He really did not want to talk about it.

Nor did he want to think about it now.

But, at last, here was the De Souza truck. Frankie waved and Louie flashed his lights. He veered sharply out of the traffic as he approached the library and came to a flourishing halt. Frankie jumped into the passenger seat and submitted himself to Ray Davies's boisterous welcome. Then he sat back and breathed out gustily. His heart was pounding, as if he'd run some distance to catch the truck. Somehow Louie made the simple act of picking you up seem as though you were participating in the getaway from a bank heist.

"How're you doing, little bro?" said Louie, punching Frankie gently on the shoulder. "Nice hoodie."

"Got it yesterday," said Frankie. "Got these, too." He pointed to his jeans. "Uncle George's card. Okay, enough now!" Ray Davies was practically giving him a face wash. Frankie put his hands gently around Ray Davies's muzzle and held them there until the dog settled down on his lap.

"Uncle G's credit card!" said Louie. He banged the steering wheel. "Those were the days. Why can't I have Uncle G's card anymore?"

"You *have* money," said Frankie. "You have heaps of money."

"Never enough," said Louie. "*C r e a m,* Frankie, *cream.* You know what the song says."

Cream, Frankie knew, stood for "cash runs everything around me." It was a song by Wu-Tang Clan, Louie's truck band. Louie's taste in music was mostly retro, but in the truck he played exclusively rap. He said it kept him pulsing and alert in the city traffic, which was, apparently, pure psycho territory.

Riding in the De Souza truck was certainly an experience. Frankie felt as if the truck drove according to interior rap rhythms. It was like sitting inside a pumping artery with accompanying breakouts from the horn; Louie was very fond of tooting. And if Louie played Dangermouse, Ray Davies started up, too. There was something about Dangermouse that drove Ray Davies crazy. He stood on the seat and barked frenziedly at the stereo. Louie said Dangermouse was way too intellectual for Ray Davies, who was a simple dog, possibly even a philistine. He preferred Wu-Tang Clan; he liked their piano samples.

It was Wu-Tang Clan playing now. Ray Davies had settled into his patch between the seats, dozing on Louie's old blue baby blanket.

"What's the first stop?" asked Frankie.

Despite Mr. A's theory, Frankie actually knew a good deal about Louie's work, mostly because Louie liked to talk about it in exhaustive detail. He had told Frankie about the various characters he worked with at De Souza's. There was Gregor, who had big gaps between his teeth and carried toothpicks in his pocket; Munro, who was Irish and probably ex-IRA; Darius Littlejohn whose middle name was *Mary,* for heaven's sake. Louie liked to tell Frankie about his circuit around the city, about his favorite cafés and shops, and especially about the cute girls he met at all the offices he called on. Frankie knew, for instance, that Louie's favorite cute girl was called Rosie Reed, that she was part Vietnamese, and that she was the receptionist at Benson Galloway, the big law firm, and that unfortunately Benson Galloway only needed their secure bins changed fortnightly.

Somehow, he doubted any of this was the kind of thing Mr. A was looking for in his report.

"Done two already," said Louie. "Why I was late. Some idiot parked me in at Hatchets." Hatchets was a printing company that produced vast truckloads of wastepaper. Louie picked up bins from Hatchets at least twice a week, but there were no cute girls at Hatchets, apparently, just a hatchet-faced woman — ha! — called Beverley Surridge.

"Teals, Farmers, College of Ed, Postal Services Center, something else" — Louie scrabbled for the clipboard on the door of the truck and shoved it at Frankie — "that'll probably be the morning, then back to the depot. Might be time for you to see some shredding."

Frankie smiled. It was really Louie who loved the shredders. Frankie had seen shredding in action and it was fun enough, but Louie became quite starry-eyed when he watched those machines, the paper worms pouring forth. He was like a little kid watching planes take off and land.

A kid with muscles, though. Louie had muscled up big time since he'd started at De Souza's. Hefting the bins was as good as a workout at the gym, he said. But he did weights after work, too. He and his roommates had a mini gym in their living room. They bench-pressed and cycled and watched the sports channel. Even the female roommate, Mishana, worked out; she was a prop for the St. Colomba girls' senior rugby team.

"How's the apartment?" said Frankie. He'd heard Louie updating Uncle George just two nights ago, but plenty could happen in Louie's life in forty-eight hours.

"Humming along," said Louie. "But DJ's leaving in a month—Perth—and Mishana might go to Japan with the team."

"To play?" said Frankie.

"Nah, to eat sushi," said Louie witheringly. "Of course, to play."

"To play women?" said Frankie.

"Who else?" said Louie.

Frankie thought of Mishana. She was six foot three with shoulders like a butterfly champion; she had broad forearms and a killer instinct and she annihilated everyone in arm wrestling. He thought of the Japanese women he saw around town in tourist groups.

"But they'll be so . . . *small*."

"Yeah," said Louie, "they'll be pulverized. Imagine packing down against Mishana. Anyway, she might be going, and Elvis might have an offshore job, so Eddie and I'll have to find new people." Louie gave a sudden blast on the horn and yelled out the window at a guy leaning against a lamppost, smoking. "Nichols! Wake up, you turkey! Tomorrow's already here!"

The guy turned his head slowly and waved a sleepy hand. Frankie saw he was Hunter Nichols, Louie's oldest friend. Louie had practically lived at Hunter's house in his last year of school.

"Dozy bastard," said Louie fondly. "He's started at the university, but he's morning barista at Havana. He's good, too. I might poach him when I start up my coffee cart."

Louie turned down Rimmer Street, then reversed into the back entrance of Teals Department Store. Frankie climbed down from the truck and followed Louie into the store, wishing for about the millionth time that he had just a tenth of Louie's swaggering assurance.

It was interesting to watch Louie at work. Frankie had been in the De Souza truck plenty of times, but only ever after work was finished; he'd never done a day's route with Louie, seen him in action. Nor had any of the family. Uncle George had demanded a full Technicolor report over dinner.

Louie wore heavy boots and green overalls and a photo ID on his breast pocket. In the photograph, he looked like a trainee mafioso; he'd had a number-two buzz cut and his expression was dour. But in reality, Louie was curly-haired, perpetually grinning, and everyone's mate.

He knew the name of every person they passed by and seemed always to have some connection with them, no matter how minute. He knew someone they played Touch with, or who went out with their cousin, or roomed with their sister or had just dumped their brother. If he hadn't gone to school with them, then he'd seen them just last Saturday at a club, or at the River Market, or the Mall, or up the coast at a party. He knew if they were skaters, skanks, stoners, gearheads, hot dancers, thugs, musicians, or had religion. It didn't matter if they worked in stores or reception or management; Louie had a wave or a shout or a joke for all of them. If they were girls, he stopped to chat; he leaned on their desks and flirted shamelessly with them.

"That girl in the office," said Louie when they were backing out of Teals. "She used to go out with Jester. She's a kleptomaniac. A genius kleptomaniac."

"She steals things?" said Frankie, alarmed. He was constantly worried Louie might revert to his semi-delinquent habits.

"Clothes, makeup, medications, groceries. But mostly clothes and makeup. She never gets caught. But Jester couldn't cope with the stress—being at the Mall and places with her, you know—so they broke up."

"Wilson, the guy in menswear," said Louie, when they were hoisting the Farmers bin into the truck. He secured the bolt and walked round to the driver's side.

"He's getting married," Louie shouted. "But she's pregnant with some other guy's kid."

Frankie waited until he was settled in the truck. "Does he know? How do *you* know?"

"He knows," said Louie. "Everyone knows. He's on some hero kick. But he's a good guy."

At the College of Education, the receptionist offered them cheese scones, left over from morning tea. She was someone's mother, but Louie still flirted; he was dedicated to charming all females, no matter their age.

"Frankie," said the woman after Louie introduced him. "Don't let your brother corrupt you."

"Too late, Natalie," said Louie. "It's Work Experience, so he's getting the whole truth and nothing but. I'll tell him about you when we leave."

"Get thee behind me," said Natalie, but she seemed pleased to Frankie.

"Natalie's a good old girl," said Louie when they were driving to the National Library. "She can *dance*."

"She's old," said Frankie.

"Thirty-seven," said Louie. "She had Georgia when she was sixteen. Then her old man went off. She's with that guy Richie from Steven's Security now and he's okay."

"How do you know she can dance?" asked Frankie.

"Georgia's twenty-first. She *owned* the dance floor."

Between the College of Ed and the Postal Services Center they went to Havana and sat outside under the heater lamps, waiting for hot chocolates. Ray Davies had to stay in the truck because the Havana wait staff fed him cake, which Louie said was bad for beagles.

Frankie liked Havana because the sparrows were particularly sociable. Sometimes they hopped onto the tables and swiped crumbs. He liked to study them close up, without binoculars, and didn't get the chance with many birds—maybe the occasional wood pigeon, drunk on berry juice and uncaring about humans, or a hungry thrush focused on a worm. Or parrots, of course.

(Gigs's family had an African gray called Albert, who was forty years old, a legacy from Chris's grandmother. Albert had once had a wide vocabulary, but he didn't say much these days except, *"Life is real! Life is earnest! / And the grave is not its goal,"* some lines of poetry Chris's grandmother had been fond of reciting. Frankie had tried many times to cajole Albert into further ruminations but the best he'd ever gotten was, *"Monica speaking! Jesus loves you!"* Chris's grandmother had been religious.)

"If sparrows could talk, what do you think they'd say?" Frankie asked Louie. He crouched beside the table, his chin resting on top. He was eye level with two grubby sparrows; they pecked at a white marshmallow he'd placed near the edge of the table. Louie crouched and rested his chin on the table, too, studying the birds.

"Where's the money, bozo?" he said, speaking out the side of his mouth like Bugs Bunny. *"Ya said ya'd get it here by six."* The sparrows' heads bobbed and lurched, exactly as if they were snatching a furtive conference. *"Listen, half-wit—it's not so easy. The old lady's watching m'every move. . . ."*

Frankie giggled. It was dead right. And it occurred to him that Louie was a bit like a sparrow himself—pecking, bobbing, chirping, and chatting, on the go and on the make.

"Ya shoulda ditched that old bat years ago. She's crampin' ya style, bozo . . ."

"Ahhh, shut ya face!"

Frankie walked two fingers gently across the table, but the sparrows were unconcerned, still jabbing at the sweet.

"If Gordana was a bird, what do you reckon she'd be?" he asked Louie.

"Something merciless that eats small mammals," said Louie.

Frankie let go a laughing sigh and the sparrows darted upward, startled by the draft.

"A sparrow hawk," said Louie. "Or a kestrel. No, no, meaner and more brooding—a barn owl." He grinned, pleased with his own meanness. "On her good days, maybe a heron . . . or a crane."

Frankie could see this. Gordana had long legs, and she could just stand there sometimes, staring off, ignoring you.

"What about when she's arguing with Uncle George?"

"A magpie?" said Louie.

"No," said Frankie, thinking about it. "A screech owl. They're really high-pitched."

"Ha," said Louie. "What's Uncle G?"

"Easy," said Frankie. "A penguin, emperor, king, Adélie—"

"A *puffin!*" said Louie, thumping the table. "They're fat and childlike."

"He's not fat," Frankie protested. "He's well built. He could be a pheasant, maybe. They're kind of big. And noble."

Back in the truck, Frankie sneaked a marshmallow to Ray Davies, and Louie fiddled with his shuffle, moving through his playlist for just the right song. The shuffle made Frankie think of

Sydney. He burned to know how it was going in the kitchen back home.

"Next stop, PSC," said Louie.

"What about the Aunties?" said Frankie. They were driving around the north perimeter of the Botanic Gardens, past the children's park. Nellie had taken Frankie there for regular swing sessions and had once been knocked out by a renegade swing going backward at speed. Frankie had been just five at the time but he could remember the incident very clearly. Nellie had recovered quickly but the woman pushing the swing had become completely hysterical. Finally, Nellie had bought everyone large ice creams to calm things, and the woman had chosen orange chocolate chip, which was Frankie's all-time least favorite flavor. It was peculiar, he thought, the details that stuck in your memory.

"Alma's a pelican," said Frankie. "All the chins. And Nellie's—"

"Something massive and slow-moving," said Louie. "A great auk. What about your *g f,* then? What would she be?"

Frankie ignored this. "I think Nellie's more of a partridge." He was pleased with this. Partridges were plump ground-nesters, which was very appropriate for Nellie, with all her cooking and gardening. "This is a good game. How come I never thought of it before?"

"The Aunties are all rocs," Louie proclaimed. "The roc was gigantic."

"Also imaginary," said Frankie.

"Yeah, but they're stranger than fiction. C'mon, Frankie, what about—what's her name? Is she a swan? A flamingo? A bantam?"

"Shut up," said Frankie.

"*Not* a bantam," he said after a moment, which made Louie laugh. "And she's not my girlfriend."

"She want to be your girlfriend?" asked Louie.

"Of course not," said Frankie. Privately, he decided that Sydney was a parakeet. Or a woodpecker. She was small and brightly colored and very insistent.

At the Postal Services Center, Louie made himself comfortable in the office. Apparently he and the receptionist had once been on a school ski-trip together. The receptionist's name was Quetchin Brooker. She had blue-black hair in a most severe cut and black fingernails. She wore dark eyeliner and a very short skirt. Frankie was just thinking she was like the femme fatale in a Bond movie, when she winked at him, and he blushed furiously.

While they chatted, Frankie began a list of words and phrases in his notebook. *Mobile shredding truck. Destruction Center. Secure bins. Licensed employee. Pulverizing. Shredding. Canceled checks. Legal records. Closed-loop process.* He could have made an alternative list, he thought, full of bird names and gossip. He could have truthfully told Mr. A that gossip was a vital part of Louie's work.

Back in the truck, Louie banged the steering wheel and let out a big sigh. "Queech Brooker," he said. "We all fancied her like crazy at school, but turns out she's strictly for the girls."

"She's a raven," said Frankie. And when they arrived at the District Court, he thought one of the men behind the counter was a vulture, and the female office manager some sort of wading bird — a plover or a curlew. The entire world was becoming avian. "You want to see the shredding or do the Istanbul?" said Louie. He was clipping the District Court bin into place on the truck platform. *Trolley. Platform. Elevator. Crane mechanism.* A group of guys stood on the steps of the courthouse, huddling a little, smoking and murmuring. *Marabou,* thought Frankie. Across the road, three elderly ladies with perfectly white, freshly set hairdos sat side by side at the bus stop, a purse each on their ample laps. *Snow bunting,* thought Frankie. A couple of young women passed by, in and then out of earshot, talking fast, waving their hands, shrieking. *Jays. Shrikes.*

"What do you think Ma is?" said Frankie suddenly.

"What?" said Louie. "C'mon, we'll do the Istanbul. I'm starving."

Frankie tried again while they waited at an intersection. Ray Davies was nosing his pocket, marshmallow hunting.

"Ma?" he said. "What kind of a bird would she be?"

Louie was jiggling his legs, banging an erratic rhythm on the steering wheel, fiddling with the mirror, and checking his face for zits, all at the same time. He hated waiting for the traffic lights to turn green.

"Hah! Did I tell you Ilir's got another DUI?" he said. "He'll lose his license this time, for sure." Ilir was the owner of the Istanbul. He was Muslim and not even supposed to drink alcohol.

For some reason Louie was deliberately ignoring Frankie's question about Ma. Instead, he began to recite the catalog of Ilir's driving offenses, which was long and not at all interesting. When the light turned green, he revved ostentatiously and roared across the intersection.

Frankie looked over at Louie talking on and on. It reminded him of something, though he couldn't put his finger on it. Instead, he tried to think what sort of a bird Ma might be. A yellow-throated warbler? They made their nests in dense undergrowth, hidden from the world. Maybe she was a songbird. A linnet or a lark? Sometimes Ma hummed the Russian opera bits when she was baking. Plus, she got up early, like the lark.

A dove, perhaps? She was certainly very peaceable. She cooed and billed, trying to calm things when the rest of them were arguing. But she wasn't snow white like a dove; she was small and dark. More like a blackbird.

But none of these were precisely right, not in the way a puffin's absurdity so suited Uncle George. What kind of bird had all those other birds' qualities but was also very quiet, very private, almost secretive? What kind of bird could be so absorbed, so lost in concentration, that sometimes it seemed as if it weren't there?

Louie was parking, right outside the Istanbul, still rattling on about Ilir. He was on to Ilir's extended family now, his cousins who owned a kebab house in the suburbs and had built a mansion in the hills.

Perhaps Ma was simply a house sparrow.

And then it came to Frankie what Louie was reminding him of. Himself, him, Frankie. Himself babbling away to Sydney, going on and on and on about the Aunties that day, trying desperately to fill the air between them with words, any words, to summon up a cloud of words so big, it shut out the intensity of her focus, deflected her questions about his times at the Aunties' house, her inevitable questions about Ma.

Clearly, Louie did not want to talk about Ma. But now Frankie saw more than that, too. Now, sitting here in the De Souza truck—staring through the windshield at the neon sign above the Siren Strip Club, pallid in the midday light—sitting there not listening to Louie's stream of information about Ilir, Frankie knew, as if for the first time, with an extraordinary little stab of illumination, that he had not in fact once in his twelve years *ever* had a conversation with Louie about Ma.

Not once had they ever discussed the startling fact of their family life: that their mother stayed permanently and irrevocably—and, who knows, maybe unnaturally—at home; that she had not left their property for nine years or more; that she seldom ever left the four safe walls of their house. They had never discussed the extremely odd fact that their mother had not, for nine years, been in a car, a bus, a shop, a movie theater, an airplane. That in this long time, she had never been to the beach, the library, the art gallery, the Aunties', the doctor, the dentist, a café, or a kebab house. How could they never have talked about this? Frankie could hardly believe it.

"You coming in?" said Louie. "You want me to get you a chwarma? We can eat them in the truck, give the boyo some treats."

Frankie looked at his brother. He looked at Ray Davies, who was standing expectantly, his tongue lolling, a long drool of saliva hanging.

"Wake up, Frankster," said Louie, leaning over and snapping his fingers in front of Frankie's eyes. "What do you want? Chwarma? Falafel? Dolma? Kofte? Lamb or chicken? Nah, nah, don't tell me. No chicken. You might get campylobacter . . ."

A thin heat crawled up behind Frankie's ears. At the same time, everything in the truck seemed to slow down just a little—Ray Davies's panting, Louie's hand-tapping and leg-jiggling, the movements of his face.

"Maybe Ma's a *house* sparrow," said Frankie, very deliberately. He turned to look at Louie, tried a weak smile.

Louie went very still and stared straight ahead, through the windshield. It was so odd for him to be utterly immobile that Frankie felt almost afraid. Ray Davies gave a little whine and burrowed into Louie's armpit.

After a long while, Louie said, "She has to be a caged bird, doesn't she?" He kept looking ahead. "Something that's had its wings clipped. Something really pretty, but a bit sad."

Louie's hand slipped sideways, feeling for Ray Davies's head. He rubbed behind the dog's ears, slowly, thoughtfully.

"A chaffinch," he said. "Or a lovebird. Or maybe a canary."

Ray Davies gave a low, pleased growl.

"Yeah, a canary," said Louie. "One that doesn't sing much. Doesn't sing at all."

"She sings," said Frankie in a small voice.

"But not really," said Louie. He finally turned and looked at Frankie.

"Lamb chwarma?" he said.

It was never completely dark in Ma's bedroom, even when she'd switched off the bedside light. A diffused glow came through the window from the street lamp directly outside the front gate. Ma never drew the curtains; she liked the glow from the street lamp.

Frankie had been listening for the click of the bedside light; sometimes he preferred to ask questions in the dim color of that outside light.

"Are you still awake?" he whispered.

"Yes," Ma whispered back.

Frankie laid his head back on Uncle George's pillow. He liked its smell—apple shampoo (which Louie said Uncle George had been using since 1977) and Uncle G's aftershave; he always shaved last thing at night, to save time in the morning, which was why in the evenings, if he was there at dinner, he looked even swarthier, and slightly disheveled.

"Everything all right?" said Ma, turning over and sitting up a little.

"Yeah," said Frankie. He looked at the woman in the painting, but only her hair gleamed, the rest of her swallowed up by the night.

"Solly Napier's cousin died. At his school. He was thirteen."

"That's terrible," said Ma. "How?"

"Hole in his heart," said Frankie. "No one knew. They were playing soccer."

There was a loud thump on the roof, followed by the skittering of claws on metal. The Fat Controller. Her night was just beginning.

"You haven't got a hole in your heart, Frankie," said Ma.

"I know," said Frankie. "I'm just saying. Solly went to the funeral. They had a soccer ball on the coffin and it rolled off during the service and bounced down the aisle."

"Oh," said Ma. Frankie could tell she was trying not to giggle.

"The Bolshoi Ballet is coming," said Frankie. "The greatest ballet company in the world." He'd read this on the poster at the town hall. "They're doing Sleeping Beauty."

"I love that music," said Ma.

They lay there, silent, listening to the sounds outside the window: the occasional passing car, a door slamming, the Fat Controller arguing with next door's cat, Colin.

"Did you ever see the Bolshoi Ballet?" Frankie asked.

"On video," said Ma.

Colin-next-door was Burmese. His mournful whine rose and fell, an unearthly music that set Frankie's teeth on edge. The Fat Controller's response was a kind of gruff meow, no-nonsense, pitiless.

"Wouldn't you really like to go?" said Frankie.

"Yes," said Ma, after a pause. "But you know how it is."

The two cats continued outside the window, an eerie drawn-out duet. It was more mysterious than Russian, Frankie thought, untranslatable—except for the Fat Controller's final exasperated yelp-yowl, which Frankie interpreted as buzz off. There was more thumping and rustling and then a long quiet.

"I wish you could just go," said Frankie. "We could get you a ticket as a birthday present."

He knew he shouldn't be saying this; he hadn't said anything like this to Ma for a very long time. Not since the time he'd given her a handmade birthday voucher inviting her to see the nest of yellowhammer fledglings he'd discovered up in McCullough's Reserve. Ma had cried that time. She'd stood at the bench in front of the electric beater, shaking; tears had rolled down her cheeks and pinged off into the cake mixture.

"Maybe, you never know, maybe it would be okay this time," said Frankie. It was an old hope, one he'd almost forgotten about. For ages now he'd told himself not to think like that.

"I'm sorry, Frankie," said Ma. Her voice was just a whisper.

They both lay still, listening now to the muted kitchen noises that signaled Uncle George's arrival home. The fridge door opening and closing. The bang of the kettle against the sink. The pipes shuddering as the hot tap ran.

The bedside clock showed 10:15 p.m.

"Sorry," Frankie said. He kissed Ma on her cheek.

"I'm sorry, too," said Ma softly.

"It's okay," said Frankie, sliding off the bed. "One thing," he said from the doorway. "I definitely don't want a soccer ball on my coffin. Or a cricket ball. No balls, okay?"

"You're not going to die," said Ma. "Not till you're extremely old."

He really didn't know how adults could say things like that. It was preposterous. Not to mention virtually a lie. How could they possibly know?

"'Night," he said, and closed the door.

FIVE

Tuesday, April 11

The day began in the worst possible way. Twice. First, it began at 3:49 a.m. when the Fat Controller jumped through Frankie's bedroom window with a rat and proceeded to do a presentation juggle on the floor in front of his bed. Frankie knew this was happening even before he turned on the light. It had happened before; he recognized the particular sounds of this tumbling act. It was as loud as forty Cossacks and accompanied by the Fat Controller's very peculiar deep-throated meow of triumph.

This was enough to make Frankie queasy. But when he snapped on the light and saw that the Fat Controller's trophy was a bush rat, he almost barfed on the spot. There'd been plenty of mice in the FC's hunting career, and any number of birds, but this was the first rat Frankie knew of. The rat was large, dirty brown, and utterly repulsive, with an alarmingly long tail. As far as Frankie could tell it was dead. But maybe it had merely been terrified into unconsciousness. Either way, he decidedly did not want it in his bedroom. The Fat Controller had so effectively eviscerated her last victim (the world's tiniest gray mouse) that

Frankie had used an entire bottle of laundry soap eradicating the blood and entrails from the carpet.

But removing the Fat Controller wasn't easy, since she became ferocious and most uncooperative if her hunting celebrations were interrupted. Since Frankie couldn't bring himself to pick up the rat (in case it was still alive) and since the Fat Controller couldn't be persuaded to leave the rat, he *had* to pick up the Fat Controller — no mean feat, considering her body mass — with the rat in her mouth, and cart them both down the hall, out through the kitchen, and into the backyard, all as quietly as possible and holding the growling cat at rigid arms' length in case any part of the rat brushed his skin and he somehow contracted bubonic plague. The back section was creepy at night and doubly creepy when the wind was up. The black-boy peach tree, the grapevine along the back fence, the garden bench, the trellising on the side of the garage, all took on most sinister aspects, shape-changing and seeming almost to mutter at him. The walnut tree hung over the garden shed in an especially threatening way, a malevolent giant, swaying heftily. Even as Frankie thought this, walnuts rained down on the shed roof and the clatter startled him so much, he dropped the Fat Controller. She gave a prolonged growl and bounded under a garden chair, the rat still firmly in her jaws. Frankie raced back across the damp grass and into the house, banging the back door behind him.

He was exhausted and disgusted in equal parts by the time he returned to his room. He shut his window and fell back into bed. But a minute later, he leaped out again, remembering that when she had prey to display, the Fat Controller attempted entry to the house by any means possible. He spent the next ten minutes securing all the other open windows — honestly, the house was a burglar's paradise — though he didn't dare go into Gordana's room. Gordana was quite capable of raising the entire house if someone entered her bedroom during the night. But, Frankie reasoned, her bedroom was upstairs, and though the Fat Controller did have a quite astounding ability to launch herself through windows from the most awkward angles, he was confident the force field of disdain hanging about Gordana would be felt by the cat even at her most distracted.

Back in bed he tossed about, trying to get comfortable. He was too hot (thinking of rat innards), then he was strangely chilled (thinking about Ma, how bothered he was by Louie comparing her to a canary), then, somehow, hot and cold both together (thinking how *unsettled* he felt these days, how not-on-top-of-things). Finally, he distracted himself by trying—as he had for the last two weeks—to decide definitively what kind of bird he might be.

Secretly, he wanted to be something intrepid and hardy, a storm petrel, say, or tough and streetwise and lippy, like a jackdaw. Or a swallow; they were like great one-day bowlers, Frankie had often thought—dressed in colors, swift, graceful, and able to catch things in flight. He loved ospreys, too. They were kind of piratical with those dark stripes around their eyes, swashbuckling and athletic. It was annoying how easy everyone *else* was to match with a bird. (Gigs, for instance, was a merganser; his stepmother was a laying hen; Mr. A was a harrier hawk; Bronwyn Baxter was so obviously—he loved this—a strutting pouter pigeon.)

Frankie turned over yet again and checked the clock: 4:15 a.m. He banged his pillow about, getting it thick at the bottom the way he liked it, and plunged his head back into it. The window rattled. It was definitely colder these nights. Autumn in earnest—that's why the Fat Controller's hunting was accelerating. Two weeks till camp. He had a horrible feeling he might be a hummingbird, sort of small and incessantly wing-beating, hovering anxiously.

But just as he was dropping off, it came to him, like a gift to make up for the rat. A kingfisher. He could be a kingfisher. Perched on a power line, still and watchful. Spying out the land and the water. Waiting.

The morning began for the second time, at 6:45 with a thunderously slammed door, followed by shrieking from Gordana. It interested Frankie that you could be more or less asleep but still able to accurately identify particular sounds and the people making them. The shrieking seemed to be right outside his bedroom door; it seemed pitched directly at him.

"Ohmygod!" she was wailing. "That disgusting, *disgusting* feline! Ohmygod, she's like a serial killer! She has no human feeling—"

"Of course she doesn't have human feeling," said Uncle George, who was somehow also outside the door. "She's a sodding cat. She's supposed to do this. For God's sake, keep your voice down, Gordana."

"Why should I? I feel *sick*. I want to wash myself all over, except I *can't*, can I! And why can't you ever wear underpants, for God's sake? No one wants to see your repulsive parts." Wail, stomp, wail, stomp. Gordana was apparently flouncing back upstairs in the loudest possible manner.

"Thanks very much," said Uncle George, to no one in particular.

Frankie moved sleepily out of bed and opened his door. Uncle George was standing there wearing only his "Partially Bling Man" T-shirt, which stopped just above his genitals. It was his favorite piece of clothing, though it was a joke against him. The T-shirt had been a present from Louie and Gordana two birthdays ago following a very unfortunate proofing error that had landed Parsons Porritt in big trouble with a client. The client was the Blind Institute, and somehow—*"How? How? How, in Christ's name!"* Uncle George had raged—somehow, in the publicity pamphlet Parsons Porritt had designed for them, the partially blind had twice been referred to as the partially bling.

The T-shirt was black and had a drawing of a man with elaborate pieces of bling decorating one side only of his body. In the early morning and late evening Uncle George often wandered around the house wearing nothing but the tee.

"Sorry, old man," he said to Frankie. "Thought a fire must have broken out." He crossed his legs, tugged down the bottom of his T-shirt and made a gasping O with his mouth. It was so silly, Frankie couldn't help smiling.

"What is it?" said Ma, coming down the hallway. She was in her bathrobe and Chinese slippers, looking very sleepy, her hair plastered against her head like a little black cap. Frankie had one of those odd flashes of memory that seemed to visit him at quite inappropriate times. He recalled Ma in her old bathrobe, walking up and down this same hall at night, talking to herself, reciting Russian vocabulary over and over. That robe had been leaf-green and brocaded, almost like a pretty coat. For a long time it had been Ma's principal outfit.

"The big girl's been busy," said Uncle George, gesturing to the closed bathroom door. "She's left a little present, and worst luck, Gordana saw it first."

"I don't think I want to see it," said Ma. She turned and went back down the hall.

"It's a rat," said Frankie. "She brought it into my room last night." He'd overlooked the bathroom window.

"It *was* a rat," said Uncle George, opening the bathroom door and pointing to the shower stall. Frankie's stomach turned over but he felt compelled to look at the deposit on the no longer pristine white bath mat.

"You've got to admire the technical skill," said Uncle George, looking down at it, too. "The precision really is magnificent. And then, it's render unto Caesar—"

"Okay, o*kay*," said Frankie.

The Fat Controller had left a perfectly cleaned rat kidney and one complete rat eyeball. Her best work yet, Frankie noted with one part of his mind, even as he shuddered at the revoltingness of it. The kidney was a deep red-black, tiny and delicate as a semiprecious stone. It had the look of something licked to a high polish. The eye seemed almost to shimmer under the bathroom light; it was like a slightly squashed, flaccid marble, shiny brown, with black speckling. Frankie was sure he could see an almost pleading look to it.

"Bit much before breakfast," said Uncle George.

"She's just following her instincts," said Frankie feebly. His own instinct was to go back to bed, pull the duvet over his head, and stay there for the day. He felt enormously tired. But even as he stood barefoot and chilled on the bathroom tiles, considering the bits of the brown rat's inner self, he remembered that it was Tuesday, April 11, and that was (a) the day the Science Fair results were announced, (b) the day they must hand in their work experience reports, and (c) Sydney's birthday, and she had invited him to her house for book project and cake. He'd decided—with Gigs's approval—to give her a starter list of Chilun vocab as a present.

"It's so early," said Frankie. "Why is Gordana up early?" Uncle George had wrapped a towel around his middle and was on his knees scooping up the Fat Controller's little present with toilet paper.

"I'll make pancakes," said Uncle George. "Damage control."

Pancakes would be good, thought Frankie. They hadn't had Uncle George pancakes in a while. These were legendary and more or less like Uncle George himself: big and thick and buttery, and slathered with excessive toppings. The downside was that Uncle George obliterated the kitchen when he cooked. He was even worse than Gordana. Raw mixture actually hit the ceiling. And other people—usually Ma or Frankie—were always left to clean up.

Frankie dressed and gave his work experience report a final check. He wasn't at all happy with it. There was a good enough description of Louie and his different routines, and then of the afternoon with Uncle George. (This had consisted of listening to Uncle G on the phone much of the time, first speaking very testily to a supplier, then mollifying a client, then swearing heartily about both client and supplier to his partner, Joe, who was somewhere at an airport and couldn't hear properly.)

Frankie had his vocabulary list and he'd managed a tolerable description of the workplaces. But when he'd come to write the portraits of Louie and Uncle George, his pen had seemed to seize up. He couldn't understand it. It should have been so easy. Uncle George and Louie were the most colorful and amusing, the most *entertaining,* characters in his life. He should have been able to write pages and pages about them.

Instead, the more he tried to capture them in words, the more they seemed to recede from him. It was as if he was watching them both through the wrong end of a telescope while they slowly diminished into the distance. At one point, disturbingly, it seemed he couldn't even think what they looked like. He'd actually gone upstairs to look at the family photo in Uncle George's office, but the more he stared at the picture, the less easy it seemed he could make them out. He'd stared at Gordana, too, and felt the same thing. She was both infinitely familiar and oddly unrecognizable. It had made Frankie feel so strange, he'd spun around and left the office. He hadn't wanted to look at himself and experience the same sensation.

He put the report in his backpack, resigning himself to a poor mark. Mr. A had a genius for spotting a halfhearted effort. Gigs would get an A. He'd ended up having a whale of a time with a weed-eater at some mansion out in the country. Sydney, too, would get an A. She'd written pages; her vocabulary list was four columns. She'd shown Frankie her report but the same unnerving feeling had come over him when he began reading Sydney's portrait of Ma. The words did and did not make sense. Ma seemed to dissolve as he read.

"It's great," he'd said colorlessly, and Sydney had bulged her eyes at him. Her eye-bulging could convey a number of emotions. In this case, Frankie knew, it was skepticism.

"I wish I could write as well as you," he said, trying to make amends.

"A portrait can be a drawing," was all Sydney had said. So he'd tried that. He'd sat down at his desk, selected a Faber-Castell 3B, opened up the music box, and begun sketching. But the feeling had come over him again and he'd ended up drawing a puffin and a sparrow. As sketches went, they were good, but he didn't want to put them in the report.

In the kitchen, Gordana was bent over the table, paintbrush in hand, daubing a pair of jeans with pink paint. Frankie leaned in to see what she was painting, then turned away quickly. Gordana appeared to be putting the finishing touches to a nipple. The jeans were decorated at intervals with naked breasts.

"Don't ask," said Uncle George to Frankie. He was fully clothed now, pouring pancake batter into the frying pan.

"If you must know," said Gordana, "it's Saint's Day. Saint Agatha. Virgin and Martyr. Put to death by the Romans. Rolled on live coals. Tongs et cetera, et cetera, et cetera. Patron saint of fire and earthquakes."

"Why breasts?" said Uncle George. "Or are you just being provocative?"

"They sliced off her breasts," said Gordana. "*Torture.* She's the patron saint of breasts, too."

"You're kidding!" said Uncle George. "A patron saint for breasts. Are there saints for other body parts? Eyes, ears, tonsils, testicles?"

"Shut up," said Gordana. "She's the saint for breast *diseases.*"

Frankie leaned over the bench, watching the pancake develop dimples and bubbles all over its surface. He wondered if there was a patron saint for rashes. He or she might be worth a prayer. He'd measured his rash again last night and it had definitely spread. But, worst luck, he didn't really believe in saints.

"Who wants the first pancake?" said Uncle George.

"Me," said Gordana. "I deserve it. I'm still traumatized by that disgusting liver."

"Kidney," said Frankie.

"It's ready," said Uncle George. "Get a plate, Gordana."

"Can't," said Gordana. "I'm in the middle of this nipple. Get me a plate, Frankie."

"Get it yourself," said Frankie, hating her.

"Don't be childish," said Gordana.

"Stop bickering, please," said Ma, coming into the kitchen.

"Can you get meat?" she said to Uncle George. "Aunties tonight."

"Lamb, beef, pork?" said Uncle George. "Let's have lamb! Lamb filets with oregano—"

"Shut *up!*" said Gordana. "How can you even think about meat after finding offal all over the house—"

"It was hardly all over the house," Ma began.

"And I'm *sick* of the Aunties. Why do we have to have them week after week after week? Why can't we—?"

"It's only every other week," said Ma. "And they love it. They love to see you."

"If only it was mutual," said Gordana. She flicked the brush with her fingers and sprayed an arc of little pink dots over the waist of the jeans.

"Pancake," said Uncle George, putting a plate down in front of Gordana. "Sour cream and maple syrup, the way you like it."

"Careful!" said Gordana. "Don't smudge the paint." Neither Uncle George nor the plate were anywhere near the jeans, Frankie observed.

"Is it the eleventh?" said Uncle George. "If it's the eleventh, I'll be late. We're wooing a new client. Big job. Frankie'll get the meat, won't you, old man?"

"I've got my book project," said Frankie. "At Sydney's." He wasn't going to mention her birthday in front of Gordana.

"Gordana?" said Uncle George.

"Nope," said Gordana, her mouth full of pancake. "I'm going to Ben's indoor cricket."

"Oh," said Ma. But she never queried Gordana's after-school schedule. Instead, she looked at Frankie. "Could Sydney come here?"

And quite suddenly, Frankie was outraged. He felt it like a flood, rushing through his body, making him almost unsteady on his feet. *No*, he wanted to shout, *no, she could not! Why should she?*

"She won't mind coming here," said Gordana. "She worships at Ma's altar."

"Shut up!" Frankie yelled, swinging round on Gordana. "Shut your ugly screech-owl face!"

"Dear, dear, *dear*," said Gordana. "Someone give the child a pill."

Frankie wanted to weep with fury and frustration. He hated Gordana for provoking this response in him.

"Enough! Calm down, everyone!" said Uncle George. He flipped a pancake and caught it neatly in the pan. "Can you help me out here, Frankie?"

Frankie looked at Uncle George. His face had a light dusting of flour and there were oil spots down his Partially Bling Man T-shirt. A flick of butter rested in his eyebrow.

He looked at Ma, standing alongside Uncle George. She was dressed and ready in her baking gear—a faded cotton skirt, white T-shirt, low shoes. Her clothes were fresh and immaculate. As always, she seemed even more petite beside Uncle George. She looked like a girl, Frankie thought, a pale, delicate girl from another time. Her face wore the expressionless look it took on when this sort of arrangement was being discussed. It was as if she were somehow transporting herself away from the conversation, waiting for it to be over. Frankie couldn't bear that look.

"I'll get the meat," he said.

"Good man," said Uncle George. "Pancake?"

"And the code word is, fellas?" said Cassino.

It was Gigs's week. "Palwankar Baloo," he said. He was having a phase on famous Indian cricket teams.

Cassino actually laughed. It was exactly like a rock face trembling. "For real?"

"For real," said Gigs. "Nineteen-oh-five, nineteen-oh-six to nineteen twenty, nineteen twenty-one. Thirty-three first-class matches. Left-arm orthodox spin."

"Fair enough," said Cassino.

"You should be on some quiz program," said Frankie when

they sat down. "Gigs Angelo. Subject: obscure cricketers."

Gigs took out his breakfast. It was savory rolled pancakes.

"Huh, we had pancakes, too," said Frankie. "But Gordana was a cow, so it was ruined."

"What's new?" said Gigs. "When wasn't she a cow? I can't remember."

But Frankie could—barely. Gordana had been more or less tolerable until . . . He thought back, but it was hard to pinpoint. A couple of years ago? Till Louie left home, maybe. Yes, it had been all downhill since then.

"It's because of her name," said Gigs.

"What?" Frankie rolled up his ticket and poked it into the seat back. He surveyed the installation critically. The sad fact was they were running out of room.

"It's a *man's* name," said Gigs. "Her personality's warped because she's got a boy's name. She's kind of in a permanent bad mood about it. Whose was it again?"

"My grandfather's. Gordon Osbourne."

"The one who died in the car crash?"

"Yeah," said Frankie. "His name was Gordon and her name was Pearl. She was the Aunties' little sister."

"Not a very Russian name," said Gigs.

"What?"

"Gordon."

"It's not Russian," said Frankie, puzzled. "I think it's Scottish."

"But wasn't he Russian?"

"No," said Frankie.

"I thought that was why your Ma liked Russian stuff so much," said Gigs.

"She just took it at the university," said Frankie. "Then she took it again later, after she had us kids. Or something. She's very good at languages."

The bus pulled into the midtown terminal and the city kids began clambering on. Frankie thought about Ma's Russian thing. Why *did* she like Russian stuff so much? He'd never really asked. It was just a fact of her life, their family life—an odd fact, along with all the others.

"Praedictum faciitus mixtum Yendys beeday?" said Gigs. (You got the thing for Sydney's birthday?)

"Sure have," said Frankie. He'd made a list of two hundred words in cursive script with Uncle George's old fountain pen. He'd used fake parchment paper, then rolled it and tied it with string so that it resembled a scroll.

"So weird," said Frankie. "I couldn't work out how to spell some words."

"Ours is principally an *oral* language," said Gigs, in Mr. A tones, and they both laughed.

"Shakespeare spelled things all different ways," said Frankie. "Even his name."

"Yeah?" said Gigs.

Frankie was about to say that Gordana had told him years ago, when she was explaining her own wayward spelling, but at that moment the bus doors banged shut and the gears ground slowly—and Frankie realized Sydney hadn't boarded.

"Hey!" Frankie was on his feet, rolling to the front of the bus. "Cassino! Sydney's not here." Frankie grabbed the pole behind the driver's seat, steadying himself.

Cassino looked in his rearview mirror. "She's not usually late, eh?"

"Never," said Frankie. It was true. For a kid, Sydney was weirdly punctual. It was compensating for her mother, she said. Her mother didn't believe in being on time for anything. Her mother believed that people should always wait for her.

Cassino was pulling over. "We can hold five."

Frankie looked out the window, hoping for Sydney, running along the footpath, perhaps, signaling wildly.

"She's not coming," said Eugene Kearney behind him.

Frankie looked at the twins. They'd both had their heads shaved. They looked like big nubbly turnips. Thuggish turnips.

"You'll be all alone today, Frankie," said Seamus, in mock sorrow.

"What would you know?" said Frankie. Cassino was eyes front. He refused even to exchange glances with the Kearney twins.

"Nothing we're telling you," said Eugene.

"She came to the buth thtop," said another voice. It was Evie Hewitt, a little Year Four girl with a lisp. "She wath there and then her mother came in the car and she had to go away again. I think they were having a fight—"

"Oooo yes," said Eugene Kearney. "*Big* shit flying."

Frankie wondered what would happen if he hit one of the Kearney twins. Probably he'd have to go into hiding.

"I think she wath crying," said Evie Hewitt.

"Her old lady's one wack-job," said Seamus.

Cassino turned and raised an eyebrow at Frankie, and Frankie shrugged. He guessed there was no point in waiting.

"She'th nithe, Thydney," said Evie Hewitt to Frankie as the bus started up again. "She leth me lithen to her Shuffle and she told me about her thithtith."

"Yeah," said Frankie, mentally translating.

Sisters.

"Her mother'th got a Porsche like my uncle."

"Thanks," said Frankie, heading to the back of the bus. A Porsche, for God's sake. How could Sydney's mother have a Porsche?

And what on earth was going on?

* * *

The Kearney twins yelled, "ABSENT!" with excessive glee when Mr. A called Sydney's name at roll time. Frankie wondered if it was possible to have a heart attack from utter fury. Or worry. His heart seemed to have been beating too fast all morning. Plus, he felt unnaturally sweaty. He'd read once in the *Family Health Dictionary* that sudden heavy sweating could signal a heart attack.

He'd handed in his work experience project and crawled through Dictionary. Today's words seemed blessedly without heavy significance. Normally *panspermia:* pan·sper·mi·a, *n, a theory of biogenetics that states that the universe is full of spores that germinate when they find a favorable environment* would have struck him as a gloriously funny word, perfect for a rude cartoon dart about the Kearney twins. But this morning's cartoon darts had all been speculations about Sydney and what might be happening. Anything Was Possible, Frankie knew. Anything Is Possible, was Sydney's favorite description of life with her mother. Frankie always heard the phrase in capital letters.

He hadn't met Sydney's mother yet, though he knew all about her. Her name was Freya. She didn't have a surname. Not anymore. She had changed her name by deed poll. Sydney's mother's name had been Joanne Corcoran, but she had long ago declared it incompatible with her free spirit. Freya was perfect, she said, because Freya was the Norse goddess of beauty and fertility. Sydney had bulged her eyes lengthily on the word *fertility* and Frankie had rolled his own sympathetically.

"My mother believes in babies," said Sydney with a sigh. "I'm sure she's planning to have more."

"But how?" said Frankie, and earned another eye-bulge.

As well as not believing in work or school, Freya did not believe in being tied to a man.

"She believes in their money, though," said Sydney, but she hadn't elaborated.

Today, his first time at Sydney's house, Frankie had been going to meet Freya. Sydney had said, with her usual honesty, that she generally avoided inviting people to her house.

"Since sometimes it isn't even a house," she said. "Plus, parents never approve of my mother. Plus, she's just way too tricky." Frankie had already figured *that* one. He had a well-developed disapproval of Sydney's mother, despite never having laid eyes on her. His disapproval had accumulated steadily with each of Sydney's stories until now he imagined Freya as a lurid combination of the White Witch and Britney Spears, kind of cool and sexy, delinquent, unpredictable and malevolent all at the same time. Of course, he didn't let on about any of this to Sydney, and he had been curious to meet Freya. In a nervous sort of way.

Loquacious: lo·qua·cious, *n, tending to talk a great deal.*

A perfect word for Sydney, thought Frankie. She was effortlessly loquacious, anywhere and everywhere and all the time. In class she managed to talk just under Mr. A's ever-active radar, a stream of stories and forceful opinions. He was missing Sydney's constant commentary. He was missing *her.* She hadn't been absent once in the two months since she'd started at Notts. It was amazing, Frankie thought, how rapidly she'd become a fixture in his life. And she was a girl. He couldn't imagine at all now what it would be like if she wasn't there.

A paper dart crashed into Frankie's exercise book. He unfolded it and considered Gigs's mad punctuation figures. The Gigs and Frankie question marks sat in an airport lounge, their cricket caps hanging at despondent angles. Question mark signalmen stood on the runway waving flags at a bulbous plane. Hanging out of the plane was the Sydney question mark, her crazy mane blowing about her face. Gigs had framed the entire picture with small green question marks.

A rush of panic swept down Frankie's arms and a tingling broke out in his wrists. It was a familiar feeling. It happened sometimes in the night if he was woken by a loud noise. It had happened once in the city when he and Gigs, mistiming a hare-brained sprint across the road, had nearly been bowled by a bus. It happened whenever he got a fright.

Gigs's scenario was entirely possible. Frankie had been suppressing the idea all morning, but he knew that Sydney's mother could pull the plug at any time. She could *up sticks,* as the Aunties called it, take Sydney and her sisters somewhere new. She'd only done it about a kajillion times before. She'd come home, Sydney said, and announce that they were packing up, shifting out, moving on, and *now.*

"Make hay while the sun shines, ha, ha," Sydney said. "The only reliable things in my life are my father and my *oma,* and Oma's house in Amsterdam. And that's only for two months a year."

Frankie was astonished at Sydney's apparent acceptance of this situation. He couldn't begin to consider a life like that. *Everything* about his life was reliable. Constant. Predictable. Even—ha!—the rodent voice and its sadistic habits. He knew the patterns and predilections of everyone and everything in his day, his week, his year. The Fat Controller's morning meow. The Zig Zag routine. Gigs's jokes. Gordana's grumpiness. Cassino and the code word. Mr. A's classroom habits. Uncle George and Louie's silly exchanges. The Aunties' visits. The smell of the kitchen on his arrival home. Every shape and shadow in his bedroom at night. The utterly dependable presence of Ma in her bed at ten p.m.

"But she's promised you'll be here for a year," he had protested. "On your grandmother's grave!"

"Yeah," said Sydney. "But she never keeps her promises. And guess what? That grandmother isn't even dead. My mother just hasn't spoken to her for twenty years. I only just found that out."

Frankie looked over at Gigs now and gave a slow shrug. Then he opened the dictionary and stabbed the page for his last word of the morning.

Shigellosis: shig·el·lo·sis, *n, a highly infectious form of dysentery caused by the shigella bacterium.*

Just what the doctor ordered, thought Frankie with bleak humor. Yet another vile addition to his unending mental Disease-Alert Compendium.

At lunchtime Frankie asked Mr. A if he could speak to him. If he wasn't on playground duty at lunchtime, Mr. A usually went to the Lido for a swim. He said it kept him sane. Gigs and Frankie reckoned it revved him right up and gave him an extra injection of verbal ferocity. The swim also turned Mr. A's scar briefly purple and his hair into ringlets. If he was particularly animated in the afternoon, droplets of pool water flew from the ends of the ringlets and landed on the kids at the Webster table, which was in the front of the classroom.

Mr. A did not have playground duty today, nor was he going for a swim. He was going to address a problem with his Campagnolo Centaur racing bike. Mr. A biked twelve miles to school every day, and twelve miles home, no matter the weather. He lived on the edge of the city, though he called it the rural-urban interface. *Interface* meant *the surface place or point where two things touch each other or meet.* Room 11 had looked it up. Most things Mr. A said required some dictionary exploration, which was just the way he liked it.

"Walk with me, Frankie," said Mr. A. "You eat your nice ordinary lunch and I'll eat my organic pork mince and biodynamic bean sprout seven-grain sandwich with homemade self-sown plum chutney." Mr. A had told room 11 he was aiming to make twenty adjectives eventually in a lunch sandwich.

"Do you secretly wish you were having Subway?" said Frankie. "Or Maccas?"

"Secretly," said Mr. A. "And if you ever tell Mrs. A that, I'll deny we spoke."

Mrs. A's real name was Mitzi. She was a champion triathlete from Colorado, USA, and had dedicated her life to fighting processed food. Unknown to Mitzi, Mr. A had a bag of Party Mix sweets in his desk drawer.

"How can I help?" said Mr. A when they'd both finished eating. They were at the bike stands behind the staff room. Frankie leaned against a stand; he made a circle in the gravel with the toe of his sneaker.

"It's about Sydney," said Frankie. "I'm supposed to be doing our book project with her today. At her house."

"She's sick?"

"No," said Frankie. "She was at the bus stop and then she had to go home with her mother."

"And?" said Mr. A. He was detaching the front wheel of his bike from its frame.

"And she was crying. Evie Hewitt said there was a fight and she was crying."

"I think," Mr. A said, "that this is what we in education service delivery euphemistically describe as 'a family matter.'"

"It's her birthday, too," said Frankie. He really didn't know what he expected Mr. A to do. Reassure him? Ring up Sydney's house? Make it all go away? "We've got a present for her."

"Can't you give it to her tomorrow?"

"She might not be *here* tomorrow," Frankie burst out. "I don't think you know about her! Her mother's a wack-job! She could take them off somewhere. Anywhere. Saudi Arabia! Cambodia! Guadalajara! She wants more babies!" He stopped and felt his heart pumping, race speed.

Mr. A placed his bike wheel gently on the gravel and looked up at Frankie. He was squatting, the gravel grinding under his weight.

"Wack-job," he said speculatively. "I like it. Is it in the dictionary?"

"It's in the online slang dictionary," said Frankie. The conversation was veering in the way it could with Mr. A.

"Listen, Frankie." Mr. A stood up, and Frankie heard his knees creak. "There's not a lot I can do—"

"You could ring up," said Frankie. "You could make up some reason, something about the book project, or about camp, anything, you could just check that they haven't"—He stopped, seeing the look on Mr. A's face, hearing his own voice, all high and wobbly—"You know," he finished lamely, dropping his voice. "You know. You could check they haven't . . . gone."

Mr. A was silent for a while. Frankie pushed more gravel with his shoe. He pushed it into a circle of little hillocks, an empty sphere in the middle.

"Real shame you're not coming to camp," said Mr. A from nowhere.

Frankie looked blankly at him, a low-grade fright snaking down his arms. He had written "family matters" on the camp sheet but maybe he should have been more specific. Ma? Uncle George? Grandparents' ashes? The Aunties?

"It's this big eightieth," he said with desperate inspiration. "My great-aunt. She's turning eighty. She—"

"No problem, no problem," said Mr. A, waving a hand. He gave Frankie a long look.

"How's your book project going? Is it working out with Sydney?"

"Fantastic," said Frankie, a little too heartily. "She's fantastic, I mean her writing's fantastic, she's really, you know, smart, and funny, and she has great ideas—" He stopped abruptly, hearing what he was saying. And as he heard the words, he was seized with the terrible urge to cry. An ache pulsed in his throat.

Frankie was horrified. What was *wrong* with him? Perhaps he was actually going insane. Could such a thing just happen? Suddenly? In the middle of a school playground at lunchtime? He clenched his jaw and did the tooth jarring. He squeezed his fingernails into his palms. He stared ahead at a spot past Mr. A's right arm.

"Well, *good*!" Mr. A was saying. "Good to branch out, isn't it? Opens out the synapses, gets ideas flowing differently."

Frankie nodded vigorously. The throat ache ebbed a fraction. He looked at the ground and smoothed out the hillocks of gravel with his shoe. He covered the gap tidily and gave it a drawn-out tamping.

"I'm going to have to take this to the cussed bike shop," said Mr. A, picking up the bicycle wheel again. "Notice how I avoided swearing there by ingeniously using a word that actually means bad language."

Mr. A was giving him time to recover, Frankie knew. He breathed slowly, measuring the in and out.

"You guys started lunchtime soccer?" said Mr. A. "Herr Angelo marshaling all the troops?"

Frankie gave Mr. A a half smile. "He was born to be a captain."

"Damn right!" said Mr. A. "I really don't see *damn* as a swear word," he added.

Frankie turned to walk back to the soccer field. "Anyway —" he started.

"I'll give Sydney's house a call," said Mr. A. He patted Frankie on the shoulder. "Take it easy, Frankie."

"Hot damn," Frankie muttered.

Frankie and Gigs got off Cassino's bus at the midtown terminal. Gigs was meeting Dr. Pete at the Music Arcade; they were checking out trombones to buy — Gigs was graduating from rental to ownership.

Frankie was going to Sydney's. He was going anyway. Not for long, because he had to buy the meat for Ma and get back home, but he was going. He'd decided suddenly in the middle of the afternoon that this was what he would do. Why not? It was obvious. There was no law against it. Sitting on the benches in the hall, in the middle of the afternoon, in the middle of the Science Fair results, he'd decided this. It was at the exact moment of the Year Eight first-prize announcement, when a wave of pure happiness broke over him, and Gigs punched him extremely hard on the arm to demonstrate his own violent joy.

"*Pat Cat, Stress Less,* by Gigs Angelo and Frankie Parsons!" Mrs. Monaghan, the science dean, called out the results. "A most imaginative and innovative project. Well done!"

"Bong! Ga! Swet! So!" Gigs was on his feet, punching the air. "Holy cow! Hot dog!"

"Mr. Angelo! Modesty, *please!*" Mr. A was shouting from

the end of the row. But he was grinning, too. "Well done," he mouthed, clapping his hands in Gigs and Frankie's direction.

We won, thought Frankie, wonderingly. *We* won.

I'll take the present around to Sydney's house, he thought, *and tell her about the prize.*

"Going to see your girlfriend?" said Seamus Kearney when Gigs and Frankie followed the twins off the bus.

"What's it to you, Mr. Turnip Head?" said Gigs. He was in a thoroughly cocky and provocative mood, Frankie could see. It was like the time they'd won the Year Seven interschool cricket champs. Gigs had been so ecstatic and careless, he'd gone too far with Ronald and was bitten on his bowling arm.

"Where's she live?" said Eugene. "Coby Street? Rochford Towers? Hastings Street?" Coby Street was full of bed-sitters and run-down housing, and Rochford Towers was, according to Louie, where you went for drugs. Frankie gave Eugene a look conveying comprehensive weariness with a brain so tiny. Gigs gave a finger signal conveying the minuteness of a lower down part of his body. Frankie shoved Gigs in the general direction of the Music Arcade before one of the Kearney brothers could thump him.

Sydney lived in Washington Crescent, Frankie knew. But he didn't know which number. He figured he'd walk up and down the street and somehow he would intuit which was her house. Or maybe he'd see a Porsche in a driveway. Frankie wondered about that Porsche. He knew almost nothing about cars, but he was pretty certain a Porsche meant money.

It was a twenty-minute walk to Washington Crescent from the midtown terminal. He knew that because Sydney had told him she had to make sure Galway and Calcutta had eaten break-fast by 8:15 so there was enough time to get to the terminal by 8:35. Freya never rose before nine, which was when she took

Sydney's sisters to their Montessori school. Frankie had no idea what she did for the rest of the day.

It was a pleasant walk. Frankie took the route through the Hiroshima Garden, where the maples and gingkoes were in full autumn blaze. His favorite part of the garden was the ornamental pond and bridge. In the summer, he and Gigs liked to sit on the bridge, dangle their feet just above the water, and spot frogs. Frankie liked the water lilies, too, their absolute whiteness, their thick velvet down. But there were only lily pads just now, like small green place mats floating on a winking table.

Frankie had visited the garden many times when he was younger. It was in the period Teen attended ikebana courses and developed a passion for Japanese aesthetics. Frankie had trotted beside Teen while she explained the elements of Japanese garden composition, the necessity for balance, the pleasure in formality. He was only seven, but even then it was the *tidiness* that he liked so much.

Their own garden at home was a street disgrace, Frankie thought. None of the family paid any attention to it these days. Hydrangeas, flag irises, and agapanthus ranged, blowsy and unkempt, along the street border. There was a disorderly abundance of flowers for every season, and clumps of native trees — the result of Uncle George's erratic planting enthusiasm — and a permanent crop of weeds. Once, a long time ago, someone, possibly Ma, had planted perennials in terra-cotta pots: pansies, sweet william, and cascading daisies — but the plants were a sorry sight now, ragged or diseased or smothered by twitch grass. The pots were covered in moss and lichen and were massed against the garage wall like a crowd of shabby horticultural refugees. Occasionally Frankie thought he should do something about them, as he knew all about the science and maintenance of potted plants. He'd paid his dues with the Aunties' veranda display;

he'd knelt beside Teen, spooning potting mix around seedlings, patting down the soil. Was there any other twelve-year-old boy in the universe who knew the names of so many flowers and shrubs? Perhaps he should just get a job in an old people's home as soon as he left school, stay there for the rest of his life. He'd fit in perfectly.

On the other side of the Hiroshima Garden was a small shopping center — a dairy, a greengrocer, a video store, and a butcher's. Frankie intended buying the meat for Ma here, though he didn't as a rule like to patronize any butcher's shop except Wysocki's down the hill. For a start, Mr. Wysocki and his son, Peter, behaved as if it was completely natural that a twelve-year-old boy should be doing the family shopping. They didn't make the predictable lewd jokes, either, if he asked for chicken breasts or legs. Plus, they made the best sausages in town. Gigs often came with Frankie to Wysocki's because he liked to talk soccer with both father and son. The boys did Chilun for Peter's amusement. He liked to guess what they were saying, and it was interesting how often he got the gist. It was because of the Russian, Peter said. Russian was a Slav language — like Polish. Mr. Wysocki and Peter conversed in Polish when they were making sausages or chopping meat or hefting carcasses. Gigs reckoned they laughed in Polish.

The butcher's at the shopping center was called the Meating Place, ha, ha, and Frankie was served by a girl. She didn't look much older than Gordana but she sliced lamb back-straps like a pro. Frankie had never thought of girls being butchers. He hadn't thought of girls being engineers, either, until Sydney had told him about her father's cousin, Lily, a dike engineer in the Netherlands. Probably he'd spent too much time with elderly people and was doomed to think in old-fashioned ways. The thought depressed him.

Sydney wanted to be a pilot. This was just one of her aspirations, though. She wanted to be a living statue in a street theater, too, also a police-dog handler and a stand-up comic. Gigs was planning to be a professional cricketer. He was planning to get his international career out of the way before he got married. It was typical of Gigs to assume he would have no difficulty finding a wife.

But Frankie had only very hazy notions of what he wanted to be. An artist? But would he ever be good enough? Something to do with birds? A conservation worker? A zoologist? A pet shop proprietor? In his very darkest moments, he didn't know how he would be able to leave home to *become* anything. Perhaps he would be one of those sad guys who worked from their bedrooms, on a computer, guys with unwashed hair and clothes that didn't match, guys who lived with their mothers and had cats and turned out to be serial killers.

He must never buy a computer.

Washington Crescent had exactly fifty-three houses. Frankie counted them as he walked along first one side of the street, then the other. Unfortunately, it was not at all obvious which was Sydney's place. What had he expected? A geometric flag? Dreadlocked curtains? A letter box signaling Sydneyness? (On Louie's street, signature letter boxes were something of a theme. There was a letter box in the shape of a grand piano at number 37, where a music teacher lived. Number 42 had a sailing ship letter box. Louie and his roommates had fashioned one out of empty beer cans and an orange boundary cone they'd swiped from a club cricket game.)

There was no sign of a Porsche in any driveway, but maybe

Sydney's mother was out. If she did have a Porsche. Probably Evie Hewitt had that wrong. What would an eight-year-old girl know about cars? Frankie stopped outside number 28 and shrugged off his backpack, which was becoming intolerably heavy. Number 28 had a trampoline on the front lawn, which suggested kids. Maybe he could just knock on any old door and ask people if they knew where a wack-job called Freya lived with her three fatherless children. Maybe he could just stand in the middle of Washington Crescent and yell out Sydney's name. Maybe he could just forget the whole thing and go home.

But as he bent to pick up his backpack, a figure turned into the crescent, on the same side of the street. It was Sydney. She was wearing bright yellow leggings and a green tunic painted all over with flowers. From a distance she looked like a walk-ing banana palm. (It was one of her Netherlands outfits, Frankie knew; Sydney made most of her clothes in Amsterdam because her grandmother had a sewing machine.) Clothes aside, the figure was barely recognizable as Sydney. She walked slowly, her head down, her hands in the pockets of her jacket. Frankie watched her approaching. She was like a comic strip picture of dejection. Even her dreads seemed to sag. He had never seen her like this before and it made his heart sink to his shoes. It made him mute, too, so that Sydney was only a couple of yards away before she raised her head and saw him. She pulled off her earphones slowly and awkwardly, an odd sleepwalking movement.

"Huh," she said, blankly. "What?"

"What what?" said Frankie. He gave an experimental smile.

"What are you doing here?" said Sydney.

"What happened?" said Frankie. "Evie Hewitt said you had to go home."

"Yeah, Thydney hath to go home to her thithtith."

Frankie laughed, but Sydney just stared.

"So, which is your house?" he said, looking around. "I was trying to work it out."

"You'll never geth."

"Does your mother really drive a Porsche?"

"Yeth, she duth."

"Stop it," he said.

"Thtop it," said Sydney.

"Seriously."

"Theriethly."

"Sydney!"

"Thydney!" said Sydney without the slightest smile.

A car backed out of a driveway across the street and straightened up parallel to where they were standing. The woman at the wheel looked with open curiosity at the two of them. Sydney languidly raised a hand and gave her the finger. Frankie flushed and looked away.

"Nothy old thow," said Sydney in the same deadpan voice.

Frankie said nothing. He couldn't think what to say. Or do. He shouldn't have come. The whole thing was a big mistake. He felt slowed down now, too, as if Sydney's mood was an infection he was rapidly succumbing to. He felt a little sick.

"Thorry," said Sydney. "Sorry." She suddenly slapped the side of her head with her hand, as if she were clearing it of static, waking herself up. Then she stood still again, not quite looking at him.

Frankie found his hand undoing the zip on his backpack and, as if unbidden by him, removing the birthday present scroll.

Sydney turned on her heel and started walking. "C'mon," she said over her shoulder. "Our house is on the other side."

He began following her, across the street and around the curve of the crescent until they reached a house near the corner. It was white, weather-boarded, two-storied, with shuttered windows and several chimneys. The front garden was grand and elaborate. Large oak trees marked the perimeter. There were roses all along the driveway.

"Stop!" said Frankie as Sydney began to walk up the driveway. He waved the scroll at her back. She stopped and turned around.

"C'mon," she said. "My mother's taken my sisters to the gym."

"I can't," said Frankie. "I've got to get home. I just wanted to give you this present."

"Don't give me a present," said Sydney, turning back again.

"What?" said Frankie. He was confused. "It's your *birthday*."

And quite unexpectedly Sydney slumped down on the driveway. She seemed just to subside, like the side of a hill in a TV avalanche. Then she buried her face in her knees and stayed that way, unmoving. She made no sound but Frankie knew she was crying. The only sounds were from the oak trees where abruptly Frankie was aware of a rackety burst of birdsong. It was like a surging soundtrack in their own private film.

He felt calmer now; somehow it was better that Sydney was crying. It was awful, too, but it seemed as if some incapacitating spell had been broken.

It's official, Frankie thought, as he walked over to Sydney's humped form. He *did* have some sort of freakish premature aging. He wasn't scared of females crying, like most normal twelve-year-old boys. He knew what to do. It seemed as if he'd been used to it all his life — Ma, Gordana, even the Aunties. He was like one of those shrunken, wrinkled kids with that horrible disease, only his aging was on the inside.

He sat down on the grass beside Sydney.

"What happened?" he said.

* * *

"Do you have an all-time favorite cake?" asked Frankie.

Ma was setting the cake alarm. She was catering for a shared ten-year-old birthday party tomorrow. It had a Queen of Hearts theme. Thirty-three jam tarts, thirty-three Queen cakes, thirty-three gingerbread princesses, heart-shaped fairy bread and pastries, and three separate layered birthday cakes. Frankie shuddered. Thirty-three ten-year-old girls. Pass-the-parcel. Candle-blowing. Spittle on the cake icing.

"Simnel cake," said Ma. "You?"

"It changes," said Frankie. "Some years lemon ricotta, some years Christmas cake."

It was a cold night. The heat from the electric blanket seeped upward through the duvet. Frankie refused to have such a thing on his bed, in case it went faulty and the bed caught fire. Even so, he worried about Gordana's blanket, about her forgetting to turn it off before she fell asleep. Last winter he'd taken to sneaking into her room and flipping the wall switch just to make sure, but, of course, she'd woken one night and there'd been an almighty row. She'd called him Freak-Boy and demanded he see a shrink.

Sometimes, Frankie almost longed to see a shrink. Maybe it wouldn't be so bad. He could have his own personal one, just like Ma.

"I don't know what to do when I leave school," he blurted out.

Ma was rubbing lotion on her hands and didn't answer immediately. Frankie loved the smell of Ma's hand lotion. It was the oldest smell in his memory, he thought, lemony and faintly medicinal.

"There's no hurry, is there?" said Ma.

"Everyone at the Pepys table knows. Esther. Vienna. Gigs—"

"Let me guess. Gigs is going to be a star cricketer?"

"Course. Solly wants to be an art forger."

Ma laughed.

Frankie could hear Uncle George bashing around in the kitchen. He would be assembling a late-night snack—cake and chocolate sauce, or cold rice pudding and cream, or his favorite: dates stuffed with chocolate and rolled in sugar. He brought his snacks to bed and talked to Ma while he ate. Frankie liked to hear their murmuring through the wall, the clink of the spoon on the bowl.

"I wanted to be a professor when I was your age," said Ma.

"Of what?"

"Anything. I just liked the word. And my father was a professor. The Aunties always called him Prof."

"Professor Osborne," said Frankie.

Professor Parsons, world famous ornithologist. Dr. Parsons, zoologist. Constable Parsons. Reverend Parsons. Nurse Parsons. Frank Parsons, chairman of the board. F. D. Parsons, opening batsman. F. D. Parsons, cartoonist. Parsons, strange hermit guy.

"Then I found out you had to talk to large groups of people."

"So you did Russian."

"Yes."

Uncle George was singing "Abide With Me." He often sang hymns at the end of the day. No one minded, not even Gordana. Maybe she found it comforting, too, Frankie thought. Kitchen sounds and an ancient hymn, signaling that everyone was home at last, everything was safe.

"But now you're a baker," said Frankie. "You didn't even need to go to college."

"But I still like languages. Different things interest you at different times. Circumstances change. You have to adapt."

Yeah, thought Frankie. To never leaving the house.

"Tears for all wo-oes, a heart for every plea . . ." sang Uncle George. Actually, "Abide With Me" was a real downer. It made you want to fall to the floor and never get up again. Frankie preferred the one with the line "me thought the voice of angels from heaven in answer sang." He couldn't remember the name of the hymn, but it was positively jolly, as Alma would say—though clearly the writer had no idea about grammar.

"Why do you like Russian stuff so much?" he asked.

Ma screwed the cap back on the bottle of lotion. She did it very deliberately, thinking as she stared fixedly at the label. Frankie checked out the woman in the painting. He'd begun imagining names for her. Victoria? Mabel? Sophia? Annie? Gwyneth? Angelina? Keira? Linda? Peggy-Sue?

"I honestly don't know," said Ma eventually. "I like the puzzle of it, I think. Or, maybe just because I'm good at it. Why do you like birds so much?"

"Maybe because I'm good at them," said Frankie. The woman could have a Russian name; she'd fit right in. Natasha? Tatiana? Svetlana? Anastasia? How did he even know these names?

"Do you think I'm normal?" he said in a rush.

"What's normal?" Ma sighed.

"Am I?"

"Of course you are, Frankie."

"How do you know?"

"Because, I know what I see. I've known you all your life."

"But I could go strange when I'm older."

"Why would you?" said Ma.

He waited a beat. "People do," he said. He couldn't look at her.

There was silence, except for Uncle George locking the front door, closing the bathroom window, making the rounds of the rooms, and turning off all the lights. "And, though re*bell*ious and per*verse* meanwhile. Thou has not *left* me, *oft* as I left thee . . ." He was flicking the switches in time to the hymn. Through the open door Frankie could see the patches of light disappear one by one to the woeful beat.

He felt a moment of despair. Why had he said that? Now Ma could be crying, or trying not to cry. Again. He seemed doomed just lately to be unkind to her on a regular basis. Perhaps he was a budding sadist. The very worst personal future seemed eminently probable.

"Who did that painting?" he said, seizing on something, anything, wanting to fix things before Uncle George came to bed.

"Someone I was at the university with," said Ma, apparently calm. She was looking at the painting, too, no tears. "She gave it to me when I turned thirty. She's famous now. It's worth quite a bit."

"Don't tell Louie," said Frankie.

"Check," said Ma.

"If that woman had a name, what do you think it would be?"

"I know what it is," said Ma. "It's on the back. It's—"

"Don't tell me!" said Frankie. "I don't want to know. I want to keep on guessing."

Ma laughed.

"Like Rumpelstiltskin," she said after a while.

Huh, thought Frankie, sliding off the bed. You said it. He just might stamp his foot ferociously, too, shatter the floorboards; he just might explode into a thousand goblin pieces, give them all the fright of their lives.

"Hello, old man," said Uncle George, nudging open the door with his forehead. He held a wad of papers in one hand, his pudding bowl in the other, a book in his armpit. "All good?"

Frankie just stared at him.

"'Night," he said.

SIX

Tuesday, April 25

Frankie knocked on Gordana's bedroom door. There was no answer, but he knew she was in there. He could hear the muffled clicks of her keyboard, the mouse brushing over the desk. When she was at home, Gordana spent a lot of time in her bedroom with her computer. She had saved enough money from her job at the Cupcake Café to pay half the cost of a MacBook. Ma and Uncle George had paid the other half as a birthday and Christmas present combined — though Gordana said it was actually an essential educational expense and should *not* be counted as a treat. She took the computer to and from school to prove her point, but Frankie knew that at home she spent most of her time communicating with her forty-seven friends or playing games. Gordana could use the computer, her mobile, the landline, and sketch clothes designs, all at the same time.

He knocked again. The clicking stopped momentarily, then started up again.

He knocked a third time.

"What?" said Gordana.

"It's me," said Frankie.

"What do you want?"

Charming, thought Frankie. Though, really, he expected nothing less. When she was six years old, Gordana had pinned the first in a long series of signs to her door. It was handwritten and colored and said, *GRILLS ONLEE. BOYEES KIP ART.* Frankie had been too young to remember this, but Ma kept the note in her treasure box these days and Louie still liked to refer to grills and boyees to annoy Gordana. The first sign Frankie could remember was the one that said, *NO ENTRY IF YOUR NAME BEGINS WITH L OR F.* He had learned the alphabet by then and could still recall his shock on realizing that this No Entry included him. Him? Frankie? *Why?* Later the sign had been amended to *NO ENTRY IF YOUR NAME BEGINS WITH L OR F, AND YOU HAVE TESTICLES,* because of course Ma's name began with F, too. There were no such signs these days since Ben had free entry to Gordana's room, but the family was about as welcome as a dose of flu.

Lately, Gordana had taken to pinning up her art class sketches. The current door attachment was a black-and-white drawing of a naked woman with only one breast. Her eyes were lifted to the heavens, her long hair fell about her like a garment. Saint Agatha, Frankie supposed. It was a pretty good drawing.

"I just wanted to ask you something," said Frankie.

"What? Ask me." The keyboard clicks alternated with a ringing trill. *Tring!*

"Can I come in?"

Click, *tring!* Click, *tring!*

"Please?"

And now he heard an exasperated *huh* and Gordana pushing back on her wheeled office chair, sliding along the floorboards to the door. Gordana propelled her chair like some hostile snowboarder.

The door opened gustily. *"What?"* said Gordana.

Frankie gave her his most beguiling little-brother smile and proffered the box of Spaceman Candies he'd bought especially to sweeten his entry. He had a marshmallow Easter egg in his pocket, too.

"Oh, good *God,*" said Gordana. She took the box and nodded him into the room. Gordana had a fatal weakness for Spaceman Candies. Her bedroom was the largest in the house, a fact Louie had never ceased to complain about when he lived at home. There was enough room for a double bed and several book-cases and a sofa. There was a balcony, too, overlooking the back garden.

Frankie liked Gordana's room very much. Occasionally, when she wasn't at home, he opened the door to the room just to survey the girly splendor, take in its distinct fragrance.

Every room in the house smelled different, Frankie had found, and he was fond of each aroma. Uncle George's office, for instance, was pretty much stationery smells—manila boxes, cardboard, postage packaging, fresh paper—and the hot electrical smells of the computer and printer. Louie's room, now technically the guest room, still housed the paraphernalia of his childhood—trampoline and soccer trophies; papier-mâché masks; film posters; misshapen pottery experiments from school; the old cage he'd built for his mice, Beezus and Henry; and his vast collection of Kinder Surprise toys. It was two years since Louie had occupied the room, but it was somehow redolent of him still, a mix of old sneakers and toast, damp towels, mouse pee, a lingering note of Tommy aftershave.

Ma and Uncle George's bedroom was mostly Ma—hand lotion and laundered sheets and the heavy perfume of the oriental lilies that Uncle G bought Ma sometimes for the windowsill. But the closet was all Uncle George. Ma's clothes hung there too, of course, but their fragrances were somehow delicate and domestic and completely overwhelmed by the hearty, outdoor, *manly* smells that Uncle George's jackets and shirts carried with them.

Gordana's room smelled like a beauty parlor—a mix of hair product chemicals and the faintly acrid odor of singed hair (the curling iron was in constant use), of mango body lotion and cosmetics, and the sharp acetate smell of nail polish.

Gordana was nearly as tidy as Frankie. She made her bed and kept her bookshelves orderly, but she was a hoarder. Every corner of her room was filled with old toys, old projects, all the flotsam and jetsam from the past. The history of her dressmaking and craft development could be traced around the room. A sampler hung over her chest of drawers, stitched with an original Gordana poem from Year Three: *My cat is fat. Beat that.* There were pottery models from Year Four of Snow White and the Wicked Queen on the chest with various representatives from Gordana's book-character modeling phase. A series of graffitied dress patterns from Year Seven were wall hangings now. Gordana's old rag doll, Infinity (Gordana had liked the word), sat slumped in a chair with several soft toys in her lap. In the corner by the window was a model of *Apollo 9* made entirely from Spaceman Candy packets. *Apollo 9* was nearly three feet tall and had been Gordana's entry for the Old Girls' Association art prize in Year Eleven; it had placed third. No one else in the family could eat a Spaceman Candy stick for months after this, but Gordana had been unbowed.

The walls of the bedroom were a riot of snapshots—Gordana and her friends at school, Gordana and her friends at parties, Gordana and her friends as *babies,* for heaven's sake—and artwork demonstrating Gordana's particular brand of surreal portraiture. Frankie's favorites were the series of drawings Gordana had done one summer of Uncle George: Uncle G as a Saint Bernard; Uncle G as a portly dolphin, Uncle G as a baby-size Winston Churchill with a homburg and a cigar. The Winston Churchill portrait was really quite repellent but somehow arresting, too. Frankie always found his eyes wandering toward it.

"I'm busy," said Gordana. She ate three Spaceman candies at once, in her usual way, then, almost as an afterthought, tossed one at Frankie.

"Homework?" he said.

"Yes," said Gordana. "Who said, 'Fashion is architecture'?"

"Don't know," said Frankie.

"Coco Chanel, of course."

"I don't even know who Coco Chanel is," said Frankie.

"Was," said Gordana. "Who's the main designer at Chanel? Karl Lagerfeld!" Click, *tring!*

"What subject is this?" asked Frankie.

"Careers," said Gordana. "Who invented the LBD?"

Frankie just looked at her.

"Coco Chanel!" Click, *tring.* "What is the LBD?"

"A drug?" said Frankie.

"Little Black Dress, idiot."

"Are you *on* drugs?" said Frankie. He sat down on the bed.

"Don't sit down," said Gordana, eating three more candies. "What do you want?"

"How is this Careers?" said Frankie.

"It's a fashion quiz. What do you *want?* I have to get to fifty points before dinner."

Frankie had seen Gordana like this before. She had these kinds of jags, which was how Uncle George styled it, and Uncle George would know, because he too had jags. In the past they'd sometimes had them together. Jigsaws, for instance. Frankie could recall the jigsaw jag very vividly, because the giant puzzles had taken over the dining-room table. For months there had always been a puzzle-in-progress—a half-completed picture surrounded by dozens of waiting pieces, random arrangements that took on a kind of independent sculptural life—spread across the length of the table, so that the family was obliged to eat meals at the very edges. When a puzzle was nearing its completion, Uncle George would bring home a new one; he would prop the box up on the end of the table, both enticement and threat for the two fanatics as they approached the homestretch.

The rest of the family participated intermittently. Ma liked to study the pictures between cakes, complete a small patch perhaps; Louie specialized in moments of casual genius, strolling past and lighting suddenly on the piece that had eluded everyone else for days; Frankie, too, would find himself seduced from time to time, teased by a tricky bit of sky or grass, staring at pieces with shadings so subtle they seemed to disappear if you blinked. But Gordana and Uncle George approached the puzzles with the ferocity and purpose of warriors fronting up to the enemy; they beat those puzzles into submission; they gave war cries when they found a home for a piece; they set themselves targets for evening bouts and vied always with each other for most completed pieces.

The puzzle jag had ended as suddenly as it had begun. Gordana, frustrated by a fifteen-hundred-piecer of *The Last Supper* by Leonardo da Vinci, had discovered six puzzle parts, comprising the left-hand marble column, hidden inside the bowl of Louie's under-fourteen trampoline trophy. A protracted battle had broken out and distracted everyone thereafter.

Frankie sighed. He missed those times, when Louie had been at home and domestic life had been rowdy and occasionally startling, and everybody had been somehow more *present.*

"Who invented the miniskirt?"

"Coco Chanel?"

"Wrong," said Gordana. "Mary Quant." Click, *tring.*

"What is a Paddington?"

"A bear?" said Frankie hopefully.

"A *bag*! By Chloe!" Click, *tring.*

"Who brought message T-shirts into the mainstream?"

"Adolf Hitler?"

"Very funny. Katharine Hamnett." Click, *tring.* "Yes! Complete this phrase: Posh and . . .?"

"Becks!" said Frankie. "I know that!"

"Doesn't count," said Gordana. Click, *tring.*

"Why doesn't it count?"

"Obviously you know that 'cause of the soccer."

Frankie lay back on the bed and let his head sink into Gordana's voluptuous royal-blue duvet. How could knowledge count *against* you? Oh, but who really cared? He had other matters on his mind. And he was preoccupied with how to raise them with Gordana.

"What are you going to do next year?" he said. This was a warm-up line. "Are you going to the university? Or work?"

"Oh, good *God, I* don't know," said Gordana.

"Are you going to stay at home?"

"Maybe, maybe not," said Gordana.

"Do you believe in work?" Frankie asked.

"What *is* this? Twenty questions? Is this what you wanted to ask me?"

"But, do you?"

"*Believe* in work? I like *doing* it; I like being busy; I like earning money. Is that believing?"

Frankie took a long breath. "Sydney's mother doesn't believe in work."

"Does she believe in being hungry?"

"Not exactly," said Frankie, wishing Gordana would *listen.* Not just to what he was saying, but to what he was not saying yet. Ma was very good at that. It made talking so much easier. Ma heard what was in the silence. But he didn't want to talk to Ma about this.

"How *is* your gf?" asked Gordana.

"She's not my gf," said Frankie automatically.

"You have a fight?" said Gordana. Click, *tring*, click, *tring*.

"She's a *friend*," said Frankie.

"Sure, sure," said Gordana. "You wouldn't believe how much I know about shoes. It just seems to have always been in my head. For instance, do you know what a kitten heel is?"

"No, and I don't really want to," said Frankie.

"I even know who popularized it. I know about you and Sydney, too, by the way."

Frankie shot upright and stared at Gordana's back. She sat very straight at the computer, tensed up and alert, like a bird of prey. Ready to swoop down on fashion facts. Click, *tring*, click, *tring*.

"What do you know? There's nothing to know."

"I know that you both skipped camp. Living dangerously, little brother. There'll be trouble."

"How do you *know*?" Frankie couldn't believe it. He didn't know which surprised him more — Gordana taking the slightest bit of notice of anything he did (or didn't) do, or her keeping quiet about his deception.

"My spies are everywhere," said Gordana.

"We went to school every day," said Frankie. "We worked in the Year Seven class."

It was quite true. While room 11 had been at camp, Frankie and Sydney had sat at the back of the Year Seven class reading and working on their book project. At lunchtime, they'd sat on the bench outside room 11 and talked and talked; there had been so much to talk about. When they were exhausted by talk, Frankie tested Sydney on her Chilun vocab.

"But how do you know?"

"Think about it," said Gordana. So Frankie did and in a few seconds he had it.

"Suzie Newcombe," he said with a sigh. Of course. How could he not have thought of this? Suzie Newcombe was the younger sister of Jilly Newcombe, one of Gordana's forty-seven friends.

Frankie Parsons is in our class, she would have said, *and the weird girl, the one with dreads and the nose stud.*

So, how come your brother didn't go to camp? Jilly would have asked Gordana. Her spies *were* everywhere, for heaven's sake.

"You can't tell Uncle George," said Frankie. "Or Ma. Please."

"What will you give me, you sad fashion disaster?" said Gordana. "That new hoodie's a horrible color, by the way."

"A marshmallow egg?" said Frankie, pulling it out of his pocket.

"Oh *yum,*" said Gordana, twirling around on her chair. "But I was kidding, you idiot."

"I don't care, anyway," said Frankie. "It's too late for them to do anything."

"I don't care, either," said Gordana. She unwrapped the Easter egg from its tinfoil and began picking the chocolate off the marshmallow, which was her marshmallow-egg-eating practice. "I know why *you* didn't go," she said. "But why didn't your gf go?"

"She's not my—" He stopped. "How do you know why I didn't go?" he said.

Gordana batted the question away with her hand. "How come Sydney didn't go? She an indoors kind of girl?"

And suddenly, there it was, the exact opening he'd wanted, the way he could tell Gordana, the way he could understand, *clarify.* "It's complicated," he said, which was both true and not true. Gordana was concentrating on the Easter egg, expertly detaching chocolate slivers with her long Ming-blue fingernails. Miraculously, she seemed to have forgotten she wanted him to hurry up and go away. She was practically being nice to him, for heaven's sake.

"She was supposed to go," Frankie began. "She *wanted* to go. She's *not* an indoor girl, and she really wanted to do rappeling. She wanted to do everything." He paused, getting the sequence right in his head.

"It was her birthday," he said finally, speaking very deliberately. "She didn't come to school. . . ."

Frankie thought he must have been in some kind of shell shock following his visit to Sydney's. He was like a puppet, wound up tight, his movements jerky and random. His brain seemed made of wood, too. He'd ridden the number 40 bus home, his head full of pictures and words, but no actual *thoughts* occurring. He simply stared out the bus window, his eyes passing over cars and pedestrians and city landmarks but not really registering any of it. At home he had practically thrown the dinner ingredients at Ma, then run out the door and down to Gigs's house. He felt a great need to tell Gigs everything he'd learned.

Gigs was in his bedroom, tenderly nursing his new trombone, a proud parent with a goofy look on his face. It *was* a beauty, Frankie acknowledged — so gleaming, so silvery. You could see your face in its shining surface, elongated and vaguely monstrous. Frankie listened to Gigs play "Beautiful Dreamer" and "When the Saints," but then he could wait no longer.

"Stroshky no weesack stupends," he said. (Serious info to pass on.)

Gigs lowered the trombone. "Huh? Oh, man. Sydney. I forgot. Did she like the present?"

"In the end," said Frankie, thinking about how Sydney had

eventually unfurled the scroll of Chilun vocab and then cried all over again at the immensity of the gift. She had particularly plump, wet tears, Frankie had noted, with the strange part of his brain that carried on heartlessly observing during moments of emotional calamity.

"But she was crying so much," he said. "Because of the fight. With Freya. And other stuff."

"Crying," said Gigs. "Sydney?" He looked incredulous.

Frankie was idly rearranging the platoon of soldiers on Gigs's desk. There was a score of them now. They were Fimo and Gigs had been making them for a couple of years—a bohemian and strictly democratic army of bizarrely dressed multinational mercenaries. They were all second lieutenants and all called Fox: Second Lieutenant Fox (British), Sottotenete Fox (Italian), Fanrik Fox (Finnish). Frankie's very favorite was Anthypolokhagos Fox, who was Greek. He loved that name, and he loved the Second-Left Army. Normally, it could cheer him up in a flash, but not today.

"But *crying?*" Gigs repeated. Frankie knew what he meant. It did seem an impossible notion, Sydney crying. Until you'd actually witnessed it.

"It was about camp," Frankie said. "The fight was about camp. You know how much she wanted to go. But next thing, her mother says she can't, there was no money for it—even though she'd promised ages ago—and Sydney's dad had actually sent the money."

It seemed easier, somehow, not to look at Gigs, to get the words out while his eyes were fixed on the army. Frankie started placing the soldiers in a two-by-two formation, Sottotenete Fox and Podporucznik Fox (Polish) in the vanguard, because their accessories were the most dashing.

"But Freya spent the money," he continued. "She's—she does it all the time, so mostly Sydney's dad pays for things straight, like school fees. He pays the school, you know, so she can't get it. He pays her dance teacher for the lessons; they send him the bills . . ." He was rushing through it and jumbling it up, but it was hard to be orderly —

"But that's . . . *mean*," said Gigs. "That's taking money from a *child*." He sounded like a child himself, his face screwed up, as if someone had just swiped his sweets. They looked at each other, both imagining the same thing, Frankie knew—the awfulness of such a parent.

"Worse, though," said Frankie, putting Tweede-Liutenant Fox (Dutch) on the left flank. He had a wooden leg. "The *other* reason she can't go to camp is that she has to look after her sisters—at night, sometimes *all* night—she has to be home at nights to look after them. She has to look after them all the time. Freya goes out at nights, stays out—"

"Working?" said Gigs. And then he remembered. "But she doesn't work."

"She goes out with guys," Frankie said quickly, looking steadfastly at the Fox formation. "That's how she gets money."

"They give her money," he repeated, meaningfully. He stole a look at Gigs, saw him taking this in, saw the full dimensions beginning to dawn. Gigs's eyes grew very round, and he seemed to draw the trombone close to his chest, hugging it.

"Is she a . . . a . . . ?" His mouth began forming a word, but he stopped, shocked, frowning disbelievingly at Frankie.

"I don't know," said Frankie. "Sort of. Maybe. But . . . maybe not really. I don't think so." In fact, he didn't know what he thought. He felt utterly confused. "Sydney says they're actually her boyfriends, but they're always rich, and they pay for her houses, for travel, for her clothes. That's how they live. She's a genius at having rich boyfriends. This guy right now, he's given her a Porsche.

"Well, lent it," he amended. "She's . . ." he searched for a suitable word, and failed. He still hadn't met Freya, but now he never wanted to. There was hatred in his heart.

Gigs was clasping the trombone tighter still, his face busy, his thoughts almost visible. Frankie could just about hear him mentally assembling the parts of the equation. It was how he'd felt all the way home on the number 40 bus, his brain creaking and avoiding. It was how you felt when two plus two was adding up to a very indigestible four.

"But Sydney's not old enough to look after them at nights," said Gigs finally, fastening on something they both knew for a fact. "She's not old enough to babysit anytime. You have to be fourteen. It's, it's . . . child *labor*." They knew about child labor. They'd done a project on it in Year Six, but all the child labor had been in other countries.

"She's been doing it for years," said Frankie.

"Bonga," said Gigs. He made it sound like a sorrowful curse.

They sat there in silence for a minute, each preoccupied with his thoughts. Frankie picked up Shao Wei Fox (Chinese) and studied her. She wore a miniskirt and a beret and carried an elaborately jeweled dagger. He placed her beside Luteni Wa Pili Fox, from Tanzania. He was very tall with shiny black skin and wore a magnificent red cloak and top hat. His weapon was a delicately fashioned slingshot. Really, Gigs should consider a career in Fimo.

Gigs loosened his embrace of the trombone and raised it almost absentmindedly to his lips. He played low, somehow thoughtful notes, pushing the slide slowly, as if he were half asleep.

"But can't Sydney live with her dad?" he said, halting momentarily. "Can't she go to Holland—she loves it there—she could just live with the O." Sydney's dad's name was Theo, pronounced *Tay-oh,* but Sydney called him the O as a joke. Usually it made Frankie and Gigs laugh, but right now neither of them could raise even a lip curl.

"That's what I thought, too," said Frankie. "But Freya won't let her. She gets more money from the government—the more kids she has, the more she gets. Plus money from the O. She goes through a lot of money."

"Plus she needs Sydney to babysit," he added bitterly.

Gigs was leaning forward on the edge of the bed now, head down, the trombone between his knees. He blew the first notes of "When the Saints." The pace was so funereal, it sounded both mournful *and* comical. Frankie imagined a robot choir with waning batteries: *Oh. When. The. Saints. Oh. When. The. Saints. Come. Mar. Ching. In . . .*

Gigs tried again. "But couldn't she tell the O? Couldn't she tell *someone*? She has to. Welfare or something? They could go to court, you know. He could get—what's it called?—custody, like Victor's granddad."

(Victor Bowyer sat at the Roget table in room 11. He was very skinny, with a number-one haircut and a tattooed ring finger. He was shy, too, almost never speaking, but he was mildly famous at Notts anyway, because his mother was dead and his grandparents had been granted custody of him over his father in a court battle. And also, of course, because he arrived at school each day on the back of his granddad's massive Moto Guzzi Jackal.)

Frankie sighed. "I said that, too. But she doesn't want to leave Galway and Calcutta. And if she says stuff about her mother, they could get taken away from her, her sisters—put in foster homes. She's scared about all that."

"She really likes those sisters," said Gigs, the notion quite foreign to him, Frankie knew. Probably Gigs would have liked nothing better than some government agency helpfully whipping away his siblings. As if this thought had somehow penetrated the bedroom walls and communicated itself to Gigs's twin brothers, they knocked that very moment on the door. They made a habit of this whenever Frankie and Gigs were sequestered; it made Gigs crazy.

"Albert wants to see Frankie," said the twins in singsong tones. Frankie and Gigs listened to them giggling and shuffling, banging Albert's cage against the door and provoking indignant squawks from the long-suffering parrot. Frankie smothered a smile. The twins were called Jock and Barty. They were six years old, with red hair, freckles, and gap-toothed grins, and Frankie found them very entertaining, though he was careful never to show too much enthusiasm for them around Gigs. He played checkers with them sometimes, or sat dutifully while they performed inexpert card tricks. He did birdcalls for them and drew episodes in an ongoing cartoon he had devised for their amusement, called *Herbert Pterodactylis*. Gigs didn't plan on taking any notice of his brothers until they developed decent batting stances.

"Albert can say *Where's Frankie?*" chorused the twins. "He really can!"

Gigs rolled his eyes operatically. He crossed the room, opened the door, blew a strident trombone note in his brothers' faces, and shut the door again.

"Monica speaking! Monica speaking! Monica speaking!" Albert squawked. The twins laughed hysterically and ran away.

Gigs thumped down on the bed and resumed his somber tooting. Frankie put Letnan Dua Fox (Indonesian; disguised as a nun; weapon: exploding rosary beads) at the rear of his troop, beside Segundo Tenente Fox (Brazil), who bore a strong resemblance to Mr. A. He had shoulder-length white hair and a livid facial scar; his weapon was the dictionary.

"So," said Gigs minutes later. He stood up and put the

trombone back in its case. "Yendys vist nottam willynets. *Bonga!* You skipped camp and now Sydney's leaving. Great."

"Sorry about that, chief," said Frankie, like Maxwell Smart. They both managed a small laugh.

"But Sydney," said Gigs. He sat back heavily on the bed. "Man."

Frankie leaned back on his chair and assessed the Second-Left Army. What a deranged crew. Could they actually win a fight? Maybe they would simply disarm the enemy with their unlikeliness. The enemy would be rendered stationary with shock and awe by the lunatic costumes and weapons. The enemy would lie down and laugh.

"Any new Foxes?" Frankie asked. He was feeling immensely tired.

"Yeah," said Gigs. He rummaged under his desk and pulled out a model-in-progress. "Molazem Thani Fox from Jordan," he said. "I think I'll give him a musket. What do you reckon?"

Molazem Thani Fox was bald and seemed to be wearing a Speedo. They were definitely getting weirder, Frankie thought. Everything was getting weirder.

"There are no second lieutenants in the Indian Army," said Gigs. "I wanted to do a Sikh."

"He could be a Sikh from another country," said Frankie. "He could have grown up somewhere else." Funny the way they could just keep talking about other things.

"S'pose," said Gigs. "And there's no Japanese Army at *all.*"

"We have to do something about Sydney," said Frankie.

"We could kidnap her," said Gigs. "*No,* kidnap Freya. Hold her for ransom. Make her do . . . Make her *promise* . . . something . . ." His voice trailed off.

Frankie lay Molazem Thani Fox facedown on top of Gigs's dictionary, a sacrificial offering on a high altar. He slid the dictionary across the desk so it was in the path of the oncoming Second-Left.

"Something," he murmured. "Huh."

"But what *can* we do?" said Frankie to Gordana. He was full of doubt now.

Gordana faced him, the fashion quiz forgotten for the moment. She had finished the marshmallow egg.

It was 5:57 p.m. according to Gordana's computer screen; soon, the Aunties would be here. It was beef Stroganoff tonight, with rice and string beans, meringues and raspberry sauce for dessert. To be followed by a game of Shogun. It was Nellie's birthday and Louie was coming, too.

Frankie couldn't bear, sometimes, the way the rest of life just rolled predictably on and on — school, homework, soccer practice, Aunties, birthdays, the dull inevitability of *meals* — when other crucial matters were so consuming, so upsetting, so un*solved.*

"Zip," said Gordana. She frowned at Frankie, rotating with clockwork precision on her office chair, left, right, left, right . . . "Zero. Nothing. You can't do anything."

"But why not?" said Frankie. "It's *wrong*. Making Sydney look after her sisters is *wrong*. Using her money — it's *her* money — it's *wrong*. Getting welfare money is *wrong*. Getting money from those men is *wro —*"

"Right, Reverend Frankie," said Gordana.

"Shut up," said Frankie. "*You* think it's wrong."

"Maybe," said Gordana. "Probably. But who knows? Maybe she's got reasons. Maybe she's just trying to survive."

"I hate her," said Frankie.

"Maybe she can't do anything else," said Gordana. "Maybe

she's just looking out for her kids — you know, like a lioness or a vixen with their cubs, going for the main chance."

"Looking out for *herself*," Frankie's voice had risen. "She's a —" But he choked on the word. He hadn't been able to say the word at all, not even in his head; it seemed somehow unkind to Sydney.

"Do you think she's a . . . ?" He left it there, the word hanging, unspoken, in the mango-scented air of Gordana's bedroom.

"A hoo —"

"Don't *say* it," said Frankie. It came out like a moan.

"Oh, good *God*, Reverend *Mother* Frankie." Gordana slid off her office chair and strode over to the closet. "Don't be so feeble. Not saying *hooker* won't change anything."

Frankie ground his face into the duvet.

"Hooker," said Gordana mercilessly. "Ho. Prostitute. Call girl. Whore. Trollop. Slapper. Scrubber." She was on a stool now, reaching up for a box on the shelf above her clothes.

It was a fact, Frankie thought. Mere words *could* make you nauseous.

"I'm giving you aversion therapy," said Gordana. "You say the bad things and then they don't — aha!"

She turned on the stool and tossed something across to Frankie. Thanks to years of throw-downs, his arm shot up reflexively and caught it before he could even think. A packet of Spaceman Candies.

"I just remembered I had these in my bird flu emergency box," said Gordana, more packets in hand.

Frankie pulled a sick face at the box.

"Oh, good *God*," said Gordana. "She's probably not a hooker. She's just kind of a kept woman. Think of her like that. Like kings' mistresses, way back. The kings gave them castles. Her boyfriends just pay for her favors."

"What's the difference?" said Frankie miserably.

"Depends how you look at it, I s'pose," said Gordana. She was making a diamond-shaped stack on her desk with the candy sticks.

Frankie opened his box and looked at the candy. When he was younger, Spaceman Candies had been called Spaceman Cigarettes and had been painted pink at the tip. On the Saturday bus to the library, he and Gordana had smoked them before eating — inhaling and blowing out with hilarious extravagance. Not calling them Spaceman Cigarettes *had* changed things.

"But why *can't* we do something?"

"Number one," said Gordana, "it's not illegal. She can get a heap of money from her boyfriends if she wants to. It's only illegal if she gets welfare, too, yes, yes, *which* she does. . . . But number two, you said the kids could get taken away if anyone turns her in. Number three, Sydney would probably never talk to you again. Think how it would be for her."

Frankie admitted silently that of course she was right. Gordana always put things very *clearly* — even when she was in a rage. Though, right now she was actually being friendly. Almost kind. Amid his misery, Frankie registered a small warm gratefulness.

"Number four," said Gordana. "Freya would probably just move away; she could leave the country. Doesn't she do that?"

"Yes," said Frankie, infinitely depressed. "She promised they'd stay here a year, but she lies." He said this as if enumerating yet another in a dark catalog of sins. In his head Freya had grown horns and a tail and malignant black eyes. Frankie had begun imagining punishments for her: broken limbs, hair loss, knee-capping, the electric chair . . .

"She's such a *liar*," he said.

"Poor old Franko," said Gordana, looking at him. Her voice

was softer. It was a long time, Frankie reflected, since she'd called him Franko. It had been all Freak-Boy for months.

"You shouldn't worry so much," she said.

Frankie grunted. *What* an original thought. If only it was minutely possible. He lay back on the bed again, the despair fingering his neck.

Downstairs, the front door banged and the Aunties' combined *yoo-hoo*s rang out. Soon Louie would arrive and Ray Davies would sniff the trail leading to Frankie. Frankie smiled faintly, thinking how nice, if somewhat damp, Ray Davies's enthusiastic greetings were. But time was running out; he wanted to make the most of Gordana's rare tender mood.

"Here comes half the Fat Ladies' Choir," said Gordana. She began droning a dismal tune, dragging it out comically. It was one of Uncle George's late night hymns. *"O* God *our* help *in* a-*ges* past . . ."

"Hard not to worry," said Frankie into the duvet, but Gordana didn't hear him.

She stopped singing. "Hey, Franko."

He rolled over. Gordana was standing slouched, her thumbs in the belt hooks of her jeans, eyes narrowed, a candy stick stuck to her lips. It was her old Cowboy Smoking pose. Frankie giggled.

"But really," Gordana said, straightening up, slurping the stick expertly into her mouth, "it's just not the same now, without the pink ends. Why'd they have to change the name, for God's sake? Ruin kids' fun. *Typical.*"

"I've got this rash," said Frankie.

Gordana looked lengthily at him, then gathered her features slowly into Long-Suffering Face and rolled her eyes. It was so long since Frankie had seen her do this that he felt like hugging her.

"Oh, good *God*," she said as Frankie lifted his T-shirt. She peered at his chest for some seconds.

"Jock itch," she pronounced.

"It's on my *chest.*"

"You can get jock itch anywhere," said Gordana with great authority. "It's just a fungus. Sporting types get it. Ben gets it in his armpit, plus his actual jock area."

"Don't tell me that," said Frankie. "I don't want to think about your boyfriend's private bits."

"That's sad for you," said Gordana, and they both giggled. "Put some of Uncle George's athlete's foot stuff on it," she said.

"Foot cream for jock itch on your chest," said Frankie. It made no sense. Nothing made sense. "Are you sure it's that? Really sure? How do you know?"

"Frankie." Her voice had the familiar dangerous impatience, but at least she wasn't calling him Freak-Boy. "Put the cream on and see. It'll take about three days, then it'll start going away. Guaranteed." She began sliding the office chair backward to the computer.

But he couldn't feel relieved yet. Not until he saw the evidence. If only it could prove one less thing to fret about.

"Hard not to worry," he said again, low.

Gordana paused mid-swivel. "You would know," she said.

"Don't you *ever* worry?" said Frankie. It came out like a bleat.

"One," said Gordana. "What's the *point*? Things might never happen. Waste of head space. Two, I'm not wired for it. I'm like Louie. We didn't get the gene." She slid off her chair and walked over to the balcony doors, pressed her nose to the glass. It was nearly dark now, but a headlight raked the room. "Speak of the devil," said Gordana.

"The gene?" said Frankie, looking down at the floorboards. But he knew what she was going to say. He did and did not want to hear it. He knew it would make him feel sick. He studied the varnished black-borer trails, those nosing tendrils, roads to nowhere.

"You know," said Gordana.

"No," said Frankie. His voice was just a whisper. He wanted Gordana to say it.

Downstairs, Louie and Ray Davies clattered through the front door. They would come up any moment, he knew, and, again, he did and did not want them to. He wanted them to save him from himself, from his own inexplicable compulsion to hear something that would make him feel bad. But he wanted Gordana to carry on talking.

"What do you mean?" said Frankie.

"Oh, good *God,* Frankie," said Gordana, turning around from the balcony doors, a sudden heaving thundercloud. "You know what I mean. The Freak-Out gene. You have it. Ma has it. You're exactly like Ma. You freak out at things. You *know* you do." She reached across the bed and pulled the light cord that hung from the ceiling; instantly the bedroom lit up like a fairground.

Frankie squinted in the brightness and drew back from Gordana, who seemed larger now, looming before him, her eyes firing, pink spots burning on her cheeks.

So, thought Frankie. She had said it. It was out, in the bedroom with them, a stealthy demon whose presence he'd been trying so hard to ignore.

He had always known it, he supposed. It had been there always, alongside the rodent snarling, the knowledge that Louie and Gordana were like Uncle George—bold and carefree, fearless, *joyous.* And he was like Ma; he was timorous and beset, a hostage to dark imaginings, cowering somehow, waiting always for the chopper.

Funny, thought Frankie, even now momentarily arrested by

a passing notion, he wasn't actually freaking out about it, ha, ha, now that it had been said. He had no desperate urge to recite batting statistics or anything. And the thing *was* . . .

"But Ma *doesn't* freak out at things," he said. Ma was sad sometimes — "wobbly" as she called it — but mostly she was composed, even tranquil. She floated, somehow, in and out of the family racket, an eternal presence, calming things. Sydney had said that, too.

"Oh, *no?*" said Gordana. "She doesn't freak out? Only at the teeming world outside the front door." She stood with her arms folded, regarding him fiercely. "Ma's calm like a stagnant pond, Frankie. She's just opted out, hasn't she? She's been having a slow, silent, *secret* freak-out for the last nine years. *That's* normal?"

And then Gordana's hot green eyes filmed over, suddenly full and lucent under the ceiling light. She blinked hard, but too late; two tears fell straight down her face, and she flicked them away exasperatedly.

Absurdly, Frankie had a vision of the last time he remembered Gordana crying. She had been fourteen and her first boyfriend, Caspar Trugly, had gone away to Camp America. Gordana had stood, then, behind Ma, clinging to her like an overgrown papoose, crying into the back of Ma's neck. Now she stood, defiant, in front of Frankie, two more tears snaking downward.

"Oh, good *God,*" said Gordana furiously. She sat down in the office chair and wiped her hands roughly across her face. "Stupid to cry. There's no point. It's just the way it is."

The words on the computer screen seemed to pulse at Frankie. *Cuban, Louis, Stiletto, Spool.* He should have left Gordana to do her quiz, left things as they were. But he didn't seem able to do that anymore. Something was making him pick at scabs these days, disturb all the surfaces.

"At least it's better than it was," said Gordana. She was

talking almost to herself, looking at her bare feet now, twining them roughly around the chair's circular base. Gordana's feet were very white and long, and her toenails were painted the same Ming blue as her fingernails. The longer you looked at them, Frankie thought, the more her feet looked like two quite separate creatures. Elegant marine reptiles.

"At least she's happier these days," said Gordana. "Stable. That's a big improvement."

A parade of images walked quickly through Frankie's head: half-caught scenes, like snatches of an old dream. Ma crouched down in the corner of the kitchen, her fists tight, sweat beading on her forehead. Ma's face fixed in panic, her tentative two-step back and forth from the front door. Nellie in Frankie's bedroom, packing his clothes and toys, stuffing Kidder in his backpack, knotting a scarf around his neck, *what fun* they were going to have, she was saying. Louie in the backyard, dribbling a soccer ball, going around and around in ever widening circles, a ceaselessly spinning top. Ma sitting on the sofa in her green brocade robe, an open book beside her as she waited, her soft hands and her breath as she pulled him close to her.

And here was Ray Davies on his way up the stairs. His unclipped nails made a crazy chatter; he was whimpering in anticipation as he climbed.

"Can you remember?" said Frankie quickly. "Can you remember when Ma used to go outside?"

"Some things," said Gordana, still inspecting her feet. "Shopping. Going to the library. At the Aunties', way back. Walking to school."

"I can't remember," said Frankie. "Not anything. I can only remember all that time at the Aunties', going places with them, staying there, and then seeing Ma sometimes, but only at home."

Ray Davies was launching himself at the door, making a loony song with his whining and barking, but Frankie and Gordana remained on bed and chair, mesmerized briefly by those old, sad times.

"We used to visit you at the Aunties'," said Gordana. "Me and Louie. Uncle George brought us over because we missed you, ha."

Gordana had lain beside him on the bed in Frankie's room, he remembered. She had read aloud to him.

"The Urchin and Little O," said Frankie. He could recall all *that* quite clearly: the Japanese paper kite suspended from the ceiling, a giant painted bird whose wings undulated gently when the window was on the latch; the sound of that latch, rattling in the easterly wind; the rise and fall of Gordana's voice, her exciting proximity and school smell, her long braids and colored hair ties. The Urchin and Little O were brother and sister, too; it was an old book from Ma's childhood. Frankie had stared at the blond children in the drawings, yet had somehow seen black-haired Louie and Gordana; he had longed to be in their games, then and always, back at his real home.

Ray Davies's entreaties subsided temporarily into a thin whine. He would be standing in front of the door, Frankie knew, staring hopefully, slobbering with excitement.

"Aboly, jaboly, B T Piggle," said Gordana, smiling a little.

"Big O and Little O," Frankie capped the line. It was from the old paperback.

"Oh, good *God!*" said Gordana as Ray Davies flung himself once more at the door. "Let the idiot in."

But the door opened wide before Frankie could rouse himself, and Louie walked in. He was listening to his Shuffle and playing air guitar, his face contorted in mock ecstasy.

Frankie lay back on the bed and yielded to Ray Davies's moist attentions.

"Meine Schwester und mein kleiner Bruder!" said Louie. For some reason, Louie often greeted them in German. He said it was the only thing he'd retained from school. *"Guten Tag!"*

Imagine being Ray Davies, thought Frankie as the dog slurped and nuzzled him. What a great life. Perpetual enthusiasm, zero worry.

"Hey, Louie," said Gordana. She had turned back to the computer. She had ruled a line under their conversation, Frankie knew, tidied it off. "What is a Novak?"

"Pass," said Louie. *"Deine grosse, grosse Tanten* are downstairs, and they've brought fudge."

"A limited-edition bag," said Gordana. Click, *tring.* "By Alexander McQueen. Go to the top of the class, Gordana."

"C'mon," said Louie, lifting the dog off Frankie. "Your breath stinks, boyo. Give the guy a break. Frankie! I have a cunning business plan. You're gonna like it."

Frankie sat up slowly. His head was spinning, his skin gluey with dog lick.

"Franko!" said Gordana. She rotated the office chair like a miniature merry-go-round. "Last one, last one, I'm on forty-nine. Where does angora fiber come from? Which animal?"

"Rabbit?" said Frankie tiredly. It was a guess. Gordana halted her spinning abruptly and banged her hands on the desk.

"Correct!" Click, *tring.* "Not so stupid after all," said Gordana, snapping shut the lid of her MacBook.

"Ein kleiner Bruder is a clever Dick," said Louie.

Oy sey, Sarlick amit Knarfie gribins Naipsac nemschie, Frankie said to himself. (Oh yes, Frankie is a prince among men.)

If only, if only.

* * *

"Have you ever done anything really bad," said Frankie. "I mean, really?"

Ma didn't answer immediately. She almost never did. Frankie liked that about Ma.

"I shoplifted," said Ma. "With Mary-Lou Haines. We shoplifted six lipsticks from the Styx Pharmacy. The Aunties were mortified."

"Worse than that?" said Frankie. He was on top of Ma's bed, hugging the winter quilt, his breath making weak clouds in the bedroom air. He could see his breath because the moon was full tonight, the uncanny light filling Ma's room.

Ma had been reading Doctor Zhivago. Again. She read it every year. The book had slipped from her hands and she had just turned off the light when Frankie tiptoed in. He picked up the book now, inspected it, though it was well known to him. The cover was silver, the title in black curlicue letters. The broad spine was creased with countless tiny wrinkles. When Frankie was first learning to read, he had thought the author's name was Boris Pancake because of the P and the K in Pasternak. He still liked to think of him that way.

"I've thought bad things."

"Like what?"

"Too private," said Ma, after a moment.

"Thought doesn't count, anyway," said Frankie.

"Count for what?"

"For my question."

"I suppose I've never been tempted," said Ma. "Or I've been too scared."

"Same," said Frankie. "I'm too scared to shoplift."

"Good," said Ma.

Frankie squinted at the woman in the painting. He had decided she must be in an asylum, a very grand asylum with canopied beds and maid-servant nurses. Could there be such a thing? Why not? It was his version of her story. Maybe she was called Hannah. Or Ruth. Or Deborah. He knew all the Biblical names. Nellie had read him Old Testament stories when he was little.

"Naomi?" Frankie asked, nodding at the painting. He asked Ma every night now, whole lists of names, exactly like Rumpelstiltskin, ha.

"No," said Ma.

"Rachel, Rebecca, Bathsheba?"

Ma laughed. "Sorry."

"Basically, you have to be brave to be bad," said Frankie.

"Is there something on your mind?" said Ma.

"Probably," said Frankie.

"Can I help?"

Probably not, he thought, but he said, "So, we're finishing The Valiant Ranger over the holidays."

"You pleased with it?" said Ma.

"Pretty," said Frankie. "Uncle George'll laser print it. It's not due till the fourth week of next term, but Sydney wants to get it done."

"A woman of action," said Ma.

The distant sound of a siren reached them through the bedroom window, which was opened to the night. Ma liked night air in her room, she said, even when it was cold.

Then why not go out into the actual night? Frankie wanted to say. Just step outside. Look at the stars. Check out the full moon. Lately he imagined these rebel questions just popping out of his mouth sometime, being spoken aloud without his bidding. They were bad-tempered, insistent questions, like the croaking toads that spilled from the mouth of the princess in the old story.

The siren grew louder. The Queen Victoria Hospital was just down the hill, so they heard sirens regularly. Frankie stole a look at Ma. Her eyes were closed. She hated sirens. Uncle George had told them years ago that siren sounds were the only thing Ma could remember about her parents' car accident. Ma had been in the car, too, and unharmed, but she could remember nothing, just that high-pitched, unrelenting wail and the flashing lights.

"Sydney might be leaving," said Frankie, to distract Ma. This was *not precisely true, nor was it exactly untrue. But it was, currently, Frankie's number-one anxiety. Ma opened her eyes.*

"Oh, Frankie," she said. "Why?"

"Who knows," said Frankie. "Her mother gets itchy feet."

"Tell me what her mother does, again?" said Ma. The siren was fading now. Frankie imagined it racing out to the western suburbs, a straight arrow to some disaster.

"She reads to the blind," said Frankie. This was the only thing he knew for sure.

"That's a neat thing to do."

Somewhere in a reasonable corner of his brain, Frankie conceded it might be a good thing, but he refused to rearrange his hostility toward Sydney's mother. He hated her and that was final.

"But all that moving around," said Ma. "Must be hard on Sydney and her sisters."

He was irritated at Ma for stating the obvious. But he said, "They're used to it. And Sydney goes to Holland in September anyway."

"Maybe she won't go before, though," said Ma.

Frankie said nothing. The moon had risen higher, well above the windows now, and the light in the bedroom had diminished. The painting woman had receded in the way she did every night, just her hair showing, lustrous and abundant. Prudence, thought Frankie; that was an old-fashioned name. The Aunties had had a school principal called Miss Prudence Fanshawe.

Gertrude. Ruby. Garnet. Faith.

"Gertrude? Ruby? Garnet? Faith? Hope? Charity?" Frankie asked.

Ma shook her head.

"What's up, Frankie?"

Everything, *Frankie thought.*

"Nothing really," he said.

SEVEN

Tuesday, May 9

Frankie sat in the riverside bus shelter, massaging the end of his nose, which stung with the cold. He imagined it red at the tip and shiny like freshly cut beef. It had been that way since he'd woken this morning, his bedroom frigid. He'd half fallen out of bed, dragging the duvet around him, and trudged to the window. Rivulets of moisture ran the length of the pane and pooled beneath the window frame. He rubbed the glass with the side of his fist and peered out into the backyard; the grass was white and solid with frost. Winter, *for real,* as Gigs would say. Frankie liked a frost, though. He liked the raw morning air that came with frosts and the blue sky that followed. He liked the excuse to wear his Wolverhampton scarf to school.

But there was no school today. It was the second day of the vacation and he was going over to Sydney's house to work on the last two chapters of *The Valiant Ranger.* They were working at Sydney's because Ma was having a visit from Dinah, her psychiatrist. (Gordana called Dinah the Shrink, in an overtly hushed tone, which Frankie thought unfair because, actually, Dinah was kind and reassuringly brisk. In the past she had come every month, and even Gordana conceded that fewer visits meant things had improved with Ma.)

Yes, he liked Dinah fine, but all the same he was uncomfortable being in the house when she and Ma were talking, though they did it in the sunroom, with the door closed. Frankie felt self-conscious somehow when Dinah was present, as if his movements around the house were slightly spastic, as if his breathing, his very *thoughts,* might somehow be visible and damning.

Sydney was looking after her sisters, which was another reason for working at her house. Freya, apparently, had appointments with the blind. Frankie doubted this very much. He was convinced now that Freya's reading to the blind was, ha, *a blind.* He was sure she really went shopping or to the movies — or worse. But Sydney, who was ruthlessly realistic about her mother, seemed to believe that Freya would in fact be sitting in elderly blind people's houses, reading to them for hours at a time. Gigs agreed with Frankie, though; they had speculated about it endlessly.

Frankie missed Gigs. He always spent the first week of vacation at Brass camp, and the second week at his mother's house down at the very south of South Island. Right this minute, he and ten other trombones would be warming up in Section Rehearsal. In the afternoons there would be Individual Lessons, then Full Band Rehearsal. (Frankie had poured over the camp brochure with Gigs when it had arrived. He had simultaneously envied Gigs *and* been thankful that he did not play the tuba or the cornet or anything else that would oblige him to lie his way out of another camp.)

On Saturday night the students would present Brass Gala, which Frankie was attending with Chris and Dr. Pete. Frankie went to all Gigs's performances. He liked to watch him flourishing the trombone, all red-faced and sweaty and transported. He liked the lines of trumpeters, standing tall, their horns lifted sky-ward like medieval heralds. Best of all he loved the music. True, there were lullabies and love songs — sometimes slow, sometimes sorrowful — but most often it was busy, triumphal music, the sounds diamond bright, *heartening*.

Back at home Ma was at work in the kitchen, a cake in the oven, several others in progress. Frankie had inspected the bowls while he ate his Just Right. Orange almond cake. Blueberry polenta cake. Ginger loaf with crystallized ginger. Something unfamiliar involving Brazil nuts and dried cranberries, which turned out to be a gluten-free fiftieth-birthday cake. Very unappe-tizing, Frankie thought. In his backpack he had a container with a wedge of day-old Mistake Cake. Mistake Cake could be any flavor and any shape, and was rarer than you might have wished. Gordana had come up with the name in the early days of Ma's business when she was experimenting and failed cakes were a little more common. The Mistake Cake in Frankie's backpack was a dark German chocolate torte that had unexpectedly sunk in the middle. He had delivered some of the cake to Gigs's house on his way to the bus. The rest of it was for Gordana, who was decamping to Ben's.

"I may be some time," she said.

"Why?" Frankie asked.

"The Shrink *and* Aunt Invasion," said Gordana. "Ask your-self." She gave the front door an emphatic slam behind her.

But, Frankie reflected as he waited at the bus stop, things had been minutely better with Gordana in the last couple of weeks. Frankie felt sure he could detect the very faintest softening in her exchanges with him. Merely *having* an exchange was a soft-ening in itself, in Frankie's view. For instance, on the weekend, Gordana had inquired — in a distinctly Gordana-ish way — about his rash.

"How's your galloping jock itch?" She was lying with her legs hooked over the back of the sofa and her head hanging just above the floor, texting several of her forty-seven friends. Uncle George and Louie were sitting at the dining-room table, trying out designs for Louie's new business card.

"Jock itch?" said Uncle George. "What's going on, old man?"

"You done something filthy?" said Louie.

But Frankie was impervious to embarrassment, because the jock itch rash *was* better. It had faded and shrunk. He had applied Uncle George's foot cream as instructed by Gordana, and the rash had visibly improved. He could hardly believe it—something actually going right. Of course, history had taught him that the minute one thing went right, something else immediately went very wrong, so it was certainly just a matter of time before a new worry was born. Still, just now, sitting at the bus stop, holding his cold nose and enjoying the dog-walkers on the other side of the river, he could, for a few moments, feel pleased about his rash.

There were four dogs being exercised across the river, but Frankie's eyes were on his favorite: Yeti, the Saint Bernard, who was as big as the proverbial monster and shortsighted to boot. Yeti moved very slowly, which was just as well because his owner, Mr. Scully, was elderly and also shuffled along at a glacial pace. Frankie found it very funny that Mr. Scully and Yeti looked so alike; they both had long shaggy hair and solid bodies. He watched them now, inching along the riverbank path toward a bench, where they would sit while Mr. Scully fed the ducks. They did this several times a week, though Frankie and Gigs usually only saw them on Saturdays while they waited for cricket or soccer pickups. Sometimes Mr. Scully and Yeti crossed the footbridge and walked along the other side toward the hospital, which was when Frankie and Gigs got to make a fuss of the big dog, who stood, stolid and patient, while they patted him.

Mr. Scully liked to have a chat. He talked as slowly as he walked—about the government, about Mrs. Scully, who had passed on, about the river traffic, and about his garden, which was the pride of Riverside Drive. Years ago, in his semi-delinquent phase, Louie, assisted by Hunter Nichols, had stripped Mr. Scully's garden of opium poppies in the dead of night. Mr. Scully had never known the raider was young Frankie's brother, but Frankie had been ashamed anyway. Mr. Scully was a nice old guy. He was kind to boys and animals, and his dog never chased the ducks.

Dogs and ducks made Frankie think of *The Valiant Ranger*. The hero of their story was a nice *young* guy who was kind to animals and also owned a dog. The ranger, Hank (Sydney had named him after her dead *opa*), had found his dog, abandoned in the countryside. Microsoft (he was undersized and fluffy, a mutt with teaspoons of beagle and terrier) had been a starving puppy at the time, left at the side of the road by owners who'd had second thoughts. The fearless duo chased bird-smugglers through bush and small town and city. Hank had trained Microsoft to carry birds in his muzzle without damaging them. In the final chapters of the story, Microsoft would round up Anders and Goldberger, the bird-smugglers, and nose out the rare and endangered "aral" bird, which the two thieves had stolen from her protected nesting site and were hiding in their tree house.

(There was really no good reason Frankie and Sydney could think up for two criminals to have a tree house, but they had one anyway. Frankie wanted badly to draw a big gnarled acacia with a perfect cubby house in it. The Aunties had just such a tree in their backyard, and Frankie had dreamed often about a splendid structure of corrugated iron and building offcuts curtained by the yellow blossoms. That was the good thing about writing and drawing, he and Sydney agreed. You could have all the things you yearned for but could never achieve. Including easy solutions.)

Frankie was really very pleased with Microsoft and the aral bird. He had sketched them over and over, trying out different features and expressions, different coats and feathering. Microsoft needed to look both adorable *and* fierce, so Frankie decided there might be pit bull somewhere far back in his mongrel genealogy. He had given him a set of menacing teeth.

The aral bird was a quite brilliant creation, he thought, an eighth wonder of the world—with an exquisitely fine beak (like a hummingbird) and an orange underbelly (like an oriole). The male aral had cute tufts about the eyes (like a burrowing owl), which lent him a comic aspect. The female aral had wing feathers that turned creamy in nesting season, making her highly visible to predators. She laid deep red-brown eggs (like a speckled warbler) in a most delicately wrought nest (like a chaffinch's). Frankie imagined the arals so vividly when he was drawing that occasionally he forgot the species was an invention, a perfect composite of all his favorite bird bits.

An ambulance drove along the river road, toward the hospital. No flashing light or siren, so no emergency, Frankie supposed. The paramedic in the passenger seat gave him a friendly wave and Frankie raised his hand in return. He tried to imagine being a paramedic or a nurse or a doctor. It would be all disease and crisis and never-ending information about symptoms; he'd be catatonic with terror by the end of the first day. It was bad enough merely visiting hospitals, which Frankie had done when Gran Parsons had been sick. He had gone with Uncle George and Gordana, who had both held Gran's purple hands and chatted to her though she was practically a corpse, propped up on pillows and thin as a stick, with only one side of her mouth smiling. Frankie had stood at the foot of her bed, trying not to breathe in the ward smells, looking away, and never touching anything, including Gran, which had made him feel like a terrible grandson.

"Oh, good *God,* Frankie," Gordana had said afterward. "Strokes aren't *infectious.* And neither is old age."

Uncle George had said, "Ahem, *correction,*" explaining that old age was 100 percent infectious because eventually everyone caught it. He and Gordana had laughed like idiots at this splendid witticism, but Frankie had imagined Ma, Uncle George, Louie, Gordana, and the Aunties, one by one becoming brittle sticks on big white pillows, and he had felt desolate.

Across the river, the ducks swarmed at the bank as Mr. Scully began throwing his toast crusts and stale Chelsea buns. Frankie came out from the shelter and perched on the fire hydrant to watch the mayhem, his head turned slightly, catching the pale sun on his cheek.

Sydney's sisters were playing War when Frankie arrived. He stepped into the hallway, and a small figure wearing swimming goggles and a woolen balaclava darted from an adjoining room and brandished a furled umbrella at him.

"Hilt!" said the figure.

"She means halt," said Sydney.

Frankie stood obligingly still.

"Calcutta," said Sydney, pointing to the child.

"No, it's not!" growled Calcutta.

"Who are you, then?"

"That man you said."

"Nelson Mandela?"

"No."

"Pablo Picasso?"

"*No.*"

Sydney screwed up her face, thinking.

"Robinson Crusoe?"

"Him!"

"So Frankie's Man Friday, then," said Sydney.

"No!" said Calcutta. "That's Galway."

"What*ever,*" said Sydney, turning away. "And that's Galway — I mean Friday." She gestured up the stairs and Frankie saw a second small figure watching them guardedly from the corner of the half-landing. Galway was wearing a crumpled Stetson and a Wonder Woman cape and holding a hairbrush. Frankie wished Gigs were there. Sydney's sisters were just like human versions of the Second-Left Army.

"Yo, Friday," he said tentatively. He raised a hand but Galway didn't respond.

"She's shy," said Sydney. "Calcutta's the boss, even though she's younger. Come on," she ordered.

Frankie followed Sydney down the passage, making his way through a jumble of furniture. A sofa minus its cushions had been inverted to provide a tunnel; a drawerless dresser had soft toys strung up on the struts. There was a procession of chairs, two deep, back to back. Bedding and pillows filled every space in between.

"They like everything out," said Sydney. "We shifted it all when Freya left. She hates it, but too bad. If they have everything out, they'll play for hours and they won't bother us, except for food."

"We can bribe them with chocolate cake," said Frankie.

"Geznady propotkin!" said Sydney, which meant "Damn fine." Sydney was making good progress with Chilun, though she said it lacked logic, unlike German or Dutch, so it was much harder to remember.

"It's not regular," she said. "It doesn't have enough patterns. It's unpredictable."

"Just like life, then," Frankie had said, and they had smiled weakly at each other.

There had been many such exchanges during camp week, while the rest of room 11 had been away. While the rest of room 11 had been scaling rock walls and trekking across rivers, Frankie and Sydney had talked themselves ragged. They talked while they worked in class. They talked while they ate lunch on the bench outside room 11. While they walked to the bus. On the bus. On the phone. At Frankie's house . . .

Sydney's abrupt tearful confession in the driveway of Washington Crescent had changed something, Frankie knew. Sydney herself had bounced back, more or less. She was still full of restless energy and inquiry. She still rolled on her feet and cartwheeled and made Frankie laugh a lot. But there was something different about her, too, something at once careless *and* resigned.

As for Frankie, the change seemed seismic. It was as if the very coordinates of his life had been reorganized. Sydney's revelation had had the magical effect of unplugging his own banked-up secrets. It seemed as if from that moment, his dread of her pesky questions had evaporated; now he practically *invited* them.

He had pondered this change to and from the village shops one afternoon, all the way down the hill with the empty burlap bag, then back up again, tilting to the right under the weight of the groceries. On his return, he had leaned on the bench in the kitchen, watching Ma make the preparations for a batch of Russian kulich. As she worked, a new understanding had seemed slowly to suffuse him; it had spread like a warm bath, *inside* him.

He watched Ma measure the yeast into the warm water and he thought about the way Sydney's presence had worked on him over the last few months. He watched Ma blend the yeast, dried fruit, and spices into the flour, and then knead the mixture, pushing and folding and turning, until the dough was smooth and elastic. His voice was telling Ma about Mr. and Mrs. Owen at the dry cleaner's, but all the time he was thinking, too, how Sydney had prodded and probed him, knocked him out of shape sometimes, given him sleepless nights for heaven's sake, with her incessant inquiries. And now he was like a proved dough, he thought, extremely pleased with this fancy and wishing he could hand it to Mr. A for a big fat A+ in literary arts.

He was like the Russian kulich loaves when they came out of the warming cupboard. He had bloomed; he had risen up and started talking; he had leaked out his worst rodent fears.

But here the promising metaphor had run dry and his moment of glorious insight faded a little. Later, he had looked at the row of round kulich loaves, golden brown and sticky with icing, lined up on the bench with the pots of pashka, and he had thought sadly that, for all that, talking still wasn't enough. His leaked-out secrets had not—would not—actually *change* his life. Telling Sydney everything had not magically eliminated, or even quieted, the rodent voice. It had not relieved him of any of the domestic tasks he longed to hand over, or his great feeling of responsibility for Ma. Nor had it stopped his vigils in Ma's bedroom, his never-ending inventory of gnawing worries, brooded over and confessed haltingly during the nightly visits. It certainly hadn't suddenly enabled him to go to camp.

It hadn't changed Ma one bit.

Frankie had tried to express some of this to Sydney during camp week. They'd been sharing cake one lunchtime and inventing a perfect cricket team. Sydney had stared out at the junior girls swarming and squealing on the hopscotch ground. She ate Granny Warren Cake with noisy fervor.

"Isn't it perfect?" she said. "*My* mother never stays in one place and *your* mother never moves."

This tidy but depressing notion had already occurred to Frankie. He waited for Sydney to say something else, something helpful. He waited for her to endorse his new insight and offer a solution. He had begun to think she could, somehow, do this—that she might somehow, someday soon, come out with *the* answer. Something simple and obvious and blindingly right.

But Sydney had just carried on eating cake and staring at the hopscotch girls. And Frankie had put his thumbs between his first two fingers, which was his new charm against the possibility of Sydney ever leaving.

Now, in the dining room of Sydney's house, Frankie pulled the Mistake Cake from his backpack and handed it over. He took out his sketches and put them on the circular table, which stood in the big bay window recess. He looked around the room.

Like the exterior of the house and the front garden, the room was rather formal and furnished in a way that made Sydney seem quite out of place. The room did not at all match Sydney's purple vest and patched jeans. It certainly did not match her dreads. It was a room for stiff-necked people, people who ate meals with extremely good manners and talked in considered tones, not a girl with a nose piercing and a chaotic home life.

There was a glass-fronted cabinet with teacups and crystal bowls and china figurines. There was a large fireplace with old-fashioned fire irons and a beaten copper fireguard. Above the mantel hung a heavy gilt-framed portrait of some distinguished gentleman in a wig, St. Paul's Cathedral looming behind him.

Frankie knew it was St. Paul's because he had seen pictures of the building often enough—the Aunties were mad cathedral buffs. They had toured all the great English cathedrals in their time; he had heard them discuss the various merits of Salisbury and Norwich, of Ely and St. Paul's. Along with all the other use-less old-lady knowledge lodged in his brain was a bunch of random facts about cathedral history and architecture.

"Who's he?" said Frankie, not really caring.

"Some bishop," said Sydney. "This isn't our house, you know."

It was true. He knew that Freya rented the house from some rich family living overseas—no, no, correction, Freya's *boyfriend* rented the house from the rich family because Freya needed *looking after* . . .

This happened quite a lot, Sydney had told him. As well as living in caravans, inner-city apartments, leaky bungalows, shacks by the sea, communes, and refurbished warehouses, they had also quite often lived in swanky houses. Freya liked to try out suburban living every now and then, Sydney said. She liked to do the soccer-mom thing. Sydney had actually called it that.

Freya had a lot of acts, Sydney went on, counting them off on her fingers: dreamy artist, soccer mom, caring charity worker, solo mother with a tragic past, worldly nomad, hot blonde, exhausted highflier having time out. Her whole life was like a series of stage plays, Sydney said, with Freya in the starring roles. Even reading to the blind was acting; she got to do different voices and accents. She was actually very good at it.

They had been walking in the village after school when Sydney had told him this, and Frankie had flung himself face-down on the grass in exaggerated horror. It was too much for him. He couldn't believe it. It was bananas.

"She is so *crazy*!" he said, banging the grass with his fists. *"Craaaazeee."* He made a big thing of rolling back and forth with his hands either side of his head.

But when he stood up again, laughing, brushing himself down, Sydney had been looking at him in a distinctly wintry way.

"Well, she *is*," he said defensively.

"Maybe," Sydney said, drawing out the word. "But maybe she's no crazier than a person who never leaves the house for nine years."

Frankie was shocked. He had gone as still as stone, but his heart had leaped up inside him and begun thundering. He felt both foolish after his grass antics and astounded that Sydney should say such a thing about Ma.

"Shut up," he said. It came out like a whip crack. "Shut *up*." He had turned and walked away from Sydney, down the main street toward the Green, but not really knowing where he was going. He passed Owens', Wysockis', the Post Office, the dairy, Cut Above, and the Unitarian Church without seeing any of them, and walked the perimeter of the Green until he reached the Centenary Clubhouse. He sat down heavily on the bottom step and stared into the distance, waiting for the storm in his chest to subside.

In a while his heart returned to normal and his face cooled, but he still felt very upset. Freya *was* crazy, he told himself stubbornly. She did *not* behave like a mother. She behaved, she behaved—he searched for the word . . . *outrageously*. He looked out over the Green, at the band of pin oaks on the other side, at the orange leaves floating slowly to the ground, cradled by the breeze.

Ma was a good mother, a *great* mother. And she wasn't crazy, not the tiniest bit. She was fragile; that was how the Aunties put it. There was a difference. A big difference. Frankie kept sitting and staring and turning over these thoughts, these *facts,* until Sydney plunked herself on the bottom step beside him.

"Thorry," said Sydney.

Frankie counted the pin oaks. Two, four, six, eight—

"Really. I am."

—fourteen, sixteen, seventeen.

"But you should be, too," she said.

Huh, thought Frankie, and kept looking ahead, counting the pin oaks again, to make sure.

Sydney began pulling grass out in clumps, a quick tearing sound.

"I guess we can't say those things about each other's mother," she said. There was a rhythm to her plucking. Pull, pause, pull, pause . . . Frankie counted the trees singly, in time to her beat.

"Other people should never say those things," said Sydney. "Even the O's not allowed."

Seventeen again.

"But you were so *upset,*" Frankie said at last. "About camp, and the money. And the . . ." He trailed off, not wanting to say boyfriends.

"Boyfriends," said Sydney. Frankie looked at her, but her head was down, she was concentrating on her outspread hand. She lined up blades of grass very carefully on her palm. One, two, three, four . . .

"You get upset," said Sydney.

Yes, thought Frankie. *But it's quite different.*

"So?"

"So." Nine, ten, eleven, twelve.

"So, we'd better go," said Frankie.

"S'pose," said Sydney. She looked at her watch. "Thirty-two past four." But neither of them had moved.

"Sorry," Frankie said after a long pause. Then Sydney had thrown her grass blades to the wind and they had gone to the dairy for chocolate raisins.

Later, lying on his bed, Frankie had gone over and over the afternoon episode, worrying away at it, bothered by the quick fury that had sprung up between them. It was quite different from a fight with Gigs. He didn't really fight with Gigs. They just occasionally went quiet, almost by mutual consent. But Sydney didn't do quiet. He saw them both, on the footpath, their *punch, punch, counterpunch,* their springing apart like surprised boxers.

"First fight," he said aloud to Morrie and Robert Plant, and then he'd covered his face with his pillow, needing quickly to smother his blush.

Frankie had been warier since then. He had saved his anti-Freya comments for Gigs and his own perpetual interior conversations with himself. When Sydney and he were together, he listened to her moan about her mother, he sympathized, sometimes he made kindly suggestions, but he did *not* lie down waving his legs in the air like a cast spider and shout, as he longed to, *Nozdoreeshna! Your mother is a wack-job. Someone has to* do *something!*

Looking up now at Bishop Whoever and the dome of St. Paul's in Sydney's latest dining room, Frankie said, "Tow shilly factium primo?" (What shall we do first?)

"Eat the cake," said Sydney. She was already scooping out a fingerful from the container. "Let's not give the kids any of this. They can have cereal. They like it dry, in bowls. They pretend they're kittens having Whiskas. This is good, so *moist.*"

So they ate some cake and then settled to work. Frankie showed Sydney his latest batch of drawings, and she said once again how lifelike Microsoft was, how she almost expected him to bark at her and lick her hand. Sydney was in love with Microsoft. She wanted a real dog exactly like him. Frankie found it very gratifying.

"I've just got a bit more," she said, "and then you can read it all."

She put her head down and wrote quickly and busily, in her usual way. Frankie tried to solve a picture he'd been having trouble with. He wanted to show Hank driving at great speed in his truck, Microsoft's head out the passenger window, ears pinned back, tongue hanging, his dappled coat ruffled by the wind. Microsoft was easy, but Frankie was no good at vehicles. He didn't know why; they ought to have been a whole lot simpler than birds and four-legged creatures, all straightforward shapes and predictable bits. But he wasn't that interested in vehicles. They just didn't spin his wheels, ha, ha.

He looked up at the big oil painting and found the bishop staring directly at him. That was interesting. He got up and went over to the other side of the room and stood in front of a big wooden dresser. It had a dinner set displayed like one in the Victorian Life section of the museum. He turned quickly, as if catching the bishop out, and once again found him looking steadily back. He walked from the dresser to the door, all the while holding the bishop's gaze, and all the while the bishop held his right back. It was a kindly gaze, on the whole. The old guy wasn't smiling, but the set of his face seemed somehow benevolent. Frankie closed his eyes and opened them again. Yup. Still looking at him.

"What are you doing?" said Sydney.

"It's one of those pictures," said Frankie. "The eyes looking at you, no matter where you are. How do they *do* that?"

"We had a Jesus of Nazareth picture like that, in my Irish school," said Sydney. "Spooky."

"Why do you say Jesus of Nazareth?" asked Frankie. "Like there might be another one."

"I just like saying *Nazareth*," said Sydney. "I've been there, by the way."

"Sydney of Nazareth," said Frankie, and they laughed, but then Frankie had to put his thumbs between his fingers again.

He sat back at the table and tried the truck once more. He entertained himself with the paraphernalia on the deck of the truck, dreaming up unlikely objects (an old armchair, a stack of comics, a rubbish sack with intriguing bumps and bulges), and ignored the actual vehicle. Beside him, Sydney huffed and snorted and clicked her tongue in her odd way, and every so often loudly screwed up a piece of paper.

"I like dogs," said a little voice behind Frankie. Galway.

She stood slightly to the side of the chair back and pointed to Microsoft with a small pale finger. It was like a white worm. Everything about her was white: her long thin hair, her eyebrows, her small face.

"You hungry, Friday?" said Sydney.

"Meeeoouuw," said Galway, very convincingly Frankie thought. She stretched her mouth and showed tiny pebble-white teeth.

For the rest of the morning, Galway and Calcutta were kittens. They crawled on all fours. They licked each other and had play fights. They ate all their food from saucers. They were really very adept, Frankie thought; they used their little red tongues with great skill, slurping up cereal, or maneuvering cheese and crackers to the side of the saucer so they could suck them up into their mouths. They ate quartered apples, muesli bars, and raisins that way. They drank chocolate milk from bowls that Sydney placed side by side on newspaper in the corner of the dining room.

"It's their favorite game," said Sydney. "It keeps them happy for hours." She sounded fond and indulgent, like an actual mother—like Chris when she was talking about Jock and Barty. Frankie tried to imagine that sound in Gordana's voice, but all he could hear was, *It's his favorite game; he's a major Freak-Boy.* Still, he *could* remember Gordana making peanut-butter-and-banana sandwiches for him when he was little, and helping him build LEGO towers. He could remember her supervising his bath, too, shaping giant bubble mountains with shampoo.

The little girls played being kittens, and Sydney continued to write and screw up paper and write some more. Frankie sketched and shaded and sneaked the occasional glance at the watchful bishop. And all the while, he was preoccupied with how extremely *odd* Sydney's life was, how utterly different from anyone else he'd ever known.

She had been to Nazareth and Nice, to Dublin and Darwin and any number of places in between; she lived in a rich person's house but her mother spent her camp money and suddenly there was no cash. She had a grandmother she loved and a grandmother she wasn't allowed to meet. She was some kind of independent spirit, *and* some kind of part-time mother. Sitting side by side at the table with her while Galway and Calcutta crawled in and out of the room, Frankie thought that they were, all four of them in this moment, like some undersized, underaged version of a nuclear family. He was kind of the dad. This caused Frankie to blush so much he had to bow his head and absorb himself in his drawing.

At precisely the moment Frankie's stomach commenced gurgling, Sydney pushed back her chair and stood in triumph.

"*Voilà! Hier is het!* And, *Plikney si tenset!* (Here it is! Here it is, *and* here it is!)" She thrust a sheaf of papers at Frankie.

They had argued for three weeks about whether the ending should be in Anders and Goldberger's tree house or high on a cliff in the bush. Sydney favored the cliff, the bird-smugglers clinging for dear life and Microsoft nibbling at their fingers; she wanted the satisfaction of saying it was a cliff-hanger, ha, ha. Frankie appreciated the joke but he wanted the tree house because (a) he loved it almost as much as the aral bird, and (b) he wanted to draw Microsoft cornering the two men so that they bulged from the tree house windows like oversized humans in a dolls' house, like a picture he remembered from *Alice in Wonderland.* In the end Frankie had prevailed, though Sydney declared this was *absolutely* the wrong way around because the writer was the boss of the story.

Frankie read this last chapter now and Sydney put more food in the little girls' bowls. She put a packet of bread and a block of cheese on the table.

"Cheese sandwiches," she said. "Make your own." She did a handstand against the wall in the gap between the dresser and the china cabinet. She recited Chilun vocab softly.

Frankie read and read, and as he read, he grew increasingly troubled.

Finally, he set the papers down. He looked at the cheese and bread. He looked up at the bishop, who faithfully met his eye. He was bewildered—yes, that was the word, *bewildered.* Sydney had set the final chapter in the tree house, just as they'd agreed, but she had written three different endings, three *alternative* endings.

"It's a Choose-Your-Own-Ending ending," Sydney said, seeing the look on his face. "The readers get to choose. You can have (a) a completely happy ending, or (b) a half-happy, half-sad ending, or (c) a completely sad ending."

Frankie looked at the pages and pages of writing, Sydney's big round letters, the fever evident in her script as she came to the end of each ending.

"But," he began, and then stopped, not really knowing what he wanted to say.

She continued, "And that way, the reader is part of the story. It's interactive, like computer games. It's like the reader makes the story, too."

"You don't even like computer games," said Frankie irrelevantly. "And I thought the writer was the boss of the story." The idea of three endings not only bewildered him; it irritated him. It was extremely unsettling; it was *untidy.*

"Exactly right," said Sydney, bulging her eyes. "I *am* the boss. So I'm making three endings—no, *we're* making them. Don't you think it's a nifty idea? Especially if we can't decide. Which, actually, I can't." She lifted the lid of the cake container and sniffed it appreciatively, then closed it again.

"You can be like the reader, too," she said. "You can choose your favorite ending."

"I don't want to choose," said Frankie. He knew he sounded petulant. "I want it to be already decided. *By the authors.* Like a proper book."

"So, you decide the one you want." Sydney cut a fat slab of cheese and stuck it between two slices of bread. She took a bite. "And that's your definite ending. *Voilà!* You want one of these?"

He shook his head. He was too disturbed to eat. "But the ending's supposed to be good. It's supposed to be happy, *victorious.* Aral birds safe, baddies go to prison. That's what we said."

Frankie had imagined a final drawing like the procession in *Peter and the Wolf*: Microsoft in front, policemen leading the hand-cuffed Anders and Goldberger, Hank bringing up the rear—and overhead, the aral birds, liberated and joyful, *chirping merrily,* just like the bird in the story.

"*So,*" said Sydney, getting impatient now, "that can be *your* ending. What's the problem?"

In Sydney's half-sad, half-happy ending, the aral birds were rescued but Microsoft was caught in a possum trap and had his front right leg amputated. In the completely sad ending, Anders and Goldberger were arrested but Microsoft lost his leg *and* the aral birds died of shock. Frankie was aghast. Injuring Microsoft was bad enough, but killing off the aral birds felt like brutal murder. How could Sydney even contemplate it?

"But it won't be my ending—it won't *seem* like the ending if I know those other endings are there." Frankie's voice climbed, urgent and a little wavery. He knew this was the reason; this was why he found it disturbing. "It's like the other endings will *infect* my ending, by just being there. In my ending the aral birds will be safe, but somehow they won't *really* be, because in another ending they will have died. Or Microsoft will have a terrible three-legged life, for heaven's sake. The other endings will be hovering there, like, like, *poison*."

He slumped back in the chair. He almost felt like crying.

Sydney stood with the bitten cheese sandwich in her hand, her mouth half open.

"Jeeze Louise," she said finally.

There was a short, tense silence, and then Frankie giggled. He just couldn't help it. It was that idiotic exclamation, more ridiculous than *Bonga Swetso* and *hot damn* and somehow always funnier in Sydney's unplaceable accent. Giggling seemed to send his outrage into retreat.

Sydney giggled, too, and took another bite of her sandwich.

"Is there a fight?" Calcutta and Galway were in the doorway, two-legged now, their white eyebrows knotted in frowns.

"Nah," said Sydney. "An artistic difference." Frankie nodded vigorously, and the little girls returned to the feline life. Sydney sat down again and finished her sandwich, chewing thoughtfully. Frankie exchanged a long look with the bishop, wondering what he should say next.

"We'll just have your ending," Sydney said. She was making another inelegant sandwich. "I don't mind. Really. It's more important to you."

Frankie's stomach gave a juicy gurgle as if in thanks.

"Cheese Louise," said Sydney, and they both laughed again. She pushed the cheese toward him and bulged her eyes.

Frankie cut slices of cheese and positioned them with pedantic care on the square of bread so that the surface was covered edge-to-edge. Now he was embarrassed by his outburst. He was like some lunatic thermometer these days, his mercury leaping and diving in unruly fashion. It was disconcerting how unpredictable and vehement his reactions had become. Hot words shot out of his mouth; his heart ran marathons at a moment's notice. There really must be something wrong with him. Perhaps he *did* have a cardiac condition. Perhaps he had that syndrome where people shouted and laughed and swore uncontrollably. He stuffed a wedge of sandwich in his mouth to prevent any looming eruption.

"You ever thought of getting a tattoo?" asked Sydney. She was tipped back on two legs of her chair, scooping up cake again, sucking it off her finger.

Frankie tried to clear his head, adjust to Sydney's swerve. Some things didn't change.

"Gordana's got one," he said, which wasn't really an answer. "A green sea horse. On the back of her neck. You can only see it when her hair's up. She had it for two months before Ma and Uncle George even noticed."

"What would you get?" Sydney asked.

He'd really never thought about it, and secretly the idea of a tattoo needle gave him the "screaming ab dabs," to quote one of the Aunties' more outlandish sayings. But now that he *was* thinking about it, he knew exactly what it would have to be.

"Something to do with birds." Wings? A beak? Claw prints? An actual bird?

"I'd have a word," said Sydney. "Or words. But I can never decide what."

He could have a word. He could just have *bird*.

"And I can never decide what language."

Oiseau. Uccello . . .

"What's *bird* in Dutch?" said Frankie.

"Vogel," said Sydney.

Vogel. Ave. Fagel.

"Thirty-seven past one," said Sydney. "Freya's late. Surprise, surprise."

Dribski. That was Chilun for *bird. Dribski* would be good. Maybe a tattoo would be okay. Frankie felt himself warming to the idea. Gordana said it hadn't really hurt that much.

"You know," said Sydney, "I actually don't mind sad endings."

"What?" He was trying to remember the Polish word for *bird.*

"I'm kind of used to them," she said. "Like, every time I have to leave Holland, it's a kind of sad ending. And when we move."

"Half sad, or completely sad?" said Frankie. It came out sarcastic.

"Half sad, I suppose," said Sydney, appearing to think about it. "Completely sad was when my *opa* died. And when we left Ireland, because Freya said she wasn't going back there any time soon."

"But why have a sad ending in a story when you don't *have* to?" Frankie instinctively stuck his thumb between his fingers. He didn't really want to hear any of this. Talk of Sydney's many departures set his spirits on a decline.

"Don't really know," said Sydney. She brought the chair back onto four legs and leaned on the table, chin in her hands. "But heaps of books have sad endings. For instance, *Charlotte's Web.*"

"Yeah," said Frankie dolefully. He couldn't bear the end of *Charlotte's Web.*

"And *The Snow Goose.*"

"Huh." Mr. A had read them *The Snow Goose* in February. Frankie had hated the end of that, too. At least the bird had been all right. It had survived and *flown in a wide, graceful spiral round the old light . . .* Frankie had memorized the words. And then, on the next page, the old light had been bombed to oblivion.

"And *Seven Little Australians.*"

"Never heard of it."

"And *Mary Poppins,*" said Sydney. She was on a roll, almost enjoying this, Frankie thought. "Mary Poppins always leaves at the end of the books."

"That is why," said Frankie, squeezing his fingers tight around his thumbs. "That is why *Harold and the Purple Crayon* is the best book ever. It has a *happy* ending. And so will *The Valiant Ranger.*"

"You know what?" said Sydney musingly. "All your ma's books, those Russian ones, they all have *completely* sad endings. She told me about them. They're totally *tragic.*"

Frankie stood up and began tidying his sketches. "So?" He was suddenly agitated, the pleasant interlude debating tattoos wiped out. "So?"

"So nothing," said Sydney. "But I suppose she doesn't mind sad endings, either. Maybe she even likes them."

Frankie felt the familiar, horrible surge down his arms, the rush of pins and needles. His heart started up its pounding. Little black dots swam in front of his eyes.

"Well, that's her!" he said. His voice was abruptly loud once more, very loud—quite without his seeming to be in charge of it. "Who cares what endings she likes? It's got nothing to do with anything!"

Even as he shouted this, Frankie wished something would stop him, but a great sore need seemed to be welling up. It was propelling him from the inside and he couldn't be quiet.

Sydney was very still, but her eyes blinked rapidly.

"I—" she started, but he wouldn't be interrupted.

"We're not the same!" he spat out. "I'm me and she's her!

Hear that? *I'm ME and she's HER!*" It sounded absurd, he knew it. Even in this once-more instantaneous wound-up state, he could hear the words, enraged and plaintive and absurd. The words began reverberating, like a strident playground chant in his head. *Me Her Me Her Mehermehermeher* . . . The black dots swam across his vision and a horrible taste filled his mouth.

And then the front door opened in a rush. That's how Frankie remembered it later—much later when he looked back on the dreadful tableau, the beginning of the end, as he thought of it. There was a painful, charged silence, there was Sydney's stricken face and the little girls shrinking in the doorway, and then there was the gust as the front door opened and Freya's voice, the almost mythical Freya calling out.

"Spring is here *and* spring is here! Mama's home, little kittens. Get out the suitcases!"

All the echoing loudness and fury dissolved in an instant, and everything in the oddly grand dining room seemed to hiccup and then restart. That's how Frankie thought of it later. He would see and hear it all in a long, drawn-out moment: Sydney's face slowly emptying, her elbows sliding along the table until her arms were flat and her head could drop onto them; the little girls meowing hello; Freya's disembodied, unexpectedly sweet voice talking mother cat nonsense; and Frankie himself, slumping into the chair again, emptied out now, and looking up at the bishop, who looked back implacably, giving away absolutely nothing.

Frankie lay in his bed. He lay facing the wall, his eyes open, but seeing only blackness. His entire body ached. He wanted to cry but it wouldn't happen. His insides were dried out somehow. He was prickly and withered and exhausted.

His head throbbed and there was a jagged pain behind his right eye; the rodent voice told him this was probably a brain aneurism, just as minutes ago it had insisted his aching muscles were meningitis.

He had been mentally reciting batting shots (cover drive, on drive, off drive, straight drive) *to keep the rodent voice at bay* (square cut, forward defense, back foot defense) *to prevent thoughts about madness* (edge, pull shot, French cut) *to shut out the future, which seemed to be worsening by the day.* (Block shot, leg glance, sweep shot, reverse sweep.) *And there weren't enough to get him through the entire night, even if he repeated them over and over, which he already had.*

So, now he was on to birds (canary, budgie, parrot, macaw, mynah, nightingale, Philomel, bulbul) *because he really wanted to stay in his room, not leave his bed in that shrinking way and move, groping, down the hallway, to Ma, ever ready and patient* (lark, thrush, throstle, mavis, blackbird, linnet) *or asleep, and then climbing out of sleep, still patient and soothing* (plover, peewit, pigeon, ringdove, turtledove). *He wanted so much to stick it out, brave it, beat down the rodent voice* (woodpecker, jay, magpie, jackdaw, rook, raven, crow). *He wanted to crawl out from under the despair of Sydney going* (goldfinch, chaffinch, blue tit, wren, robin, cuckoo, yellowhammer, wagtail, sunbird, weaverbird). *He wanted to cease worrying, to feel different once and for all, to calm down, chill out, be released*—wader, stork, crane, heron, spoonbill, ibis, swan, teal, mallard, diver, dipper, grebe, martin, petrel, swallow, swift . . .

EIGHT

Tuesday, May 16

Frankie woke with a rinsed-out head and wobbly legs. It was an important day. He knew this just as surely as he had absolutely no idea what the day would hold.

It was the second day of the second week of vacation. In the middle of the previous night, he had made a decision.

At 2:07 a.m., and for the seventh night in a row, he had been wide-awake and sweating, alternately opening his eyes and squeezing them shut, alternately viewing the dark forms in his bedroom or the rainbow of pulsing colors inside his head. For the seventh night in a row, his head swam with words—it was roiling with conversations, dictionary definitions, song lyrics, old nursery rhymes, and lists, endless lists: lists of cakes, of school projects, of book titles, of birds, of four-legged animals, sports stats, batting shots, bowling actions, Chilun vocab, flowers, trees, cathedrals, paint colors—*anything* that would stop his mind from straying into uncontrollable territory and his body bolting down the hall. He had been utterly weary, and wearily amazed that a body and brain so desperate for sleep could still fail to achieve it.

In the middle of this seventh sleepless night, Frankie felt

nearly resigned to his new state. Probably he would never sleep again; probably he would have a permanently slowed-down half-life now, even though he was only twelve and three quarters. He felt almost intrigued by his monumental exhaustion, by the strange new deadweight of his head and his limbs, the peculiar buzzing sensation that seemed to have settled over his entire skin.

At 1:39 he had switched on his lamp for the hundredth time and picked up *Asterix and Cleopatra*. In the past Asterix had been a reliable soporific, not because he was dull, not at all. He was as comforting as an old friend, funny and pacifying. But now the well-loved jokes and exchanges seemed to shout inside Frankie's head; the pictures bulged and strobed. He tried to read the words very, very slowly, but then they were being spoken by the rodent voice, and he had to put Asterix down and stare hard at Morrie for reassurance. The absurdity of looking for comfort in a skull did not escape him, but in his new sleepless world everything seemed absurd. Or pointless.

Frankie hadn't been able to see the point in anything much since the terrible episode at Sydney's house. For the last week, he had dragged himself around, pushing drearily through each day as if through stiffened porridge. He wasn't hungry and he couldn't sleep. He couldn't be bothered talking. He seemed to have lost his capacity to laugh, too. Louie had been around twice and neither he nor Ray Davies had stirred the faintest hint of mirth.

"Frankie's lost his mojo," Louie said.

It was after dinner on Sunday. Louis and Uncle George were playing backgammon at the table. Frankie slouched on the sofa beside Gordana, looking at nothing. Ma was in the kitchen. At dinner she had put her hand on Frankie's forehead to see if he had a temperature, but Frankie had shaken her off.

"Does one *have* mojo at Frankie's age?" mused Uncle George.

"Don't be repulsive," Gordana said.

But Frankie didn't care. He didn't care what any of them said.

"You do look undead," said Gordana. She rose and stood over him, her hands on her hips. She scowled; she was like a humorless matron, assessing a backsliding patient. "You've got massive pits under your eyes. And your hair's all lank." She leaned into him and sniffed. "And it smells."

He hadn't washed his hair. He couldn't be bothered. He couldn't see the point. And what was the point of soap? He just stood under the shower each day and let the water pour over him. Nor could he be bothered drying himself afterward; he wrapped a towel around and stood at his bedroom window, staring into the backyard, which looked suitably dismal now that the trees had lost most of their leaves and a general dampness had descended.

"Everything all right, old chap?" Uncle George asked.

But Frankie had just shrugged and left the room, closing the door on Ray Davies's hopeful face. He could hear them all as he walked away.

"Definitely in love," said Louie.

"More like crossed in love," said Uncle George.

"Like you two would know," said Gordana.

What would any of them know? Frankie had thought, trudging down the hall. They didn't have a clue.

But later that evening Gordana had come into his room. She came in without knocking, which had always been her habit, though she hadn't come near his room for months and months. Frankie was so surprised that a flicker of something stirred momentarily in him. He was sitting on his bed, *Asterix and Cleopatra* open, waiting.

"What's the matter?" said Gordana.

"Nothing," said Frankie. It sounded pathetically unconvincing.

"*What* is the matter?" Gordana favored the broken-record technique.

"Vacation," Frankie mumbled. "Boring. You know, Gigs away."

"Why didn't you go to his concert?"

Frankie had rung Dr. Pete on Saturday afternoon and said he wasn't feeling well. He hadn't wanted to go to the Brass Gala. The thought of exultant brass music made him feel quite cold inside.

"Too tired," said Frankie.

"Where's Sydney?"

"Busy," said Frankie. "Being a child-minder."

"What's *really* the matter?" said Gordana.

She went over to his desk and lifted the lid on the music box. Plastic Lara rose creakily and began turning. The tinny tune and Gordana's gruff concern seemed to open a pit in Frankie's chest. It made him give a great dry gulp, and he thought he might cry. He *wanted* to cry. He wanted to crumple up and fall off the bed and wail, maybe even yell. But he couldn't. It just wouldn't happen; he was a rag doll without stuffing now, listless beyond belief.

"It's something to do with Sydney, isn't it?" said Gordana. "Has something happened with her mother?"

"Nothing new," said Frankie. Which was technically true.

"Have you had a fight?"

"No," said Frankie. Also technically true.

* * *

He had talked to Sydney just twice since the terrible day. His head had been playing a more-or-less continuous movie of the afternoon, all the scenes and exchanges at hurricane speed: Sydney's head-down distress at the prospect of leaving alternating with his own humiliating outbursts and the punch-drunk feeling he'd experienced when Freya had delivered her—somehow—inevitable news.

In Frankie's private film, he seemed to have burst from Sydney's house not long after that, gasping for air, desperate to get away from the confusion of feelings. The film showed him walking unnaturally fast through the streets, through the Hiroshima Gardens, standing at the midtown bus terminal, reading the timetable over and over, traveling home through the city in a strange repeat of the ride a month earlier, his head so full it was actually blank, a white noise of unspeakable thoughts, and no thoughts at all.

On Wednesday Sydney had phoned. She sounded her normal self, which Frankie found astonishing. They weren't leaving for three weeks, Sydney said. Frankie had been awake all night, dreaming up solutions. He told her she didn't need to leave at all, she should come and live at their house, in Louie's room. Or, it was possible she could live at the Aunties', in Frankie's room. He had it all worked out.

He listened to Sydney's breath, steady and even.

"Face facts, Frankie," she said eventually.

"What do you *mean*? *Why?*"

"It's easier."

He had nearly hung up then. He didn't understand her. She was too different from him, after all.

"It's not so far away," she said. "Two and a half hours by plane is nothing. You can come and visit."

Frankie was silent.

Sydney sighed. "At least we got *The Valiant Ranger* done," she said. "Do you think Mr. A will mark it before I go?"

That was when Frankie had hung up. It was an almost involuntary reaction, his body's response to the mention of their book project. He just couldn't think about *The Valiant Ranger*. His mind simply snapped shut if he considered it. It was that whole business about the endings, and his demented tirade. If he allowed his thoughts to stray there, he thought he might curl into a ball and stay bunched up for the rest of his days.

Of course he had phoned Sydney back a minute later. He had said, "Thorry" and she had laughed croakily and said she could come over the next day and bring the sketches he'd left behind. But by Thursday Frankie had had two sleepless nights and was feeling extremely strange. And he did not want to see his drawings. He'd rung Sydney and said there was a big order on. Two dozen midwinter Christmas cakes. He had to help Ma.

It was an awful lie, and also, what was he *doing*? His heart was nearly bursting with sadness at the thought of Sydney leaving, but here he was willfully not making the most of every single moment before she was gone, possibly forever.

"I can help!" Sydney said. "I'm an excellent baker's assistant; you know I am."

"Not enough room in the kitchen," said Frankie. He was sitting on the garden bench with the Fat Controller, looking back at the house. The bench was damp after rain and now the seat of his jeans was damp, too, but he hardly noticed. He was so tired, his eyes had become watery. The house blurred and wobbled in the thin morning sun.

"What's the matter, Frankie?" Sydney had said. Her voice came from a long way off.

* * *

"What's the *matter,* Franko?" said Gordana again. Her voice was distant, too.

Frankie made a great effort and focused on his sister. She wasn't looking at him. She had lifted the kereru feather from Morrie's skull and was brushing it back and forth over the top of his desk, a delicate, painterly gesture.

"Sydney's leaving," he said, and was surprised in a remote kind of way. He hadn't known he was going to say this. His mouth had just done it. Now his brain was mildly curious to see what Gordana would say.

Gordana put the feather back in Morrie's skull and picked up Agent 99 and Maxwell Smart. She stood them close together on the desk, facing each other, their perfectly shaped Fimo noses nearly touching.

"Oh, *Max,*" drawled Gordana in 99's American accent. Then in her own voice she said, "Where're they going?"

"Sydney," said Frankie.

Sydney of Sydney.

Gordana put Agent 99 and Maxwell back in Kidder's lap. "Does Ma know?"

"Haven't told anyone else," said Frankie. He leaned back against the headboard and closed his eyes.

"When do they go?" said Gordana.

"Three weeks."

The room was very quiet.

"Poor Frankie," said Gordana.

He wanted to say, "She's not my girlfriend." But he couldn't be bothered. What was the point? He kept his eyes closed. He remembered how he used to sleep with Kidder beside him in the bed; he remembered the creaky touch of Kidder's synthetic fur, his comforting smell.

"Go away," he said to Gordana, and she had gone, out of his room, shutting the door softly.

On Sunday night, Frankie had gotten out of bed and started down the hall, muzzy and unsteady. He wanted to tell Ma he was sorry for shaking off her hand; he wanted to say he was sorry for avoiding her, for hardly looking at her yesterday, and the day before, and the day before that. He had hovered at the door of Ma and Uncle George's room, shivering and stiff, faltering, his hand going up to the door handle and down again. Then he had turned and gone slowly back to his room.

On Monday there was a rainstorm, and Frankie lay in bed, listening to the wind and the thrashing tree branches. He dozed, the Fat Controller on his feet, Kidder tucked down under the duvet where no one could see him. It was so warm in bed, and his thoughts were blessedly neutral while he slept.

Sometime in the morning Ma knocked on the door and called his name softly.

"Are you awake, Frankie? It's Sydney on the phone."

He didn't answer, pretending to be asleep. He heard Ma walk away.

"I think he's coming down with something," she was saying. "It's funny: he quite often gets sick during vacation. Does that happen to you?"

In the afternoon she knocked again, and this time when he didn't answer, she came in to his room. Frankie lay very still and kept his eyes closed, but soon a pleasant smell reached his nose.

Chicken soup. Ma always had chicken soup there when he was sick.

He could feel her looking down at him.

"C'mon, Frankie, sit up. I've got soup. It's good you're sleeping, but you need to eat, too."

He struggled up in the bed and the Fat Controller moved lumpily and complained, then jumped crossly to the floor. Frankie stared at the tray on his lap. He didn't want to look up at Ma, look at her nice gray eyes, the concern or reproach that might be on her face. He hadn't looked at her at all for days; he hadn't wanted to see any kind of expression on her face. He kept his head down when she came near him, or looked away; he looked a lot at other things, everything, anything except Ma.

"I've got the flu or something," he said.

"You're probably just very tired." She stood, waiting. Frankie picked up the spoon and held it over the soup, watching the steam creep around the spoon.

"Sydney rang," said Ma. "She told me about leaving."

Frankie brought the back of the spoon down slowly on some floating parsley, submerging it.

"You're really going to miss her, I know," said Ma.

"She's not my girlfriend," he said flatly.

"I know," said Ma. "I know."

A burst of rain beat against the window. The Fat Controller yawned and began loudly washing herself.

"Would you like some bread with that?" said Ma.

"No, thanks," said Frankie. He kept his eyes on the bowl, sipping the soup.

"Frankie," said Ma from the doorway, "is . . . ? Can I?" Her voice faltered. "Is there — ?"

"Thanks for the soup," said Frankie, cutting her off, still not looking.

The door closed gently.

On Monday evening, Uncle George knocked on the door and came in.

"You not too good, old man?"

Frankie was lying on his side. He was concentrating on a memory: his first wicket in Intermediate Reps. It had been early in the season, a windy day, and though he was the smallest and skinniest, he was the one who always bowled into the wind. It was because he was so economical, so reliable.

"Go, Frankie! Frankie's our postman!" Dr. Pete yelled from the sideline. "Always delivers!"

And almost never gets wickets, Frankie had thought, turning for his run up.

But then it had happened. It was a kid from a North Island school; he had a brand-new cricket jersey and elegant strokes. But Frankie's ball had hit his middle stump and sent the bails flying. The click of those skittled bails was the most beautiful sound Frankie had ever heard.

"You awake, old man?" said Uncle George.

Frankie grunted, pulled himself away from the high-fives and cheers and the very satisfactory look of disappointment on the batsman's face. Underwood. That was his name. Good joke.

"Got the flu?" said Uncle George. He sat down on the bed, and Frankie rolled over, squinting up at his father.

"Probably," said Frankie.

"Game of Last Card?"

Uncle George always played Last Card with them when they were sick. It was the perfect game for invalids, he said, because it only demanded a tiny bit of brain and it distracted you from the throat-cutting boredom of the sickbed.

Uncle George was a terrible patient. He was hardly ever sick, but when he was obliged to take to his bed, everyone else scattered; otherwise he press-ganged you into nursing slavery. He roared increasingly precise demands from the bed: Could he have something decent to read? Some extra pillows. The radio. Some candy. Some weak tea, *weak* tea, with half a teaspoon of sugar and just a drop of milk, just a *drop*. And a Malt Biscuit. With butter. No, without butter. No, no, with just a scraping of butter and a smidgen of plum jam.

A couple of winters back, he'd had a knee operation and been confined to the sofa for two weeks. Frankie had assumed nursing duty and manfully returned the Last Card favor; he'd played every day after school and most of the weekend, though Uncle George ceaselessly disputed the rules. Frankie had finally dug his heels in over the matter of reversing jacks, and Uncle George had gone into a sulk.

That seemed forever ago now; Frankie couldn't imagine playing Last Card ever again.

"No, thanks," he said.

"I heard about Sydney," said Uncle G. He patted Frankie's hunched form under the duvet.

Frankie grunted again.

"Real shame," said Uncle George. "She's a great girl."

Yes, thought Frankie.

"So, Louie rang," said Uncle George. "This T-shirt and bandanna thing's looking good. He's found a couple of machinists. And he seems to have convinced Gordana. Wait for the fireworks!"

Grunt.

"Parsons and Parsons," said Uncle George.

Won't last, thought Frankie.

"Could be Parsons, Parsons, and Parsons," said Uncle George. "Louie's keen for your birds — big market there, I reckon. People can't get enough of native birds."

Grunt.

"Better let you get some more sleep." Uncle George patted him again. "Best medicine."

He stood, waiting for something.

"'Night," said Frankie.

He closed his eyes and saw two aral birds, dull-colored and lifeless, lumps of dusty feathers discarded on the floorboards of a tree house.

At 1:50 a.m. Tuesday, Frankie put *Asterix and Cleopatra* back on the pile beside the bed and turned the light off once more. He lay back down and closed his eyes, though he had no expectation of sleep. The buzzing sensation on his skin was becoming more and more pronounced. More accurately, it was just under his skin. It was as if a vast colony of mosquitoes had settled there and was concertedly humming.

He wondered if it was kidney disease. Or septicemia. Or perhaps the buzzing feeling wasn't there at all and he was just a paranoid schizophrenic with delusions. Vienna's older brother was schizophrenic and believed the city council was poisoning the water system. He drank only bottled water from France. His name was Julian and sometimes he came to school to pick up Vienna. Julian seemed perfectly normal to Frankie, and rather nice; he knew a lot about cricket, too, which just showed you.

Another list started up in his head, stopping thoughts of Julian and possible mental illness, stopping his feet from swinging sideways out of bed, onto the floor. *Diamond, ruby, pearl, opal, sapphire, emerald.*

In the Aunties' library was a big old *Readers' Digest* atlas. When he was younger, Frankie liked to open it out on the floor and study the maps. On one double-page spread were photographs of gems in their uncut and polished states. Frankie had been entranced by the transformation from rock to faceted jewel. And by the names of the gems; they were somehow foreign-sounding, a little mysterious. He had learned them by heart years ago, lying by the Aunties' open fire on a wet winter afternoon. *Turquoise, beryl, aquamarine, garnet, amethyst, topaz, carnelian* . . . Ma had a carnelian ring that had belonged to her mother. It was heavy, like a man's jewel. But he didn't want to think about Ma. Or her dead mother.

And then a wave of pure horror poured through his body, an icy flood that pooled around his heart, squeezed his lungs. He broke out in a fresh sweat. This was the very worst feeling, this wave. It terrified him. It propelled him, usually, straight out of bed, as if he were being pushed forward on tidal waters, down the hall to Ma.

Chalcedony, agate, moonstone, pearl, jade, lapis lazuli, onyx, amber, jasper . . . That was his favorite, *jasper*. If he ever had a kid, he'd called him Jasper. Gigs was planning to call his sons Prince and Duke. But they would have to be born completely adult, since Gigs couldn't stand actual children. *Coral, zircon, bloodstone, fire opal, beryl,* no, he'd done that. He'd have to start again, or he'd be back to Ma.

But dogs began instead. Good, there were so many dogs, dogs could last for ages. *Beagle, Saint Bernard, dachshund, Labrador, retriever, collie, setter, spaniel* . . . The Aunties had owned an old black spaniel years ago, Walt. He'd gotten sick and farted incessantly and revoltingly, and they'd had to have him put down. Frankie had wanted a funeral service, so they'd had a procession out to the back garden, with Teen holding Walt, and Frankie in front with a wooden cross. Alma had said some Latin and then they'd buried Walt and marked the spot with the cross . . .

Bulldog, boxer, borzoi, Alsatian, Dalmatian, Great Dane . . . The horror wave was receding, but only very slowly . . . *Whippet, short-haired pointer, fox terrier, Chihuahua, Pekinese, corgi, poodle* . . . *bitzer* . . . Microsoft appeared in his head, the intelligent face, the sturdy terrier legs. But then three-legged Microsoft limped bumpily across his thoughts and he abruptly wiped the image . . . *Greyhound, foxhound, bloodhound, wolfhound* . . . He ran out of dogs.

Frankie lifted his head and wished he could howl like a wolf-hound. He wished he could leap from his bed and bay and bay at the window and the sliver of moon hanging just above next-door's roof. He wanted the manic listing to end; he wanted to extinguish the horror waves and the cold fingers around his heart. He wanted the malignly insistent thoughts to be banished forever; he just wanted it all to *stop,* and he wanted so very badly to sleep.

He had to find help. He needed help—he knew it; he really did. He had to talk to someone, and soon, or he wouldn't be able to go on. Immediately, on thinking this, came a brief wash of relief and—how strange—now a tear welled, warm and pendant, in the corner of his eye. Yes, he had to talk to someone. He couldn't talk to Ma, for reasons he couldn't examine just now. He couldn't talk to Sydney because it was all tied up with her. And it was too complicated and halting somehow with Gordana or Uncle George or Louie. He must find someone else. Tears fell out of both his eyes, but he didn't care; it felt almost good, though his nose was blocking up and his head pounded, and now that the tears had started, he couldn't seem to stop them.

He reached down, found his discarded T-shirt on the floor, and blew his nose in it, which was disgusting, but who cared. He wiped his eyes, though tears just came and came. He wiped and blew and wiped, and then, like a rider approaching from a long way off, the thought came slowly through the pounding and the blowing and the tears: Alma.

He lay quite still for a few seconds, Alma's great form looming in his head, her big fat ankles, her yellow paisley scarf and fur beret, her meaty arms lifted, ready to sweep aside problems. He could talk to any of the Aunties, but he chose Alma. He would go there tomorrow. He would find Alma, and somehow, he didn't know how, somehow it would be better. Alma would save him.

And then instantly it was as if he were being pulled through the bed, through the mattress and the base and the floorboards. An immense force was drawing him under in a heavy rush, down and down and down, and he was asleep.

The Aunties lived in a big house on Old Mill Road. The original house, they said. Not the Mill House, but the mill *owner's* house. The mill owner was some character from last century called L. Cuttance Boyd, an early settler who'd made it big in the new country. There was a little metal plaque and several framed photos in the Aunties' hallway testifying to this fact: L. Cuttance Boyd and his large family (and servants) seated outside their splendid wooden residence. L. Cuttance Boyd and his workers outside the sawmill. L. Cuttance Boyd and his fine new Thoroughbred, His Lordship.

L. Cuttance Boyd was a big man with a big belly and a bushy mustache; he had lived to the age of ninety-two. Alas (Alma's word), good health and worldly success had bypassed his children and grandchildren. The Cuttance Boyd line and fortune had died out several generations back. The Aunties had researched L. Cuttance Boyd and his ignominious descendants when they had bought the house and begun restoring it to its former glory. That had been years and years ago, before Ma was born, and now the city had spread out to meet the mill owner's mansion; now you could take the bus there in fifteen minutes from the midtown terminal. The old sawmill had disappeared without a trace, but Frankie liked to think that L. Cuttance Boyd's portly ghost lingered around the area. He had always thought L. Cuttance Boyd looked rather jolly. He liked to imagine he'd been called Cut for short, which would have been perfect for a miller.

So the mill owner's house had been the Aunties' for more than forty years now, and Frankie loved the place. But it was a seesawing, roller-coaster love, a love diluted by dollops of melancholy and visiting unease. The house was a child's paradise — so many rooms, so many interesting objects and books. And outside was better still — a garden with trees and places to make your own, and a river down at the bottom. Of course, the Aunties were great pamperers and wildly entertaining and most tender and solicitous when you needed them to be, but when Frankie thought about living at their house, he seemed to remember that in the midst of all the laughing and big dinners and hilarious visitors and card games and rides in the Morris Oxford, he had been somehow quietly haunted.

All that time, he had been waiting for something; whatever it was, he had wanted it and he had feared it, too. The something was behind him or it was just over his shoulder or just around the corner, out of sight. He worried about it; it made him nervous and uncertain and sometimes sad.

It was such a cavalcade of memories, those times at the Aunties' — bursts of color and music and loud activity and discussion — and there in the middle of it all, something like a faint, insistent tune, some wordless song in a minor key that kept catching his ear.

Frankie was thinking all this as he rode first the number 40 bus into town and then the number 83 bus out to Marshlands, which was both the name of the Aunties' house and the suburb that had grown around it. The bus stopped outside the primary school where Frankie had been going to start years ago until he had cried bitterly and said he must go to the same school as Gordana and Louie. So the Aunties had taken him across town every day, except when they thought it would be more fun at home or touring around the city in the Morris Oxford.

Frankie got off the bus and sat for a while on the low stone fence that bordered the school. He'd biked down here sometimes when he was older and practiced his bowling on the school cricket strip with some of the local boys. He remembered a big kid called Simon Stanhope, whose name had sounded just like a great cricketer's. Frankie's own name was pretty good, too; hadn't Sydney said so, back on that first day, on the school bus? But he wouldn't be a great cricketer; he was just a trundler, really, accurate enough, but no flair. Gigs was planning to use his real name when he was famous. Gregory Angelo. Gordana said Gregory Angelo sounded like a slimy, afternoon soap star and he should change his name altogether. Or his career ambitions.

Frankie yawned copiously. It was warm; he could fall asleep right now, here on the stone fence. He had slept properly last night for the first time in a week, but it had only been five hours. His thoughts were a little clearer but his exhaustion was still epic. His head and torso and limbs felt as if they had fused into something amorphous and nearly immovable, a granite boulder, or a waterlogged tree-trunk beached after a storm. He had lifted himself out of bed with enormous effort and dressed as slowly as an invalid. In the kitchen, he had moved clumsily around Ma, like the proverbial bull with china. And he had dropped his cereal bowl, which had shattered in a dozen pieces. Ma had been rather sharp with him and Frankie had abandoned the idea of breakfast. He had left the house without really saying good-bye. Ma would think he'd gone to Sydney's.

He stood and stretched and began walking toward the Aunties'. It was only half a mile or so. It was Tuesday. Nearly midday. They would be long home from tai chi and pancakes with Johnny Mac. Since it was sunny, Teen might be in the garden, though there wasn't much to be done in May. Nellie would be writing letters or reading or on the phone to one of the parish ladies. Alma might be writing letters, too, or studying one of her university art books.

But sometimes on winter mornings, and before the sun disappeared over the back of the house, Alma sat in the wicker chair on the front veranda, reading, or smoking and watching the fountain. Naturally L. Cuttance Boyd had built a fountain in his front yard. It was a tiered stone structure, like an oversized cake-stand, and Alma could watch the water shooting out the middle and tumbling down the platters for whole hours at a time.

This picture of Alma was in Frankie's head as he walked the length of School Road and then Boyd Road and as he rounded the corner into Swan Road—where there were, in fact, swans gliding in regal fashion on a large pond—and as he turned into the drive of Marshlands, Swan Road, RD 1. He traipsed up the driveway, along the curving line of poplars, and he fixed his mind's eye on Alma and the wicker chair and the fountain playing in the winter sun and the pretty curl of smoke from Alma's cheroot. And the picture was so clear and settled that it made something burst warmly in his chest when he looked up and saw that very picture made real. Alma was indeed sitting, blowing smoke to the sky, her plump legs raised up on a stool, a heavy book open in her lap.

Frankie thought later that he called out, like a kitten, a wan and creaky sound. He knew that he wanted to run to Alma, but his tired, somehow elderly body was too dreary a thing now to hurry. He could see Alma, pushing the footstool aside, heaving herself up from the wicker chair and standing, immense and dependable, smiling widely, and then the smile faltering, but her arms were up and out, anyway, just as they used to be when he was small.

"How's my darling boy?" she called.

It seemed such a long way up the six steps to the veranda and to Alma's wide-open arms. He was like an albatross now, Frankie thought, wind-buffeted and injured and gasping, after a tumultuous flight. He felt like a wounded bird and an ancient human and a small boy all at once, not a twelve-nearly-thirteen-year-old, who was much too grown up, surely, to sob on the large chest of his great-aunt. But that is what he did. He flung himself at Alma and he let her gather him in, and then he cried and cried.

Frankie sat on the bed in Frankie's room, looking through his old sketchbooks. It was the first time in years and years since he'd opened them.

After their long talk, Alma had told him to lie down and see if he mightn't doze. Frankie had done so obediently, staring up at the Japanese bird kite, its washed-out colors, the paper-thin wings, and his first thought had been that before this was Frankie's room, this bedroom was *Francie's* room. Ma's room. Of course he had always known this, but now the fact seemed part of some important tapestry only just coming into focus. He let the thought lie there in his tired brain, unexamined for the moment. He couldn't doze. He wanted to look at his sketchbooks; he wanted to think about everything he and Alma had talked about.

The early drawings were all shades of purple — in imitation of Harold, of course. Frankie could actually remember doing them; he could remember the feel of the crayon under his fingers, the new satisfaction he experienced as his hand moved across the paper and the pictures sprouted beneath it. The pictures were all of his family. A dozen variations, a dozen different settings, but in every picture were Uncle George and Louie, with great nests of curly hair; Ma and Gordana in dresses, Gordana differentiated by a ponytail; and then himself, small and skinny, with a black cat—their old cat, Stanley.

The Aunties and Walt were in the pictures, too, nearby but just a little apart. There they all were—everyone at the park, at the beach, on the street. There they were, standing in front of L. Cuttance Boyd's fountain. At a zoo. At the supermarket. At the river. There were birds and dogs and fish and lions and horses, too, sometimes earthbound, sometimes airborne. They were all in there together, an exuberant confusion of people and animals, and they were—all of them, Ma included—always outdoors.

"It will be all right," Alma had said to Frankie as he cried against her chest. "It will be *all* right."

She had said it over and over, hugging him hard and patting his back. Dimly, he was aware of Teen and Nellie coming out to the veranda, patting his back, too, then going indoors again, down the long passage, back to their various tasks. He was four years old again, crying over a fall or a bad dream, or wanting to go back home, wanting to see Gordana and Louie.

He had stopped crying at last and loosened his way out of Alma's hug and they sat down together on the top veranda step. Frankie fastened his eyes on the plant tendrils fighting up through the stone path. He felt despairing again. He had no idea what to say, where to begin.

"It's times like these, you really need to be able to smoke," said Alma. "Smoking is such a good thought-gatherer. But I mustn't corrupt the young." She pulled the packet of cheroots from her sagging cardigan pocket and lit up. "I'll do the smoking and you do the thought-gathering."

Frankie breathed in the woody perfume of the cigar, and his breath turned into a hiccup. His face ached from crying. He felt as if someone had punched him in several parts of his body—his cheekbones, his lungs, his legs. Alma smoked patiently, saying nothing. A gull squawked overhead.

"Things," Frankie began tentatively, speaking to the stone path. "Things—" He stopped and closed his fists, pushing his fingernails into his palms, trying to clear his dull head with that small pain. "Things have gotten out of hand," he said.

"Yes," said Alma. It seemed like a statement of fact.

"But I don't understand it," said Frankie. "I can't talk to Ma anymore. It's terrible. I don't *want* to talk to her. I don't want to even look at her." He said this last very low, ashamed, waiting for Alma's recoil. But she patted his knee, hummed some kind of agreement.

"But all the rodent thoughts are out of control, and it's always Ma that helps me—" Frankie felt the wisps of panic rising on the back of his neck. He wanted to clutch at Alma's skirt, gather up big folds in his hands.

"Rodent thoughts?" said Alma calmly.

"It's like a voice," said Frankie, slowing down. He didn't care if Alma thought he was crazy. He knew he had to say it all. He made himself breathe evenly. "A ratty voice saying everything that I'm afraid of. Which is just about everything in the world now. It can get so loud. But if I talk to Ma, it always goes away . . . It's so *stupid.* I get into bed and the voice starts up, so I go and talk to Ma. There's always something I'm worried about, *afraid* of. I'm just always *afraid . . .*"

He felt the pressure of Alma's hand again. "This is brave," she said. "Talking like this. You know that, don't you?"

The tears sprang back. If Alma were too kind to him, he'd never get through it. He dug his feet hard into the step, pressing on.

"Ma calls it the ten p.m. question, sort of a joke, which made it seem almost all right, but it isn't. It's gotten worse and worse. I couldn't go to camp. I don't like to stay anywhere because of it — and because of Ma —"

"Because of Francie?" said Alma.

"Because she needs someone to help — and it's usually me. It has to be me because of Uncle G being busy and Gordana not being around much and Louie moving out . . . But now —" Frankie stopped again. Alma was bending with effort, stubbing out her cheroot on the side of the step. She dropped it into the shrubbery beside the veranda.

"But now?" she prompted.

"Now *Sydney's* going," said Frankie, and this time tears leaked right out. "And that's all a mess. It's been so much better while she's been here! Everything was better somehow, more bearable. She asked questions. I could tell her things, and I thought maybe everything could change after all. But she's going. And she *accepts* it! She *accepts* sad endings. That's what I can't bear."

Frankie spat the words into the air, sickened by them. Sad endings. Gulls squealed, as if in agreement. Alma waited. He tried to put his thoughts in order, work out what should come first, work out what he felt.

"It was when Sydney said Ma loved sad endings — like the Russians — that was when it all went so bad. I couldn't sleep, I couldn't stop the rodent voice, but I couldn't talk to Ma. I don't want Ma to love sad endings. And I don't want to *have* a sad ending, either. I don't want to be just like Ma, Alma! I want her to leave the house. Why can't she? Why *won't* she? Why does everyone just accept it? Why doesn't anyone ever, *ever, ever* talk about it?"

Now he looked up at Alma, not caring about the tears. She was looking straight back at him, her face puckered, her old blue eyes full of loving concern.

"Oh, Frankie," she sighed. "Isn't it hard?"

Frankie leafed slowly through the sketchbook, watching the purple drawings give way to profusions of color. The family turned all shades, and after a while, their formation changed, too. Sometimes Frankie was with them; sometimes he was with the Aunties. Sometimes it was just Frankie and Louie and Gordana. Sometimes it was Frankie with Walt and Stanley, which was funny since those two animals had never been together in real life.

His Walt and Stanley drawings were comically primitive. Looking at the careful C curls on Walt's coat, Stanley's precise but oversized whiskers, Frankie remembered suddenly the story he'd invented: *Days with Walt and Stanley*. He could remember telling himself the story as he drew the pictures. And here were the pictures. Walt and Stanley at the river. Walt and Stanley in a boat. Walt and Stanley on a swing. Walt and Stanley *in a tree house*. Dead Walt. Sad Stanley. *RIP Walt* on the wooden cross in the Aunties' garden. Good-bye, Stanley — there were no more drawings of the cat after that. Frankie remembered the line he used to say at the end of all the stories: *Don't worry, Stanley. Walt is beside you.* He'd adapted it from *Hansel and Gretel.* But poor old Walt had died anyway. He sighed and turned to the second sketchbook.

It was all ducks in the first few pages. They had been his first bird drawings, because of the ducks on the river at the bottom of the Aunties' garden. Frankie assessed them with a critical eye—the proportions were wildly askew, and occasionally the birds seemed to have more than two feet, but what could you expect from a four-year-old? After a few pages the ducks were joined by other birds. Sparrows? Thrushes? He recognized the pugnacious stance of a magpie, and that made him remember Teen's bird feeder, wrecked in a storm years ago. There were drawings of the bird feeder. Swans from down the road. A budgie in a cage. Very purple pukekos.

The drawings changed to pencil. Frankie remembered those pencils perfectly. He'd gotten them for his fifth birthday from the Aunties, a huge packet of Crayola. Fifty pencils! And the words written in a rainbow across the packet: *Super spectrum of color.* He could remember Gordana reading it to him, following her clear consonants and the rainbow letters with his finger.

Frankie pulled back the eiderdown and got beneath it. He lay back on the pillows and propped the sketchbook against his upright knees. A great crowd of memories had been waiting for him, he thought, as if behind a half-open door. Turning the pages of the sketchbook was like opening the door again and again, and after enough pages, the door seemed flung wide. The memories were pushing over each other in their hurry, so that even as he turned a page, he knew what he'd see next.

It was a picture of Ma, a long-haired Ma in a green brocade ball dress, hung about with stars of every size and Crayola hue. She was suspended, floating, in some outer lit-up heaven. She was over the page again, then again and again, in the sky, on the ground, in night and in day, sometimes with wings, sometimes not, always in the green brocade gown.

He had drawn Ma over and over, a kind of *Don't worry, Frankie. Francie is beside you.* It didn't really look like Ma, of course, but Frankie knew it *was* Ma because now he could remember doing

224 :

the drawing. He could remember showing Ma waving—
yes, there it was—you could tell it was a wave because there were
three little lines above her hand, signifying movement, like a
comic strip. He could remember when he'd first done that, how
pleased he'd been with the technique.

Frankie looked up at the bird kite. What did that wave mean?
Hello, Frankie? *Good-bye,* Frankie? *Don't worry, Frankie. Francie is
beside you.*

"The thing is, Frankie," Alma had said, lighting another cheroot,
"you must talk to Francie yourself. She must tell you how it was;
it will be good for both of you. We've been saying that to her for
years, but she doesn't like to upset you. She doesn't like to upset
herself, I suppose. And fair enough. It's hard to bring it up, relive it."

Alma fiddled with the match as she always did, digging it into
the step, flicking off the burnt carbon. She put it back into the
matchbox and looked at Frankie.

"But people keep silent for too long and then, next thing,
silence is their bad habit. Things fester."

"I want you to tell me," said Frankie.

"Happy to," said Alma, blowing smoke in an expert stream.
"But only if you talk to Francie, too. And Uncle George. Poor old
Uncle G. He never likes to ruffle the waters. He likes it all tickety-
boo, now that it's so much better—"

"But it's not better!" Frankie cried. "Nothing's really better!
Ma isn't better. Louie said—" He stopped, remembering with an
ache the emptiness of Louie's voice that day outside The Istanbul.
"Louie said Ma was a *caged bird.*"

Alma gave a small grimace, and Frankie felt the familiar
treachery. "I know Ma *is* better—"

"Look, Frankie," said Alma, seeming to make up her mind on something. "It's important to have a long view in these matters. Once upon a time, your mother was unable to get out of bed. Once, her world had shrunk to this"—she drew a wobbly rectangle in the air with her big hands—"the size of a *bed.*"

Frankie's skin pinched and contracted. He knew it was true. There were parts of that *once* that he could call up in a moment, like the daytime flash of a nightmare.

"I know. . . ."

"Now," Alma plowed on. "*Now,* she runs a business from home. She's stable; she's successful; she's . . . I . . ." Alma paused. She was choosing her words with care, Frankie could tell. "I want to say she's happy, but really, what a stupid word—it's not *useful.* . . . She's content. Content is a good ending for Francie."

Frankie looked at his great-aunt. Her face was weathered and whiskery, like an old walrus. She seemed always to have looked exactly the same. He remembered other times he'd sat close by her, inching toward her fleshy comfort.

"You used to say that Ma was resting up," said Frankie.

"So she was," said Alma stoutly. "Resting from life. Temporarily. I told you she'd be back, too.

"And I'll tell you what," she continued. "I was *very pleased* that I could say that to you, you understand? Very pleased. I couldn't say it to your mother when she was the same age."

Frankie stared at her; the terrible truth of Ma's childhood bereavement was written on Alma's walrus face. He closed his eyes, taking it in. Ma had never gotten her own mother back. She hadn't gotten her father.

He heard Alma's big chest going up and down. He heard the fountain and the gulls and Teen whistling in the house.

"Is that what did it to Ma?" he said finally. "Her parents dying? Is that what made her—?" He never liked to think the word that hovered there, much less say it. There were so many of these, the words he didn't like to think or say.

"Break down?" said Alma. She was like Gordana, Frankie thought. And Sydney. They were able to say the hard words, all of them. They didn't cower and snivel like he did, hearing and seeing and speaking no evil.

"Could be," Alma said. She looked around the garden and back at the fountain, narrowed her eyes at the falling water. "These things are so complex, Frankie. Some people are just more fragile. Look at me, and the girls. I'm an old boot, you know that, and so is Teen. Nellie's the sensitive one. She feels things more. And then there's what life throws up . . ."

"Am I wired like Ma?" said Frankie. He said it to the side, very softly, hating the thought, hating himself for hating it. "Gordana says I am."

Alma lit a third cheroot, blew out thoughtfully.

"Maybe," she said. "In some ways. But not every way. You must talk to Francie," Alma said again, very firmly. "Francie's thought about it all for a long time now."

"But it happened," said Frankie slowly. "It happened . . . more than once. It happened twice." He dug this out, like a particularly difficult splinter.

"Yes, it did," said Alma. "When you were four, and then just after your sixth birthday."

Frankie pressed his feet into the steps again, willing himself forward.

"But why did I come here?" he said, and then because it sounded rather ungrateful, he said hurriedly, "I'm glad I did. I mean, you, the Aunties, I mean it was great and everything—"

Alma put her arm around his shoulder and squeezed him. "Oh, Frankie, you are such a *kind* boy."

She grinned, remembering, too. "It *was* great—we loved it.

We loved having Francie's boy to look after." She squeezed him to her again. "And you were such a dear little boy. You *are* a dear boy. . . ." She turned and eyed him speculatively. "Not so little anymore, though. You've grown. You'll top Louie one of these days."

"You really think so?" said Frankie, absurdly pleased, and then astonished he could be diverted by something so trivial.

They sat for a minute or two, listening to the random music of the fountain. Behind them, in the house, Frankie could hear the heavy tread of an Auntie, up and down the passage, bureau drawers opening and closing.

"It was strange for you here sometimes," Alma said. "You missed everyone, even when you were happy. But we were the obvious place — you needed someone all day. And then the second time, it was because we were so familiar to you, like a second family. And Uncle G coped better with just Louie and Gordana."

The sun was dropping, the air cooler. A blackbird called roughly from its perch on the front gate. Frankie leaned his head against Alma, the hard pillow of her flesh.

"Everyone copes differently, don't they?" said Alma. She spoke slowly, as if she were thinking aloud. "Uncle G worked too much. Louie had his rebellion. Gordana got all flinty. And you —"

"I'm too scared to leave Ma!" The words bubbled out of Frankie, but he hid his face in Alma's side. He couldn't look at her. "I don't want it to happen again, and if I stay there, keeping an eye on her, maybe it won't." He began to cry again, and it was hard to speak. "But. But, I'm just getting. More and more worried. And I *hate* it. I don't want to be afraid all the time. I don't want Sydney to go. And I don't want to have to look after Ma; I don't want to. I don't want to do that anymore. . . ."

Frankie pulled the eiderdown up to his neck. It was nearly dark. He switched on the lamp attached to the headboard. He liked that old lamp. When he was six, he had thought it nifty that he had a clip-on lamp.

Nellie had brought him tea and fruitcake and told him to take it easy. He was into the fourth scrapbook. It was mostly birds now. He'd begun that book on his second stay with the Aunties. He had proper art pencils by then, another birthday present, and he'd drawn a lot of magpies. They had fascinated him, gathering in gangs on the fence around the back section, a little menacing, but tough and almost beautiful, their feathers shiny in the spring sun.

These drawings were pretty good, Frankie thought. He'd improved a lot between five and six. You really could tell the birds were magpies. And then sometime after that, he'd had an exotic bird phase — copying cassowary and fieldfare and weaverbirds from a bird encyclopedia Teen had given him, partly because he liked the words. He'd copied the nests too, and the eggs. He remembered all this as he turned the pages, and he remembered how he'd shown the book to Ma when he visited her.

That second time at the Aunties' he didn't see Ma for quite a while, weeks perhaps, and then the Aunties began taking him regularly to see her at home. She would always be sitting on the sofa and usually in her dressing gown, and he would sit in her lap and show her his most recent bird drawings. Soon he began doing the drawings especially for her, working up a new bird each time, looking forward to her delight, her gentle approval. A swallow. A nightingale because Ma said they sang beautifully. A kingfisher. A coot, because he liked the word. A dabchick, because Ma liked that word. He had found the dabchick in the encyclopedia and copied it carefully, its strange, staring, white-button eye and scruffy back feathers.

Frankie closed the sketchbook. There were two more books, but he would take them home with him, look at them later. He took a bite of Nellie's fruitcake, gulped some tea, and thought about the dabchick. It was all there in his head, the dabchick's shining eye and anxious thrusting neck, his feelings when he'd been drawing it. He'd thought the bird was a little like Ma; it was small and sweet, but ever so defenseless out there on the water. It seemed trembly, as if it knew there were threats nearby.

But when he'd shown the dabchick to Ma, she had smiled and said the bird reminded her exactly of him: it was small and dark, and looking about with its big eyes.

"My little dabchick," Ma said. She'd held him very close, and he had burrowed into her so that he could smell what he was missing, the mix of lotion and bed linen and sleep in her neck.

Ma's light was on, her door ajar. Frankie knocked softly and pushed it open. Ma was sitting up in bed, waiting for him, as Uncle George had said she would be. He had said she would be ready to talk. She had been reading, but she had laid the book aside. Frankie knew his face was like a buffeted tomato, red and puffy and going to liquid. He'd stared at himself in the bathroom mirror when he arrived home.

"Hi," said Ma softly.

"Hi," said Frankie.

"How're you doing?" said Ma.

He nodded vaguely and sat down on the bed.

"Ten-ten p.m.," said Ma, but Frankie didn't smile.

He thought, with a kind of internal sigh, that it didn't matter how much he talked, how much happened, he seemed somehow always back at the beginning. Back to not knowing where to start.

Instinctively he sought out the painting, the woman, her halo of hair, her amber eyes. Fright swept down his arms when he saw it wasn't there.

"Where's she gone?" Frankie cried, looking at Ma.

She pointed across the room. The painting was perched on the window seat, leaning against the bay window. Frankie fell back on the pillows in relief.

"I was cleaning the glass," said Ma. "Then I wondered if you'd want to look at the name. I thought you might be tired of guessing."

Frankie wanted to laugh and cry and throw up his hands in operatic despair. Ma was perfectly right. And wasn't that the problem? Ma was tuned to him. And he was tuned to her. But Alma had said their tuning had got stuck on some bad notes. They had to change their tunes, she said. He had to.

"I have to talk to you about everything," he said in a rush.

"I know," said Ma. "I know. Alma told me." She had picked up the book and was turning it around and around in her hands, as if she were measuring its dimensions by touch. Frankie read the title, The Lady with the Dog by Anton Chekhov.

"Why do you read those Russian books over and over?" he asked, though he hadn't meant to start this way at all. "Is it because of the sad endings? Do you only believe in sad endings?" Already, his voice was rising, though staring in the bathroom mirror, he had promised himself he would be very calm.

"But they're not always sad," said Ma. "It's not tragic for everyone." She paused and then put the book down again. Frankie waited, doing the even breathing.

"I think," said Ma at last. "I think it's because they're the books I know best. I first read them a long time ago, when life was more straightforward. When I was completely well."

Frankie flinched. She may as well say she wasn't well now. He hated that.

"So I find them kind of . . . comforting," Ma said. Frankie shook his head.

"But Frankie," said Ma. "The world *is* in those books. I think it's how—" She stopped and stared across the room at the uncurtained and black window.

Frankie tried to see the woman in the painting but it was too far away. She was a blur of hair and draperies. He knew what Ma was going to say.

"I can, I can have *the world that way,*" said Ma, "even though—"

But Frankie didn't want to hear the next part. He couldn't hear it. Instead, he felt roaring up in him from a long way down and a long way back the question he'd avoided all this time. It spilled from him, in a rush of tears and fury and anguish. It was a livid question, an accusation, an appeal, all at once, right into Ma's emptied-out face.

"Why can't you go out to the world? What's wrong with you? Why can't you leave the house? Why can't you just do it?"

Ma stayed very still and upright. She didn't fold up; she didn't dissolve, collapse, break down, as Frankie had always feared she would. Frankie was the crumpled-up person. He lay back on the pillows, overcome by what he had said, and scared to death of what Ma would answer.

She took a long time. She waited until his tears had subsided and there was just the nighttime quiet in the room. She took Frankie's hand and spoke quite matter-of-factly.

"I just can't do it, Frankie. I've tried and I've tried. But I can't."

Frankie's hand, cold and dry in Ma's, felt like a dead gecko. Her words were as heavy as stones, settling in his chest, gray and final.

"Staying inside is how I manage," said Ma. "It's how I keep it all okay. Outside just became more and more terrifying. Inside is manageable."

She squeezed Frankie's hand, a nervous apology.

"Dinah talks to me about changing it, but I don't want to."

She paused, and Frankie heard the words again in his head, emphatic and inescapable. I don't want to.

"I know it's not normal," said Ma, "but I've accepted that. It's very *simple. I take the medication and I stay inside and I bake the cakes, and it's all right."*

But it's NOT, Frankie's brain shrieked. It's NOT. Someone has to do something!

He sat up, his dead gecko hand suddenly alive, gripping Ma's hand. He was startled, remembering how often he'd wanted to shout those very words at Sydney about her mother.

He thought of Sydney's cool words on the phone: Face facts, Frankie.

"What is it?" said Ma.

Frankie sat back, let go of Ma's hand gently. He wanted to ask her why outside was terrifying, how it had started, and so much more, but quite suddenly he was too tired. Colossally tired. Beyond tired.

He shut his eyes to say the last thing. He knew they would talk again. He knew they could do it now. And he would talk to Uncle George. He would talk to Louie. And Gordana. It was up to him. But he had to say one more thing to Ma now.

"I don't want to be like you," said Frankie quietly. "I don't want to be terrified of the world."

"I don't want you to be, either, Frankie," said Ma. Her voice was quite firm. Clear.

They sat side by side for a while longer, quiet together. Frankie could feel the sleep seeping into him like fog.

"Last guess?" said Ma.

He smiled dozily.

"Susan?"

"No," said Ma.

"Jean?"

"No."

He fell asleep for just a few seconds. Then—

"Myrtle."

Ma chuckled. It was a good sound. "No."

"C'mon," she said, nudging him. "Before you fall asleep."

"I am actually asleep," Frankie murmured.

Ma leaned over and kissed him. "We'll talk lots more."

"Yes," said Frankie. He pushed himself out of the bed, stood dopily, swaying a little.

"Frankie," said Ma. "You don't have to watch over me. I don't need you to watch over me."

He looked at her, a small figure in a big bed.

"I really mean it," said Ma.

He nodded, turned, and walked sleepily over to the painting. He lifted it and held up the back of it to the light, squinting at the little white strip that bore the title.

"'Aurora wakens.'"

He read it aloud and looked over at Ma.

"You know what it means?" she said.

"Something to do with the sky?" said Frankie. "Or the stars?"

"Dawn," said Ma. "It means dawn. It's the name for Sleeping Beauty."

Frankie read the title again.

He walked over to the wall beside the bed and placed the painting back on its hooks. He stared at it for a moment, feeling almost sad that the guessing was over. Aurora.

"So?" said Ma.

"Hmmm," said Frankie.

He walked to the door, turned, and gave Ma a little wave.

"'Night," he said.

NINE

Tuesday, June 6

June the sixth began really quite well for Frankie Parsons. He did *not* have a dead leg from the Fat Controller sleeping on it all night, because he had banished the Fat Controller to the laundry, where her new beige and blue merino-lined pet home resided between the earthquake kit water bottles and the bird flu bags of rice and pasta. He had told her encouragingly that she was the new emergency depot commander, though he was *not* interested in seeing any rats she caught.

There was plenty of milk and butter for breakfast, plenty of everything, in fact, because as of last Friday the groceries were being ordered *online* and delivered twice a week by the super-market. This had been Gordana's brilliant idea. Apparently several of her forty-seven friends' families did it. Apparently it was the very latest thing. And, apparently, Gordana was quite happy to be in charge of it.

The newspaper had arrived, but Frankie had temporarily stopped reading the newspaper. He was taking a break from national and world affairs at the suggestion of Petrus, the guy he'd been chatting to for the last couple of weeks. Petrus was South

African and worthwhile for two reasons. One, he was extremely keen on cricket, and two, he had some quite useful suggestions for combating persistent worry.

There were plenty of crisp apples for lunch (thank you, online groceries) and a piece of leftover potato pie from last night's dinner, which Gordana had graciously foregone, since potato, apparently, was carbohydrate death and to be avoided at all costs.

Frankie stuffed his lunch bag and jacket into his backpack, then stood and mentally perused the coming day. Math (calculator, yes). Reading (*Hergé and His Creation,* yes). Language arts (*Concise Oxford,* yes). PE (shorts, sneakers, yes). Soccer at lunchtime (cleats, T-shirt, yes). Lunch (*crisp* apple, potato pie, coconut cake, washed carrot, secret-chocolate-now-hidden-behind-the-lima-beans, yes). Art (pencils, ink, charcoal, old jug, yes). Book project (two copies Version One, one copy Version Two, yes). Sydney's going-away present (signed portrait of Microsoft, yes).

"Why are you looking so smug?"

Frankie jumped. Gordana seemed to have arrived downstairs without her usual thunderous tread.

"I'm not smug," said Frankie. "I'm . . ." What was he? Organized? Satisfied? Pleased? He didn't know.

Gordana tapped his forehead with a knuckle. "As I suspected. Completely empty."

"Shut up," said Frankie mildly. He checked the other bag. He'd packed pajamas — or what passed for pajamas in their house: an old T-shirt of Uncle George's and a pair of boxers — a change of clothes, a cake tin with a lemon ricotta, a *Get Smart* DVD, and his pillow.

"What's all that for?" said Gordana.

"I'm staying the night at Sydney's," said Frankie. "It's her second-to-last night." He gave Gordana a defiant look.

Gordana flung herself on the couch and stretched luxuriously.

"So, Mr. Shrink *is* working," she said.

"He's not a shrink," said Frankie.

"Whatever," said Gordana carelessly. "He's a genius if he can get you to stay the night somewhere else. But Frankie"—Gordana dropped her voice dramatically—"this is your first night at your girlfriend's. We should have the Talk."

"She's *not* my girlfriend!" Frankie shouted, and instantly regretted it. Why did he fall for that every time?

"Well, you just have a dandy time with old Sydney," said Gordana. "And her crazy mother."

"Gordana," said Ma, coming into the living room. "*Crazy* and *mother* are not tactful things to say around here."

Frankie and Gordana looked at Ma with astonishment. She gave a hesitant smile.

"Oh, good *God*, so it's just me with the Aunties tonight?" said Gordana. She groaned extravagantly, then went to the kitchen and began banging pans and plates.

"All right?" Ma said to Frankie.

He squared his shoulders like an eager recruit.

"Fine," he said. "Really."

"Have a nice time," said Ma. She kissed him on the cheek. "Say *bon voyage* to Sydney."

"You should take Ludo," Gordana called out. "Or Monopoly. Some nice board game. I can lend you the Game of Life."

Ha, ha, thought Frankie. Very comical. Hilarious. Side-splitting.

He opened the front door, looking back at Ma. "Have a good one," he said.

"I will," said Ma.

"Seriously, Frankie," said Gordana, appearing with an egg in each hand.

"What?" said Frankie. He gave her his most derisive look.

"Tell Sydney good luck from me," said Gordana.

Gigs was waiting for him at the top of the Zig Zag. He was leaning against the Forsythes' fence, peering at something in his cupped hand.

"Look at this." He opened his fingers a little, and Frankie leaned in. It was an orange ladybug, moving tentatively across Gigs's hillocky palm.

"I thought they were only in summer," said Frankie.

"This one's tough," said Gigs. "She's a survivor."

"It's good luck to have one land on you," said Frankie. "But only if you let them go."

"Who says?" said Gigs. "She likes me."

"No, you have to say the rhyme and let them go." Frankie could remember Teen doing this in the Aunties' back garden. "*Ladybug, Ladybug, fly away home,* you know . . . and something something something about children."

Gigs opened his hand and blew gently on the ladybug. "Just to give her the general idea," he said.

In a second she was gone.

"Better move it," said Frankie.

There was a frost this morning and the shadier parts of the Zig Zag were still a little icy. But Frankie and Gigs liked to live dangerously in the winter, so they jogged down the path, holding a handle each on Frankie's extra bag. It swung heavily between them.

"What's *in* here?" said Gigs.

"*Not* Ludo," said Frankie.

"What?"

"A dumb Gordana joke."

They gave perfunctory pats to Marmalade, banged Mrs. Da Prini's letter box without ceremony, and dispatched Ronald as quickly as possible.

Ernest Burrows was icy, too, but they leaped up onto the seat together and came down off the back with almost balletic precision.

"We're good," said Gigs. "We should join a circus or something."

"I'll get it," said Frankie at the bus stop. He brandished his brand-new three-month bus pass. Uncle George had gotten it for him from the bus ticket office.

At Petrus's suggestion, Frankie had made a list of all the things about the household that were (a) mildly irritating, (b) very irritating, (c) plain unworkable, (d) actually dangerous. *Unreliable source of bus fare* had been in the very irritating column. Uncle George had agreed to address columns (b), (c), and (d) promptly, and had been as good as his word, which meant, among other things, that the smoke alarm batteries were fresh and everyone (except Ma) had had a flu shot.

Gordana said she didn't see why Frankie should be the only person who got to have a fix-it list, so she had made one of her own. She had put *Uncle G walking around without underpants* in the (d) actually dangerous column.

It was Frankie's code-word week. He'd given quite a bit of thought to it, too, since it was a momentous week, but in the end, nothing had seemed particularly fitting. He'd rejected capital cities, wildcats, European soccer clubs, native trees, and names for marbles (he knew quite a few of these from the Aunties), and had settled rather lamely on candies.

"Odd Fellow," he said to Cassino, which was slightly appropriate, come to think of it. Yesterday he'd done Wine Gum, which had no significance he could think of. Maybe on Thursday he'd do Jet Plane, because Sydney would be flying out then. Tomorrow he'd be catching the bus from the midtown terminal, which would mean enduring constant filthy comments from

Seamus and Eugene Turnip Head. Too bad. Ha, he'd do Jelly Rat, just for them.

"Yendys nil presentium findefinatus chalkydom?" (Sydney definitely not coming to school?), said Gigs as they sat down.

"No," said Frankie. "Packing. But really, just looking after the little ones."

They rolled up their tickets and stared at the installation.

"Can you see anywhere?" said Gigs.

"We could squash them up some more," said Frankie.

"Tried that," said Gigs. "They won't move. I think they're fossilized."

They looked helplessly at each other.

"S'pose we could change seats," said Gigs, without much enthusiasm.

Frankie tried to imagine sitting somewhere else in the bus. Too bad what Petrus said about the danger of inflexible routines, the thought freaked him right out.

"No," he said.

"No," Gigs agreed.

"What shall we do with them?" said Frankie. He held his ticket up, looking at it with regret.

"We could save them," said Gigs. "How many months left of Notts? June, July, August . . ." He counted the months off on his fingers. "Five and a half months, minus four weeks of holidays, that's about eighteen weeks. Eighteen multiplied by five, that's ninety, multiplied by two, that's one hundred and eighty tickets . . . That's quite a lot of paper!"

"For what?" said Frankie.

"We can make a papier-mâché figure of something . . . of the bus, or the Turnip Heads, of Mr. A . . . of—"

"Of *Cassino*," said Frankie.

"*Yes,*" Gigs breathed.

They sat for a few seconds in happy contemplation of a Cassino figurine, a memorial to four years of bus rides and code words and Chilun.

"I'll look after the tickets," said Gigs. He plucked Frankie's ticket from his hand and put it with his own in the front pocket of his backpack.

They really *were* a well-oiled machine, Frankie thought. Maybe they should start a business, make millions.

But he might be going into business with Louie and Gordana. Louie had given him the hard sell, saying his bird drawings would ensure the business took off, ha, ha. Gordana was going to design the T-shirts and bandannas. Louie was going to do the selling and marketing. Frankie was still thinking about it. It would certainly be a fun way to earn money, better than a paper route or dishwashing at the Cupcake Café. And he wanted to start saving. The Aunties had said they would match him half a fare to Sydney if he wanted to go. He definitely wanted to go. Petrus thought it was a good thing to aim for.

Gigs unpacked his breakfast. "Today we have a poppy-seed bagel"—he lifted the lid of the bagel and displayed the contents—"with bacon and tomato relish, *no* greens, to be followed by an egg and banana and Black Doris smoothie."

"I'm carbo-loading," he added, biting into the bagel. "For the Pasadena game."

On Saturday Notts was playing Pasadena at Victory Park, the name of which, as Gigs pointed out in his team talk, had *not* done much for Notts in the past. So no complacency. Gigs had actually said this. And with a completely serious face. Frankie had to very strenuously not look at Sydney in case she eye-bulged and made him laugh. Sydney had been on the sideline at practice—with Bronwyn Baxter, who had come to watch Gigs, though he comprehensively ignored her before, during, and after.

Bronwyn Baxter would probably be at Victory Park on Saturday, too, but there would be no Sydney. Frankie knew this rationally, but somehow he still couldn't quite believe it.

Frankie stared out the window at the passing river. A thin mist hung just above the water, obscuring the tips of the willows. A few ducks hunched together on the riverbank. Three more months and there would be ducklings. Petrus had suggested Frankie practice thinking ahead to good things rather than bad. It was partly a matter of habit, he said; the more you did it, the easier it became. Frankie wasn't finding it easy yet. But he was practicing manfully.

For instance, next week was Ma's birthday. He was drawing her a comic strip story of Boris Pancake and his true love, Plastic Lara, condemned by the curse of Baba Yaga to a music box life except for one day a year when she could take human form and be in the world with Boris Pancake. It was a tragi-comedy with a half-sad, half-happy ending. On the whole, Frankie was finding it very enjoyable.

Frankie had hatched the idea in the week after his nut-out. *Nut-out* was, of course, a Gordana term, but he didn't really mind it. *Nut-out* seemed as good a word as any for that fevered, *desperate* time. The farther that time receded, the more it seemed like it had all happened in a gloomy cave or tunnel, some unlit Otherworld; he had been stumbling around in that place, looking for his bearings.

He had spent a lot of the week after his nut-out lying around, thinking and sleeping. He was like an invalid, depleted and dozy. Ma had fed him chicken soup.

But two days after his visit to Alma and his talk with Ma, he had rung Sydney and she had come around with the unfinished *Valiant Ranger*. Frankie had looked at the three endings and wondered at his earlier outburst.

"I think we should do it your way," he said to Sydney. "I really want to. I'll do the pictures for it. I'll do them before school starts."

"So what's been going on with you?" Sydney demanded. "Why have you been mad at *me*?"

Frankie had known she would cut straight to the chase. He had wanted her to. He wanted to explain everything, especially his new brilliant lightbulbs of understanding. He'd been tired that week, but he'd been elated, too; his head had felt perfectly clear at times, his thoughts burnished and valuable.

They had sat in the sunroom; it was warm and light and the sounds from outside lent a muffled music. Frankie had been enjoying lying there the last couple of days, looking out the glass doors at the liquidambars, the stark architecture of their branches, emerging slowly as the leaves fell.

He told Sydney everything about the last week, and while he talked in the usual messy, out-of-order way, and even though she was there listening attentively, it was right then that he began missing her, missing her busy-listening face, her eye-bulges, and her bold questions.

But Petrus had said that missing was good. Sad was good, said Petrus. Nothing wrong with sad. Frankie had glowered at him, doubting he'd ever had a sad day in his life.

"Do you think your mother will ever go outside?" Sydney asked in the sunroom.

Frankie had counted the leaves falling from the liquidambar—one, two, three, four, five—and shrugged.

"Do you think you'll ever go and live with the O?" he asked.

"When I'm older," said Sydney firmly. "When the little ones are older."

"I was so mad at your mother," said Frankie. He had been thinking about saying this for days.

"I'm pretty mad at her, too," said Sydney.

"It was *easier* to be mad at her," he said a moment later. He had figured that one out all by himself, somewhere between Ma's room and his own, two nights before.

"Like I didn't know that," said Sydney, giving him a vintage eye-bulge.

Frankie sighed now, remembering the sunroom conversation. He had nearly cried twice in front of Sydney, but he had drawn the line. He had to get a grip on that. He would rather have multiple encounters with rabid, genetically altered bull ants than turn into someone who cried at the drop of a hat. And speaking of ants, Petrus reckoned he was going to have Frankie coexisting happily with the horrible little beasts by next summer. Frankie was skeptical. But you never did know. Petrus had given him some exercises to do in the night when ten p.m. anxiety loomed, and they weren't bad. He had gone several nights in a row without trotting down the hall.

And tonight would be a good test.

He took a deep breath and let it out slowly and heavily.

"Too much *sighing*," said Gigs. "I'm counting. You want some?" He offered Frankie some dried pear. "Albino's ears," he said.

Frankie chewed the dried pear and decided its texture was working against it. It was like wet sand.

"Splontys, maximal, Yendys partil?" said Gigs. (You really sad about Sydney going?)

"Multiplyls." (Totally).

"Nixtus meesum asdys eldduc-top?" (Is she your girlfriend?)

Frankie turned and bulged his eyes at Gigs.

"Seriously," said Gigs. He had chewed all the middle out of his dried pear so that he was left with a pale rind, which he now rolled into a circle and bit.

Frankie decided to give the question serious thought.

244 :

He thought of all the things he liked about Sydney: her black eyes, her dreads, her nose stud, her bangles, her almost accent, her jokes, her clothes, her questions, her speeded up movements, her plump tears, her handwriting, her magnificent *daring*.

He thought about what Alma had said when he had been leaving the Aunties' that night. They had been on the veranda once again and she had hugged him fiercely, then stood back and looked at him, taking his chin in her smoky fingers.

"Rara avis," she said. "That's what you are, Frankie. A *rara avis.*" She had pushed him out into the night then, to Uncle George and the waiting car.

Frankie had looked it up in the dictionary the next day. *Rara avis* meant "rare bird." It was Latin. He'd been doubtful about it at first, thinking really he didn't want to be rare; he'd rather be common, especially if it guaranteed being normal.

But he liked saying it. It sounded good, rolling and majestic. After a few days he changed his mind. It was quite splendid, really. He wouldn't mind being called *rara avis,* after all, not a bit. It made him sound rather wonderful.

But now, as the bus turned into Memorial Avenue and he contemplated whether Sydney was his girlfriend, it occurred to him that *rara avis* should really be her honor. It fit her perfectly. *Somebody or something rarely encountered,* the *Concise Oxford* had said.

"So?" said Gigs, doing a rather good eye-bulge of his own. "Is she?"

"I don't *think* so," said Frankie.

"Ha! Bonga!" said Gigs, snapping down the lid on his breakfast container.

He smacked Frankie on the arm, and Frankie smacked him back and they both watched out the window as the bus turned the last corner to the midtown terminal.

Kate De Goldi has published young adult novels, short fiction, and picture books. *The 10 p.m. Question* was awarded the *New Zealand Post* Book Award in both the young adult and general fiction categories. About the novel, she says, "I wanted to write a book that explored profound personal difficulty amid the chaos of ordinary life, a book about sadness and loss and about fat, whiskey-swilling aunts, swimming pool phobia, exotic cakes, delinquent brothers, bird species, childish parents, cricket, bad-tempered sisters, cartoons, secret languages, pets with funny names. . . . I wanted to write about the complexity and hilarity in the everyday business of being human." Kate De Goldi lives in Wellington, New Zealand.